SON OF THE AVENGER

The Last Daughters of Titus Book Five

A D HUNTER

A D Hunter

Copyright © 2021 by A D Hunter

All rights reserved.

No part of this book may be reproduced in any form or by any electronic or mechanical means, including information storage and retrieval systems, without written permission from the author, except for the use of brief quotations in a book review.

❦ Created with Vellum

For Michael, thanks for the fire!

BUT FIRST, THIS...

There was a horrible sound of tires squealing, but it was too late. The grill of the car was coming at her and there wasn't a damn thing she could do about it. Vanessa opened her mouth to scream, but no sound came out. She could feel the heat from the car's radiator as it bore down on her...

Vanessa jerked awake. The dream had been coming more frequently as of late. Reliving the last moments of her previous incarnation. She knew why. It was soon time for her to change. She was going back to human form. Ebony had, finally, earned her wings and Titus would throw the mother of all parties to celebrate his latest debutante. With Ebony's blessing, he deliberately timed it so Vanessa could attend in human form. It was so exciting. Finally, the chance to hold her baby girl in her arms again. Titus didn't know it yet, but king or no king, this queen was going to be the first one to dance with her daughter as a new adult and she was prepared to fight him for it if need be. She would chuckle if she could, so a snort would have to do. *Crunch.* Footsteps. Somebody was in her stable. She sniffed the air. Blaze. It was an odd hour for him to be there. That meant one thing. He needed to talk. Something must have happened.

"Milady? Am I disturbing you?" he asked, speaking in a hushed tone.

She shook her head. Usually, when he came to vent, he'd bring her an apple and feed it to her while he talked. Not tonight. *Uh-oh. This can't be good.* She tilted her head inquisitively. He looked stricken. *Wow, what could it be?* He was still in his black suit. He'd been covering for Jared again.

He looked at her and shook his head. "Boy, I really wish you could talk to me here. I could use your input, especially since you're familiar with all parties involved."

Whoa. She double blinked. Then she nudged over a bale of hay. *Take a seat, warrior, I'm listening.*

He gave her a weak smile as he sat down. "I don't know, milady, maybe speech is overrated. What do you think?" he asked.

She nodded, then gave him the double blink again.

He said. "I think we've got a problem."

She waited patiently for him to continue.

"You know how I sometimes help Jared and his crew?"

She nodded.

"Do you remember a woman named Ileana?" he asked.

Vanessa had to think. It had been twenty-two years since she'd died as a human. There were a lot of holes in her memory. *Ileana. Ileana. Ileana.* She couldn't recall. She shook her head.

"She was a schoolteacher," he said.

Now the light bulb came on. Of course! Ileana was Miss Llewellyn, Ebony's kindergarten teacher. Vanessa nodded as the memories flooded back. The woman had practically thrown herself at Titus, but it was Trip, who would be the one to scratch that itch. Wait. Vanessa looked at Blaze and rapidly blinked. *Is this going where I think it is?*

Blaze ran a hand through his hair. "There was a plane crash, and she was on it. When I went to retrieve her, she asks me if I know an angel named Trip."

Vanessa was sure, human or not, her mouth had to be hanging open. She rapidly blinked. *Go on.*

He sighed. "I'm so glad I have you to talk to. I needed to say it out loud to somebody before I said it to him, because this? This is gonna turn his life upside down and inside out."

Vanessa blinked twice. She knew what he was going to say, and he was absolutely right. It most certainly was.

He looked her in the eye and said. "Trip has a son."

PART I: OF FATHERS AND SONS

1

Trip stared at his friend as if he'd just sprouted an extra head. After a few moments, he said, "Get the fuck out of here, dude. That's not even funny."

Blaze scowled. "Do I look like I'm laughing right now?"

Trip exhaled a gust of air as if someone had kicked him in the stomach. "Are you sure? Did you go look for yourself?" he asked.

Blaze nodded. "Of course, I did. I wouldn't drop a nuclear bomb like this on you without having my facts straight," he said.

Trip asked. "So, you've seen him?"

Blaze nodded.

Trip's eyes were wide as he leaned in. "What's he look like?"

"Brother, he looks just like you did at his age," Blaze said.

Trip's mind was running through everything that had happened that night. "But, she had implants. She showed them to me."

Blaze raised an eyebrow. "And what exactly does that have to do with the situation? Enlighten me, please," he said.

Trip frowned at him. "Not boob implants, dumbass, birth control. The ones inside the upper arm."

Blaze shook his head and shrugged. "Just goes to show how much experience I have fucking human females."

Trip wasn't in the mood to indulge Blaze's elitist attitude toward what he often referred to as the lesser species. The comment went ignored. "I've got to go get him. You think he has wing buds yet?"

Blaze raised his hands. "Whoa! Easy there, killer. You can't just show up and snatch him. Chances are he probably doesn't even know what he is," he said.

Trip hadn't thought of that. He nodded. "Okay, yeah, maybe you're right. I guess I should at least talk to his guardian first. Who's he living with now?"

"I'm not sure, brother. I just went to get a look at the boy. I didn't interact with him or the man he calls dad," said Blaze.

Trip froze. "What? He calls someone else dad?" The blond warrior didn't like that.

Blaze winced. "Yeah… a dark-skinned individual. Though, if you ask me, I can't see him making a baby the conventional way."

Trip knew who it was. "His name is Rodger. He was her best friend. And you're right, he's gay, but my son calls him dad?"

Trip had to pause a moment and let it sink in. Saying the words out loud made it far more real than when Blaze had initially said it. Holy shit. He had a son.

The big deal in Trip's situation was not so much that he had a son, but that he had missed out on seeing him grow up. Not to mention, because the boy was half-human, he would have to earn his wings. Trip had so much to teach him. He also had a lot of folks to tell, starting with Lylac. Being newly mated, he thought that she would be upset with him for not being more careful, but he was wrong. It thrilled her.

"Well, what are we waiting for?" she asked. "Let's go get him."

She was about to lift off when Trip stopped her. "Babe, no. I think I should do this alone."

She looked up at him, trying to hide the hurt. "Okay, Trip, if you think it's best."

He placed a hand on her cheek. "I do. Let's not overwhelm him. Okay?"

She nodded. "Okay, but hurry back. I can't wait to meet him."

"Absolutely," he said.

He leaned in for a kiss and she didn't disappoint as she slid her arms around his neck and kissed him like there was no tomorrow. You gotta love Venusians. They do nothing half-assed.

"Are you really going to send me off to meet my son for the first time with a raging hard-on?" He growled in her ear, cute little pointed thing that it was.

She gave him an impish grin and shrugged. "So tell him about the sexy kitten you have waiting for you at home. He'll understand."

She turned to walk away from him, swaying her hips as she did so. He couldn't help himself as he reached out and gave that healthy Venusian booty of hers a satisfying crack.

"Ooooh!" she cried out, then said. "Now, who's leaving somebody turned on?"

"Hold that thought until I get back," he said.

"Count on it, big boy," she said with a wink. "Hurry back."

Trip went to see his parents next. It was only fair that they know. They surprised him by being just as excited about it as Lylac. They made him promise to stop at their home first upon his return. His last stop was to see the king himself. He couldn't just bring a new person into the kingdom without the proper permission. It would be disrespectful.

"So, Miss Llewellyn, huh? She was beautiful and smart, so at least he's got that going for him," Titus said, teasing.

"Thanks a lot," Trip said, feigning hurt feelings.

Titus laughed, then he asked. "But seriously, are you okay? I know this has to be a shock."

Trip nodded. "That's grossly understating it. Have you seen Ebony? I'd like to tell her before I bring him back."

Titus shook his head. "I haven't seen her. Go do what you need to do. She'll be here when you get back. And Trip?"

"Yeah?"

"Remember, he has free will. You can't make him come. Respect his choice. No matter what. Understood?"

Trip nodded, bowed to his king, then bade farewell as he lifted off.

※

CALEB LAWSON WAS HAVING A SHITTY DAY. IT WASN'T enough he had just buried his mother less than a month prior. His girlfriend of two years had broken up with him that morning and she wanted him gone, immediately. Pack your shit and leave your key. In other words, get the fuck out. He couldn't blame her. After all, how many girls could say they woke up to a boyfriend screaming in terror and shitting the bed? Who does that? She accused him of being a drunk and wanted no part of it. So he gave her what she wanted. Since he had never officially moved in, everything he had there fit in two boxes and a laundry duffle. After loading it into his car, he needed a drink. Ironic? Maybe just a smidge.

He was seated at the bar minding his own business when a couple strolled in. He took one look at them and knew. The guy was abusing her. Never mind the bruises on her arms that were in various stages of healing, it was a feeling he was getting from the vibes they were giving off. He had always been sensitive to the feelings and emotions of others, and he was never wrong. According to Rodger, his adoptive father, it was something he inherited from his biological father. An irresistible drive to make things right, to stand up for the underdog. And it had gotten him into trouble on many occasions. He couldn't help himself.

He made eye contact with the woman, and the desperation he saw there almost gutted him as the familiar urge fired up. His heartbeat increased, as did his breath rate, matching her anxiety. *Not now, not now, not now!* He told himself that it was none of his business. He quickly turned his attention back to his beer, downing it in one long drag. *Leave now, stupid. We don't need this today.* The couple edged past him and the girl accidentally bumped into him.

"Excuse me. I'm so sorry," she said.

"It's okay. No worries," he murmured, averting eye contact.

They moved on, but as they were walking away, Caleb heard the man accuse her of checking out the patron on the barstool.

"I saw how he looked at you when we walked in. How do you know him?" the man said to her.

She shook her head, fear in her eyes. "I don't know him. I wasn't looking at him, I—"

"Are you calling me a liar?! I saw you!" he hissed.

As her rising tide of anxiety increased, Caleb's back

started tingling. *Fuck!* He was fast approaching the point of no return and if he didn't get out of there; he was going to end up confronting the bully.

The man gripped her up by her arm and spoke to her through clenched teeth. "You lying bitch! I'm so sick of your lies. Wait 'til we get home!"

He grabbed a six-pack from the cooler and paid, then was heading for the door, dragging the woman behind him.

What had started out as a niggling tickle was now a furiously, maddening, out and out, itch. Caleb took a deep breath, resisting the urge to scratch. Two weeks ago, scratching had helped. Now? Scratching caused his heart to hurt to the point of breathlessness. The weirdest symptom ever. *Get out, get out, get out... now!* He stood and placed a twenty on the bar.

The bartender frowned at him. "You okay, buddy? Need me to call an Uber?" he asked.

Caleb shook his head. "No. That won't be necessary. I'm good." *This is me minding my business. This is me leaving. This is me getting out.* He said to himself.

He paused to catch his breath. His back and chest were now screaming, and there was a roaring sound in his ears. Was this a heart attack? No. It was an anxiety attack. That's all. That's what the doctor told him two weeks ago, attributing it to the loss of his mother. He was fine. The feeling would pass... as long as nobody touched him. So why did the bully choose that moment to shoulder check him?

The bartender watched in shocked surprise as Caleb's eyes went from deep blue to steely grey to icy white, contorting with rage and pain. He'd been doing the job long enough to know when shit was about to go south. And it was about to hit the proverbial fan. Umbrellas open, folks. One shit storm coming up. He reached for his cell and called 9-1-1.

Caleb whirled around, fist already rising, and punched the man in the face. The woman screamed. The man's nose was bleeding profusely as he tried to counterstrike. Caleb easily dodged it and struck again. This time the man's teeth crunched under the impact, breaking the skin on Caleb's knuckles.

"Stop!" the woman cried.

Caleb heard nothing as he went to the floor landing atop of the man. Speaking through clenched teeth, he said, "If you hit her again, I'll know. Don't ask me how, but I will and I will come for you. That's a promise. Nod if you understand."

The guy nodded, horrified at the face with the now glowing white eyes leaning into him.

"Apologize to her. Now!" Caleb demanded.

The guy looked up at his girlfriend. "I'm sorry, baby. I let my temper get the best of me and it won't happen again. I promise!" He looked back at Caleb. "Yo, man, what's wrong with your eyes? Let me go!"

Caleb frowned as his eyes phased back from glowing white to their normal deep blue. "What?"

The man chose that moment to scramble out from under him, grab his girlfriend's hand, and run out the door.

Caleb stood up, shaking out his hand. His knuckles were already turning purple. The bartender wrapped some ice in a towel and handed it to him. "Thanks," Caleb said. "Sorry, I guess I'm having a bad day. I—"

"It's okay. He had it coming, but I had to call the cops. You may want to split while you can."

"Good looking out," Caleb said. But his shitty day was about to get shittier as the officers walked in, took one look at him, and pulled their cuffs.

"Everything all right here?" the first officer asked.

Caleb sighed, then placed his hands on the bar.

2

Trip was perched atop a neighbor's house, watching. Fortunately, Rodger and Ileana hadn't moved, making them easy to find. So there was that. He was about to settle in and wait when he heard the car pull up and park. He watched as Rodger stepped out, still talking, but Trip couldn't hear a word he was saying. He was waiting with bated breath to see his son get out of the passenger side. The door opened and Trip's eyes widened as a replica of himself stepped out. He was wearing a blood-stained white tee, blue jeans, and black boots. Multiple tattoos snaked up both arms and across the back of his neck. Trip shook his head as his heart swelled. Caleb was one sexy motherfucker, with those intense blue eyes, chin-length hair, and the beginnings of a full-on beard. A red one at that. Trip chuckled, oh man, his own father was going to have a field day with that.

"But did you have to beat him down?" he heard Rodger saying. "One hit would have been enough. He was bleeding all over the parking lot. And look at your hand. Are you sure it's not broken? Jesus, Chip!"

Caleb looked down at his hand. It was black and blue and

very swollen. And it hurt like a son-of-a-bitch. He could only imagine the condition of the guy's mouth. Good! "It's not that bad, Dad. He should've just left me alone."

"The guy shoulder checked you. Big deal. And you couldn't just ignore him, right? He goaded you and you fell for it."

Caleb didn't respond. What could he say?

Rodger sighed. "Even his girlfriend took his side, saying you were like a madman. Look, son, you can't keep stepping in and fighting for others."

Trip smiled to himself. *Oh, yes, he can. He can't help it. It's in his blood. Chip? What the—?*

Rodger continued. "One of these days you're gonna really hurt someone and end up in prison or worse. What if you get someone who's armed? You can't outrun a bullet, son. That's the shit that keeps me awake at night."

"Sorry, Dad. I'll try harder. I promise."

Rodger winced. "I know you will. By the way, I'm sorry things didn't work out with Brandi."

"Thanks, Dad," Caleb said, grateful that Rodger hadn't asked for details.

They went inside.

Trip took a deep breath. This was it. The moment of truth. He jumped down from the roof, walked up to the door, and just stood there. He was nervous. What if Rodger didn't remember him? What if Caleb chose not to come? It wouldn't do for his son's wings to break through in that dimension. It would classify him as a Nephilim and strand him there until he died... or worse, got recruited by the Lower Realms. Fuck. That. He knocked on the door.

"I got it!" he heard Rodger say from the other side. Then the door opened. "What took you so long, J—"

The sentence went unfinished as Rodger came face to

face with the being responsible for changing his life over twenty years ago.

"Hi Rodger," Trip said.

"Holy shit. She found you," Rodger said.

Trip frowned. "Excuse me?"

"Ileana. The timing can't be a coincidence. She died three weeks ago, and now you're here. Am I right?"

"Sort of. She forwarded a message to me via a friend and I'm so sorry for your loss, Rodger. Uh, may I come in?"

"Oh, right, yes, of course." He stepped back, allowing Trip inside.

They may not have moved, but they had renovated the hell out of the interior. It now had an open floor plan and he could see clear through to the backyard, which now had a pool. They had also added extra rooms.

"Wow!" Trip said. "I like what you've done to the place."

Rodger grinned. "Ileana received a large settlement. We never moved because we wanted to make it easy for you to find us. So we invested in a remodel."

Trip nodded his approval. "So does your en suite now have windows?" he teased.

Rodger laughed. "No. No, it doesn't. So if you need privacy for summoning, it's all yours."

The two of them were laughing when a door opened down the hall and Caleb emerged. He had changed clothes and was now wearing black jeans, black boots and a black t-shirt with the words "Steel Feather" emblazoned across the chest. His hair was neatly brushed back into a ponytail. His eyes met Trip's, and he froze. Trip's mouth went dry as he beheld his son face to face for the first time. Rodger discreetly stepped back, allowing space between the two.

Caleb spoke first, still not moving. "She wasn't kidding."

"What?" Trip said, just above a whisper.

"She said I looked like you. She was always telling me that. She told me if I ever met you, I would know who you were."

It was rare for Trip to be at a loss for words. He was always good for a snappy comeback or some smart ass remark, but he couldn't think of anything to say. He nodded toward Caleb's hand. "You should put some ice on that."

Caleb looked down at it, then absently nodded. Twenty-two years. All his life, he had known love. Lots of it. Rodger's family had accepted him as one of theirs. Nobody cared that he had blond hair and blue eyes. Nobody cared that Rodger was openly gay, but had still married Ileana, anyway. Nobody cared that Rodger and Ileana's little boy was a little strange in that he never got sick. He had felt the business end of Nanny's wooden spoon just as often as his cousins. He belonged to them just as much as any of the children Rodger's sisters had given birth to. Yet for all that love, he had still felt isolated and alone. Like there was something different about him. Something that went deeper than his skin and hair color. Was this the missing piece? He looked up at Trip and Trip did the only thing he could think of. He opened his arms. Then father and son were embracing, and Trip couldn't help himself as tears flowed down his face. He buried his nose in Caleb's hair.

"Please believe me. If I had known, I would've been here sooner," he said.

Caleb nodded. "I know. I believe you."

Rodger stood fanning himself as tears streaked down his face. "Damn, you guys! Got me crying up in this piece and wishing—" His voice cracked and trailed off.

"I know, Dad. I wish she was here too," said Caleb.

Trip wiped his son's face with his thumbs. "We have a lot to talk about and, unfortunately, not a lot of time."

"What do you mean?" Caleb asked.

Trip looked at Rodger. "Have you told him?"

Rodger shook his head. "We weren't sure if it would be a definite thing. We were hoping to see you again so you could explain. Thought it would be better coming from you. Especially since, you know, proof?"

Trip nodded. "Ahh. I see."

The front door opened and a tall, thin, dark-skinned man with cornrows walked in carrying a box. "I stopped and filled your tank, Chip. I was thinking we could—" The box dropped to the floor as his eyes widened. "Jesus, Mary, and Joseph. Trip?"

Trip looked at Rodger, then back at the young man. "Uh, yeah, and you are?"

"I'm Chip's cousin, JJ. Nice to meet you, finally." He offered his hand.

Trip shook it, then looked at Caleb, questioningly. "Chip?"

"Yeah, Nanny gave it to me. She says I have a chip on my shoulder because I, uh, kinda fight a lot."

Trip smiled. "I see. Well, I guess I should start explaining. First, let me assure you, the fighting thing is not your fault. You have Avenger blood. It comes with the territory."

"Avenger?"

Trip looked at Rodger, then at JJ.

Rodger nodded. "It's okay. He won't tell."

"Let's sit down," Trip said.

SON OF THE AVENGER

Trip, JJ, and Caleb took seats at the dining room table while Rodger made lunch.

"Sandwiches guys?" he offered.

They all nodded.

Trip said, "Look, I'm not gonna beat around the bush. You're not human, Caleb. I'm not human."

Caleb frowned, exchanging a look with JJ. "Then what exactly are we?"

"We're angels. Well, you're half, and that's where the time crunch comes in. I have to get you back to where I'm from before your wings come through. To claim your birthright you have to earn them, otherwise... has your back been itching?"

Caleb's face paled as he nodded. "Just in the past couple of weeks. Ever since Mom died. It gets almost unbearable when—"

"When somebody challenges you or if somebody is mistreating someone else in front of you."

"Yes! What the fuck? And now my chest even hurts when it happens. Is that part of it too?"

It was Trip's turn to pale. *Shit.* Caleb was further along than they'd expected. It was imperative he leave with him as soon as possible. "Yes, it is. We have to go," Trip said, standing.

Caleb nodded. "Okay. For how long? What all do I need to pack?"

"Yo, Chip, hold up. Don't you think you should get some more information first?" JJ asked in alarm.

Caleb placed a hand on his cousin's shoulder. "Listen J. All my life I have felt like I didn't belong. Like there was something missing. But now? It's like the pieces are falling into place. I'm ready. I need to do this. I can feel it."

Rodger placed the food on the table. Turkey sandwiches

on kaiser rolls with pickles and potato chips on the side. "Surely, you have time to eat first, Trip. Would that be okay?"

Trip sat back down. "Of course, but then we've got to go. There's a lot going on back home, right now. And there's stuff I can't miss."

Rodger joined them at the table. "So, Trip, how is Ebony? Her parents? Her father is the king, right?"

Trip took a huge bite of his sandwich and nodded. "Yes. There's a ball tonight. We're celebrating the return of the queen."

Caleb's eyes were wide. "Seriously? A king and a queen?"

"And princesses," Trip said.

JJ cocked an eyebrow. "So who all is welcome at this party?"

Trip laughed. "Sorry, JJ. Angels only."

"Man! Chip, you lucky dog! You'd better put in a good word for your cousin back home, bruh."

"I'll see what I can do," Caleb said.

They finished lunch and Caleb showed Trip the rest of the house. "I'm gonna help JJ finish unloading the car," he said.

"You mind if I hang out in your room?" Trip asked.

"Sure, go ahead."

Trip nodded and stalked down the hall to his son's bedroom. It was a typical guy's room with posters of cars, motorcycles, and scantily clad women. There was a TV mounted on one wall with assorted video games neatly stacked atop the stand below it. A large aquarium housed a boa constrictor named Stanley, according to a small sticker on the glass. And a smaller one contained a tarantula named Sadie. His nightstand contained only a box of tissues and a bottle of lotion. The wastebasket next to it was half full of used tissues. Trip chuckled, then opened the bottom drawer.

Not there. Top drawer? Nope. He ran a hand along the edge of the mattress. Pay dirt. Caleb's porn stash was only two magazines, but both showcased women with ample asses. Oh, yes, he was his father's son. The neatly made bed had a sketchbook lying atop of it. Trip sat down and opened it. Caleb was good, really good. The first picture was of Ileana smiling. A few more of her followed, then some of Rodger. A large thin sheet of paper folded in quarters fell out. He picked it up and opened a pencil scratching of Ileana's grave marker. It would have been nice to see her again. However, the irony wasn't lost on him. If she were still alive, he wouldn't know about Caleb. Then where would they be? He folded the paper and replaced it between the pages. There were a few drawings of cars and engines. Then he got to the last few pictures and froze. The first one to give him pause was a sketch of the neighbor's roof, right outside Caleb's window, with a being perched atop. The picture wasn't as sharp as the others. The details were shadowy, but accurate, all the same. The being his son had drawn had long black hair and golden eyes. It was the first drawing in the book that had any color. Holy shit! When Blaze came to check, Caleb had seen him. Trip turned the page. The next drawing was a little girl with curly hair laughing and riding a majestic black pegasus. Trip's mouth went dry. It couldn't be. He almost cried out in surprise when he turned the page. Even without the use of colored pencils, he could see she was a woman of color. She lay stretched out on her belly on a bed of hay. She was nude with the curve of one voluptuous breast exposed. Her long curly locks spilled over her shoulder. Her eyes were closed and she had the slightest hint of a smile on her lips. Postcoital? That's how it looked to Trip. He turned the page. This time she was on her back with one arm over her head. Still nude. Caleb hadn't missed a single detail. From the large dark nipples to the slight indent of her navel down to the dark inverted triangle of pubic hair. Trip had never seen her nude once she reached adulthood. And even though it felt strange for him to see her now, that wasn't the part that made his jaw drop. She had a small birthmark on her left hip, courtesy of her mother, and there it was in the sketch, plain as day. There was no question in Trip's mind. It was Ebony.

Caleb and JJ returned from the car with the boxes.

"You found my sketchbook?" Caleb asked.

"It was lying on your bed. Nice work," Trip said.

"Thanks."

"Umm, so who's the chick in the back of the book?"

"Jade?" Caleb asked, taking the book from him and opening it to the page.

Trip's eyes were wide. "That's her name?"

Caleb shrugged. "I don't know, but that's what I call her. Every guy has that ideal. You know?"

Trip nodded. "And she's your ideal?"

Caleb's cheeks pinked up a little. "Yeah."

JJ laughed. "Your boy here always has had a touch of the 'jungle fever'."

Caleb frowned. "Don't say that J. It's crass and disrespectful."

Trip suppressed a grin. Ileana and Rodger had done right by his son. He couldn't be prouder. "Did I hear Rodger right earlier? Your girlfriend broke up with you? What did she look like? Just curious."

Caleb took out his phone and showed him a picture of himself with a beautiful girl. Caleb had his arm around her shoulder. She was dark-skinned with dark brown hair and eyes and waist-length braids. She was well-endowed in the chest area with wide hips.

"Nice and thick. Go you," Trip said, holding up a fist.

SON OF THE AVENGER

Caleb bumped it. "I guess."

JJ sucked his teeth. "Go on, Chip. Tell him how much of a bitch she could be. I'm glad you finally came to your senses."

"Well, she broke up with me so..." Caleb retorted.

"You didn't like her?" Trip asked.

JJ shook his head. "Not for him. She was a little too bossy for my taste."

Trip looked at Caleb and made a whip cracking sound effect, which caused JJ to fall out laughing.

Caleb frowned. "Hardly."

"You sure about that?" Trip asked.

Caleb flipped them off with his good hand.

"Oy. Let me see that left hand," Trip said.

Caleb held it out.

Trip gingerly took his son's hand and turned it over, scrutinizing. "Titus can heal this. You'll be fine."

His gaze went to the ink work on Caleb's arms. Two dragons snaked their way up his left arm and disappeared under his shirt sleeve. *Dragons? Hell no.* Titus will need to fix those too. On his right forearm, the words "Steel Feather" stood out within a dream catcher; the feathers dangling down to his wrist.

"What's 'Steel Feather'?" he asked.

"Our band," Caleb said. "Me, JJ, and two friends have a band. I play drums. JJ plays bass."

Trip nodded. "You'll probably be able to keep that one, but Titus will have to fix the others. We don't do dragons. We're above that."

"Who's Titus?" Caleb asked. "And what's wrong with dragons?"

"Titus is the king. Whoo lord!" said Rodger from the doorway, fanning himself.

"Why do you say it like that?" Caleb asked.

Rodger wiggled his eyebrows. "Because I have an excellent memory."

Caleb rolled his eyes. "Seriously?"

Trip chuckled. "To answer your question, dragons are lesser beasts. They exist in the Lower Realms. We don't taint our bodies with images of Lower Realm creatures. And in Rodger's defense, the king is pretty fucking hot. Just saying."

"And how would you know that?" Caleb asked. "Wait. Are you… bi?"

Trip winked at Rodger and they both started laughing. Then he said, "Ugh! You humans and your labels. Why does everything have to have a label? Here's the deal. I like sex in any way, shape, or form I can get it." He crooked a finger at Caleb and JJ, motioning them to move in closer. "You want to know where to get the best sex in all the universe?"

They both nodded.

Trip held up his left hand. "Right here. Nobody can do you like you. Ha!"

"Aw c'mon!" JJ said. "I thought you were gonna tell us some shit we didn't know."

Trip stopped laughing, then leaned in. "Seriously, though. The best sex in the universe can be had in Hedon."

"Hedon?" All three of them said it together.

Trip nodded. "Unicorns. Remember, sex starts in the mind. You find yourself a horny-assed unicorn, and she starts winking and blinking at you. If she turns around and lifts her tail? You're done. First, she glams you. You can feel it. Like fingers reaching into your mind. A skilled one will find all your deep dark desires no matter how fucked up and kinky they are. Then she'll turn that shit up full blast. By the time she's got your imagination on lockdown, you're already inside her, balls deep. And let me tell you, unicorn pussy is all kinds of magical. They can shape-shift into whatever you desire."

"Are you for real?" JJ asked.

Caleb waved him off. "Hell no. He's fucking with us."

Trip shrugged. "Fine. Believe what you want."

"I believe you," said Rodger. The look on his face said it all. He was ready to go, even if he had to die to get there.

"But that would mean unicorns are real. Really?" Caleb was dubious.

"Shakespeare wasn't lying. There are a lot of things that exist outside your limited capacity of understanding. No offense, but it's true," said Trip.

"And you've seen this shit?" JJ asked.

Trip gave him a mischievous smile. "Seen? You guys would be shocked at the shit I've experienced. Good and bad. Let's keep this light, though. Have I ever had a unicorn? Oh, yes. Her name was Eunice, and she was just learning how to use her powers. The things we did. If I were to say she turned me out, it would be a gross understatement. I guess I should tell you now since you'll find out soon enough. Where I'm from, I'm kinda known as the resident freak."

"Because of Eunice?" JJ asked.

"Yup," Trip affirmed.

They all stood by quietly as Caleb continued to put away his belongings. When he was finished he turned to Trip and said, "It's not too late to take me to Hedon, you know. It would make up for all the birthdays you missed."

Trip put up his hands. "Easy killer. Slow your roll. We'll get there. I promise."

Caleb nodded, then yawned. Trip had been so wrapped up in seeing him for the first time, he hadn't really *looked* at him. It had been so long since he'd dealt with a preemie, a human/angel just before the transformation. Caleb had all the classic signs. Itching back, aching heart, behaviors linked with whatever bloodline they were from, and dark circles under the eyes. Some said that was the worst. Horrific nightmares that were so real they could drive one stark raving mad.

"How have you been sleeping?" Trip asked.

Caleb looked away and shrugged. He didn't want to talk about it. Inevitably, he knew the conversation would get round to the dreams, and he didn't want to go there. Ever.

"Hey, this is important. Tell me," Trip said.

Caleb swallowed and said, "It's bad. And now that you've told me that unicorns are real, it means they're real too. Doesn't it?"

JJ looked at him. "They?"

Trip said, "Are you familiar with astral projection?"

JJ nodded.

Trip continued, "Well, when you dream at night, that's what's happening. Your soul, if you will, leaves your body and goes exploring. Sometimes you remember and sometimes you don't. Sometimes you go to places and see things that are outside of your ability to comprehend. Those are the ones you don't remember, but you still remember the feelings that accompanied them. You follow?"

They all nodded.

Trip said, "Caleb, I need you to tell me about them. It's important."

Caleb's eyes were wide as he shook his head. "No way! Besides, as you said, I don't remember everything."

"You remember that it frightened you though, right?"

Caleb was trembling now. "I try not to think about it. Please don't ask me to remember," he whispered.

Christ. His son was going to hate him for what he was

about to do. Trip looked at him and said, "I love you. Forgive me."

He reached out and placed his hands on either side of Caleb's head.

The room faded, and Caleb screamed.

3

Trip closed his eyes and saw what appeared to be a nightclub…

… JJ said, "Chip, I didn't forget. We're going to the clinic. You ready?"

Caleb nodded.

"What clinic?" Rodger asked. "Caleb? Is there something we should discuss?"

Caleb rolled his eyes. "It's not that kind of visit, Dad. That rash. It's getting worse."

"Pull up your shirt. Let's see it," Rodger demanded.

Caleb removed his shirt.

"Does it hurt?" Rodger asked, gingerly touching a spot on his lower back.

Caleb winced, expecting the touch, but the spot Rodger felt didn't hurt.

He shook his head. "Not there."

Rodger moved his hands up and touched near the middle. "Here?"

Caleb roared and spun away from him. "FUCK! Yes! That hurts!" he said, teeth clenched.

His eyes were watering as he angrily tugged on his shirt and stomped off to the men's room. He stood in the restroom, trying to catch his breath. The pain was unreal. He leaned over the sink and splashed water on his face. Someone opened a stall door behind him.

"What's up, Neph?" A voice said.

British accent? He couldn't be sure. Caleb lowered his hands and looked at the guy in the mirror. He was tall and thin, dressed in black leather from head to toe and silver. A lot of silver. Truth be told, he looked like he could have been part of the band. Caleb frowned. "Excuse me?"

The guy grinned, showing a mouthful of pointed teeth. Each one filed to an insanely sharp tip. Jesus! The shit some people did to themselves just to stand out from the crowd. Tats and piercings were one thing, but this was some next-level shit. Like a permanent Halloween costume and whatnot. The guy ran a hand through his black spiked hair and Caleb noticed discolored and pointed nails. His long fingers were gnarled with knobby joints. Arthritis? The guy looked too young for it, but nowadays one could never really know. His tongue snaked out from between his jagged teeth and ran across them. Was it black and forked? Had he seen that right? To say the guy gave him the creeps would be a gross understatement.

"I said, what's up, Neph?" The guy said walking forward.

Caleb instinctively backed away. Fuck this! "I think you've got me confused with someone else, buddy," he said.

The guy smiled, sheepishly. "My bad. You remind me of someone I know. My name is Xavier. Nice to meet you." He held out his hand.

Automatically, Caleb went to shake it but stopped. Something wasn't right. He could hear and feel his heart thudding against his ribs. It hurt. Instead of shaking hands, he rubbed his chest. The guy was looking at him, expectantly? No, that wasn't it. Hungrily. Then his eyes did something über-creepy. For a split second, they flashed a silvery color. Like mercury. Yeah, no. Just fucking no! Caleb turned and ran. He could hear the guy still talking just before the door closed behind him.

"See you soon, 'buddy'," said Xavier.

The creepy cackling laughter that followed would haunt Caleb for a long time.

They all looked up when he came running out of the bathroom. Rodger frowned.

"Caleb? What's wrong? You look like you've seen a ghost."

Caleb looked back at the men's room. "I —"

The sudden pain in his chest felt like a sledgehammer to his breastbone. His breath hitched. He couldn't breathe. He couldn't breathe! The room started spinning. He got a glimpse of a blond man rushing towards him, then he heard Rodger say, "Trip?"

Then there was nothing.

CALEB OPENED HIS EYES AND LOOKED AT TRIP, WHOSE EYES were still closed in concentration.

"Please stop," he begged.

He tried to struggle, but Trip's hands were like a vise on his head. The room started fading again. And he knew what was coming. Again, he screamed...

THE FIRST THING CALEB NOTICED WAS THE SOUND OF SIRENS and he was moving. He opened his eyes. Holy shit! A pair of beautiful golden eyes stared back at him. She was stunning. A bronze-skinned redhead with the face of an angel and the body of a freaking Venus. She leaned over him, her blue jacket with its EMS badge on the one side announcing her name as "Sienna". Underneath, she wore street clothes. Oxblood leather. The top was a halter that exposed her pierced navel, while leather pants laced up the front and the sides. Steel enforced leather? It had to be because her ample bosom was stretching it to its limit and it was holding. Well! The band of her pants rested on nicely flared hips, just above the hairline. He was dead. He had to be. Only an EMT in Heaven would look like that. She smiled down at him.

"Caleb? Can you hear me?" She asked.

He swallowed and blinked. Why couldn't he talk? She looked at her partner and said, "It's wearing off. He's trying to talk."

The man came into his field of vision. He wasn't wearing a jacket, but he was in leathers. Whereas her top was a halter, his was a vest, and it was black. He had a kind face. It was the only word that came to mind. Kind. Dark wavy hair framed his bearded face and his dark brown eyes expressed concern.

"Did we make it?" Asked another voice from behind him. Whoever it was, they were stroking his hair. A dude. What in the ever-loving fuck? He tried to turn his head.

"Don't move yet, honey," said Sienna. "You're not ready."

She reached for something behind him and her chest was in his face. Nice rack with no bra and it was chilly in there. And she smelled so damn good. Yes, this was definitely Heaven. Caleb smiled as he ogled her.

Another voice, "Yo, bruh, your son's a horn dog!"

The voice stroking his hair replied, "I know, right?!"

The blond man leaned into his visual field and winked.

The EMT in black said, "Caleb. Listen to me. I don't have time to ease you into this, you're going to have to trust me. My name is Titus. I'm a king. You are an angel. The reason you're having the pain in your chest and back is that your wings are coming in. We can't have them coming through in this dimension. We need to get you back to our world to complete your transformation properly and safely. Do you understand?"

Caleb frowned and shook his head.

The blond leaned in. "Hey, listen. I'm your father. My name is Trip. I didn't know about you until recently. I got here as soon as I could. He's telling you the truth. You're half-angel and to complete your transformation you must forsake your humanity before your wings come in otherwise you'd get stuck here as a..." He paused and cleared his throat. "... a Nephilim."

Caleb's eyes widened. "Neph," he whispered. It hurt to talk. His chest felt like there was a tank sitting on it. He swallowed. "Weird dude in the bathroom called me that."

Another one, with bronze skin and golden eyes, leaned in. A male. He had long black hair and a goatee. He was wearing the same thing as the king, along with a severe scowl.

"What guy," he demanded. "What did he look like?"

Caleb swallowed and slowly told them about Xavier.

The four of them exchanged a look.

Titus ran a hand through his hair and sighed. "Fuuuuuck. Okay, Caleb, for this to happen you must agree to it. Repeat after me. I, Caleb Lawson, do solemnly pledge my allegiance to the Upper Realms. Forsaking my humanity, I now choose an alliance with my father's host and family for the rest of my current incarnation."

Caleb repeated the words. That wasn't so hard. Why all the drama?

Titus cleared his throat. Then the dark one was standing above his head. He leaned in and placed his hands on Caleb's shoulders as the blond laid a hand across his forehead. Sienna was now leaning on his thighs. Were they holding him down? What the—

The vehicle swerved and came to a sudden stop.

"Stryker? What's going on up there?" Titus demanded.

The driver joined them. Did the sun shine 24/7 in Heaven? He too was well-tanned with green eyes and dark brown hair, and damn if Sienna didn't look like she was about to melt at the sight of him. And the guy was oblivious.

"We have company. A Fallen," he said.

"Shit!" Titus said, then the rear door was being ripped off its hinges.

And there stood Xavier.

"The Neph is mine," he said, "step away and—"

The sentence went unfinished as the dark angel with long hair drew a flaming sword and advanced upon him. "He swore allegiance. You're too late, Fallen. Get thee back to the Lower Realms!"

"But you haven't completed the ritual!" Xavier said. "Oy! Neph! Did they tell you what forsaking your humanity entails? Did they tell you they have to kill you?"

Caleb's eyes widened as he started fighting. "What?!"

He looked into the faces of the angels in the rig with him.

Stryker, who was now holding his shoulders, looked at the king and shouted, "Do it! Do it now!"

Caleb heard the sharp zing! *as the king unsheathed a dagger from his scabbard and raised it over his head. The angel's eyes were solid obsidian as he started reciting an incantation in a strange tongue. The pain that had quieted was now back with a vengeance. Caleb screamed as the new wings began forcing their way through the muscles in his back. Xavier stood smiling in anticipation. As scary as the king looked, Xavier licking his lips was far more terrifying.*

Caleb tried to make sense of what was going on. The blond was his father? His father! And he was holding his head down and telling him everything was going to be all right and that he loved him. The driver, Stryker, had his full weight on his shoulders, pinning him to the gurney. And Sienna. She had to be the hottest chick he'd ever laid eyes upon, was practically sitting on his thighs holding them down. Caleb struggled to raise his hands and feet and found his wrists and ankles restrained. Jesus! They had planned this. And to top it off, whatever drug they had given him to control the pain was no longer working. His back was on fire! He screamed again as his chest seized. The king didn't need to kill him. Whatever was happening to his heart would take care of that. He was sure of it. His breath caught in his chest as he tried to inhale, gearing up for another scream. The king's eyes were now back to normal as he recited the last word, "Amen." The pain was so intense Caleb was on the verge of passing out. It was agony.

He looked into the king's eyes and pleaded. "Make it quick?"

Titus gave a curt nod as the dagger descended. The last thing Caleb Lawson heard just as that blade was about to pierce his throat was Xavier roaring.

"He. Is. Mine!"

The fallen angel dodged past Blaze. Trip stood, reaching for his own sword just as Xavier grabbed Caleb by the foot. There was a flash of blue light as Caleb, Stryker, and Sienna disappeared, leaving Titus's blade sticking out of the gurney and not one drop of blood...

SON OF THE AVENGER

. . .

Trip gasped as he released Caleb's head. Caleb fell to the floor trembling and curled up in a fetal position. Trip stared at him wide-eyed.

"What just happened?" Rodger asked. He kneeled down next to Caleb and pushed his hair back from his face. Caleb flinched and pulled away. The terror in his eyes gave Rodger the heebie-jeebies. "What did you do to him?" he demanded, angrily.

"He hasn't been dreaming," Trip said, somberly. "It's just as I feared. He's been to another dimension. He's seen things that... that would terrify anyone."

"Yo, bruh, how do you know that?" JJ asked.

"Because I was just there with him. I saw everything he saw, except from my own point of view. I was there. He's got good reason to be afraid. You said his girl broke up with him today? Why?"

JJ shrugged. "He didn't say. Just said she wanted him out right away. Like she woke up pissed off or some shit. Who knows? She's like that."

"Has he mentioned the nightmares to either of you?"

They shook their heads. Trip looked ill. He stalked over to Caleb, who was now sitting with his back against the wall, knees to his chest.

"What is going on, Trip? What has him so terrified? I've never seen him like this. Not even when he was a child," said Rodger.

"I suspect the dream he had this morning was the worst one, and she witnessed his reaction. I think he frightened her. I need to find out what it was."

Caleb looked up at him. "Fuck you!"

"I'm sorry, but—"

"I shit myself," Caleb said, quietly.

They all looked at each other.

"That's why she made me leave," he continued. "She thought I was so drunk that I couldn't control myself, and she said my eyes looked weird." He stood up.

Trip looked at Rodger and JJ and said, "Leave us." He knew a scared rabbit when he saw one. And Caleb was about to bolt.

Caleb was shaking his head and practically hyperventilating.

Rodger frowned. "I will not!"

"Rodger—"

"No, Trip!"

"I don't want to remember something that was that bad!" Caleb said. "Please, don't make me relive it."

Trip wasn't listening as he continued to address Rodger.

"It's a matter of life and death, and I'm not asking for your permission. I don't need it. This is what *I* do, Rodger. This is shit that *I* know about. And if you want him to stay safe? I need to know where he's been and what he's seen. I'll say it again. Leave. Us. I'm not asking."

Rodger stepped in front of Caleb. "Twenty-two years, Trip. I raised him. I won't allow you to come here and hurt him."

Trip scoffed. "Hurt him? Rodger! I'm trying to save him! But I can't do that if I don't know what we're up against."

Rodger shook his head. "You're going to have to go through me."

JJ stood with him. "And me."

Trip closed his eyes and exhaled. He didn't want it to be like this. They were incapable of understanding. He met Rodger's eyes. "Okay. He already told you how terrifying it was. Do you really want to see it happen to him for real?

Because that's where this is headed. And if I'm right? Whatever shows up from the Lower Realms to claim him will kill you both, effortlessly, to get to him. Is that what you want?"

"Yo, why should we believe you?" JJ asked.

Desperate times called for desperate measures. Trip opened his wings.

Caleb ran.

4

Caleb was fast, but Trip was faster. He threw his son over his shoulder and carried him to the bathroom then crowded him into the shower.

Caleb was fighting tooth and nail. "Don't touch me! Don't touch me! Get away from me!"

Rodger and JJ burst into the room.

Trip didn't even look at them as he spoke. "Please. I'm saving him. This is happening, with or without your approval. It's gonna get bad. It's gonna look bad. He may lose control of his body again. If you love him, you'll help me. At the very least? Stay the fuck out of my way."

He reached for Caleb's head, and Caleb surprised him with a punch to the nose. A good one, with his non-dominant hand. It didn't deter Trip. Blood flowed down over his upper lip as he placed his hands on either side of Caleb's head. This time when the room faded Caleb didn't scream. He fainted.

... THE STAINLESS STEEL WAS COLD AGAINST CALEB'S FACE AND *chest. He was on his belly, shirtless. He could see another slab across from him. Xavier was on it. In pieces. His head, his hands, both legs below the knee, and his torso. The stench of burned flesh hung heavy in the air. Caleb's stomach roiled, and he leaned his head over the table, releasing its contents onto the floor. He closed his eyes against the morbid sight and took in a few deep breaths. The sharp smell of antiseptic assaulted his nostrils. It was better than the smell of barbecued Xavier. His stomach lurched at the thought, threatening to heave again.*

"What about him? Titus sent him back in pieces, deliberately. You know that, don't you?" a woman's voice said.

Caleb stayed quiet with his eyes closed.

"Oh, I know. Don't you worry. I'll take care of Xavier... and our other guest," a much deeper voice answered.

Caleb's blood ran cold at the sound of it. This place, wherever it was, was bad. Really bad. He just knew it. And he was there alone. What happened to the ambulance crew?

There was the sound of movement behind him. Curiosity won out. He turned to look. The one they called Stryker was on another slab. Staring back at him. Was he dead? As if on cue, Stryker blinked and looked at him, pleadingly. He made a shushing motion with his lips. Caleb nodded. He looked around the room. It was some sort of lab. Where was Sienna? The two that were talking looked over at him.

A woman with dark hair tied up in a ribbon and wearing white robes. She looked like a goddess. Then there was the being she was speaking to, and... it couldn't be. Caleb didn't want to believe his eyes. A dragon walking upright on two legs and dressed like a scientist. It had deep blue reflective scales and yellow reptilian eyes. Caleb wanted to scream, but he couldn't. His throat wouldn't cooperate. The dragon laughed, showing rows of large sharp teeth. Then Caleb saw it had Sienna in its clutches. Its talons were digging into her skin. Caleb's back started to itch. Fuck. The last thing he needed was to try rescuing someone in this godforsaken place, but his body was not receiving the 'stand-down' memos.

The woman talking to the dragon disappeared before his eyes. Holy shit! Where the hell were they? Then the dragon was half-walking, half-dragging Sienna across the room toward a large water-filled container with something floating in it. Air bubbles floated up from the bottom of the tank, surrounding the floating object. Caleb squinted, trying to make sense of what he was seeing, then recoiled. Organs. Female organs with the external genitalia intact. What the fuck?

The dragon pressed Sienna's face against the glass.

"When Minerva gets back, you're going to be trading places with Isabel, here. What do you think of that?" *the dragon asked.*

Sienna screamed. Caleb's back was now on fire. His heart felt like it was being squeezed in a vice. His vision clouded over.

Stryker's eyes grew wide as he watched the transformation on Caleb's face. "Dude! You need to chill! Deep breaths, man!" *he hissed in a forceful whisper.*

Caleb did as he was told, but it wasn't helping.

Minerva reappeared. "Give them to me!" *she demanded.* "You've got Sienna. Honor your promise, dragon!"

"Fine. Cool your jets, Minnie."

And damn, if she didn't reach out and slap the beast. "Never call me that again, you toad!"

The dragon snarled and snapped at her, then unplugged the canister and handed it to her. She disappeared without so much as a "thank you". The beast then turned to Sienna and grinned.

"I've got very special plans for you, my dear. But first, I have these three to deal with. You'll sit there and wait for me like a good little Reaper, won't you?"

She promptly sat on the floor and didn't move. But Caleb could see it in her eyes. Sheer, terror. The pain level of his back was now off the charts. Not only could he feel the muscle separating as his wings forced their way through, but he could also hear it.

"Let her go!" he roared.

The dragon turned to him, surprised. "Oh, ho! What have we here?" He leaned in, looking into Caleb's eyes. "An Avenger! Nice. You'll make a delightful addition to my army. Once I bring Xavier back, he'll show you the ropes."

Another scientist joined them. He leaned in and also looked into Caleb's eyes. He had a handsome human face, Caucasian with short dark hair and crisp features. But his eyes. They contained black sclera with yellow-red irises, and elliptical pupils. Reptilian eyes. They were the stuff of nightmares. Caleb screamed and tried to back away. The being frowned.

"You ain't cute either, Neph," it said, then turned to the dragon. "Where you want to start? The girl?"

The dragon shook its head. "No, she's last. Prepare a new canister. I gave Minerva the other one."

The humanoid looked at Sienna, then licked its lips. "You mind if I have a go first? Hate to waste it."

The dragon shrugged. "Why not? There will be plenty of eggs once I'm done with her. Have at it. Call me when you're finished and when the new canister is ready."

Caleb's eyes clouded over as the sound of rushing blood roared through his ears. Thoughts repeating inside his head, 'Can't let them hurt her! Can't let them hurt her! Can't let them hurt her! Kill them! Kill them! KILL THEM!' There was a loud ripping sound as his wings burst through the skin and opened. Caleb didn't even feel it as he desperately clawed at the stainless steel slab trying to sit up.

The dragon and the humanoid turned to him and smiled. "Looks like you've awakened the Avenger," the dragon said.

Humanoid shrugged. "Saved me from slicing his back open." He shook his head. "Left a bloody mess, though. And white wings, no less. He's good for now. Do we have all of Xavier's parts? I can take care of him first."

The dragon nodded. "Yes, put him back together and wake him up. Meanwhile, I'm going to dismantle the Redeemer and send him back to the Upper Realms. Think they'll get the message?"

Humanoid nodded. "I say you dismantle him and her and have the Avenger deliver the parts, personally. That would knock out all of them. What's that game called when you throw a ball and knock down ten bottles?"

The dragon laughed. "Bowling. And that's called a strike."

"How appropriate," said Humanoid. "Too bad you will lose your Avenger."

"Meh, he's a Nephilim. He's expendable," said the beast.

The dragon went to a closet and returned with a scimitar sword. The thing was massive, yet the beast wielded it like it weighed nothing. It ran a talon along the blade, drawing blood. It licked the cut, then grinned.

"I think it's sharp enough."

The dragon leaned over Stryker, looking at him as if trying to decide. Then he looked over at Xavier.

"Okay, both legs below the knees, both hands at the wrist, the head, and... well, let's just say, the king castrated him before sending him back to me. If I had to guess, I'm going to say the hands went first."

Bile rose in the back of his throat and Caleb closed his eyes, only to have them opened by an invisible force.

"Oh no, Neph," the dragon said. "You will watch. You will watch and you will remember because you're going to relay everything you see and hear."

Stryker met his eyes. "My father's name is Banger. Tell him I love him and I'm sorry for failing."

Without warning and with unbelievable speed, the dragon hacked off both Stryker's hands. All went black as the angel started howling...

WHEN CALEB OPENED HIS EYES, HE WAS STANDING IN HIS shower. Normally, it would be way cool to see an extra pair of feet standing with him, but not when they're bigger than his. Strong arms were gripping him around his midsection, holding him up from behind. Then he remembered his father forcing him to recall the nightmares. He started fighting. "No! Don't touch me!"

"Stop! Stop! Stop! It's over," Trip said, stroking his hair. "You're fine. You're safe. It's okay." He placed his hand over Caleb's forehead and said, "Peace be with you."

The calming effect was immediate and better than any drug Caleb had ever tried. His eyelids fluttered as the memory faded, then dissipated like smoke.

"Yo dude! Your junk is touching my ass," he said.

Trip snorted. "I'm your father. Who cares?"

"I do. It's weird. Back up a little."

Trip complied.

"I lost control again, didn't I?" Caleb asked.

"It's okay. I was expecting it. You had good reason," Trip said.

"Did you wipe my memory?" Caleb asked. "I can't recall

anything." Even the fear had fled. Truth be told, he felt like a million bucks. It was the best he'd felt in weeks.

Trip shrugged. "Just the feelings. Your brain is doing a pretty good job of burying the details. There's no reason for you to recall it ever again, but you never know when certain bits of knowledge or information will come in handy so, it's best that I left it intact."

"So what now?"

"I still need to get you through the portal before your wings come through." Trip said. He reached for a bottle of shower gel, gave it a sniff, then soaped up his hair.

"Portal?" Caleb asked as he followed suit.

"Yes. A doorway, if you will, that exists between our worlds. I don't have the privilege of thought travel so we'll be flying and I'll be carrying you. Make sure you pack light," Trip said. He rinsed off, then stepped out. "Take your time, but hurry."

Caleb nodded.

❧

RODGER AND JJ WERE SITTING ON CALEB'S BED WHEN TRIP returned to the bedroom. Rodger's mouth dropped open as Trip casually removed the towel and started putting his clothes back on. It was one thing for Ileana to fill him in on the details, but to see it live? Yowza. And the angel had zero shame.

JJ voiced it. "No shame in your game, bruh. How's Chip?"

"Forgive me. I always forget how 'modest' human beings are. Nudity isn't a big deal where I'm from, and he's fine. Even freaked out a bit because I was standing too close." He shook his head. "Humans."

Rodger and JJ looked haunted. How much had they heard? He couldn't be sure. "You guys all right?"

They nodded. Though Rodger knew he would never forget what he had walked into after he heard Caleb screaming again. The two of them on the floor of the shower, Trip's hands on Caleb's temples, brown water swirling down the drain, and vomit in Trip's hair. But the worst of it had been their eyes, wide open and glowing, solid white. Rodger had cried out, startled. And neither of them had heard him. Whatever was going on was far above his capacity to understand as a human being. He had quietly left them.

"Guys. It's okay. Here, take my hands. Both of you," Trip said. They did. He closed his eyes and said, "Peace be with you."

Rodger and JJ jerked as if a bolt of electricity had struck them. They looked at each other, stunned. What had just happened and why were they holding hands with Trip?

"Thanks, guys. I really appreciate your help," Trip said, releasing them. "Caleb sure is taking his time. Can you check on him for me, Rodger? It's imperative we get moving."

Rodger shook his head as if to clear it. "Sure thing. Yeah, he takes long showers. Blames it on his hair."

Trip winked at him. "We know better though, right?" he said, twisting his own hair up into a bun and tying it with a strip of leather.

Rodger nodded and chuckled. "To be young and dumb again."

"Speak for yourself," Trip said, teasing.

"Oh, I see how it is," Rodger said. "What are you anyway? Like five, six-hundred years?"

Trip nodded. "Something like that. Still in my prime. Don't hate, old man."

"Fuck you, Trip."

"If only we had the time," Trip shot back.

JJ's eyebrows shot up. "Yo, you really swing like that?" he asked.

Trip smirked. "And then some."

Moments later, they were standing in the living room saying their goodbyes. Rodger embraced Caleb, inhaling the scent of his damp hair, committing it to memory. Then he was kissing Caleb's temple. He turned to Trip.

"Will we see him again? In this lifetime?"

"I don't know, Rodger. I can't say for sure and I'm sorry."

Caleb embraced his cousin. "Take care of Sadie and Stanley for me, will ya?"

JJ nodded. "Of course."

"Oh, and one more thing," Caleb said. He reached for a set of keys hanging on the wall, then placed them in JJ's hand and closed it. "Take care of her, too."

JJ's eyes were wide. "You're giving me the Bimmer? Yo!"

"I think I've got an upgrade coming, right?"

He looked at Trip, who smiled and nodded.

"We gotta roll. I've got a previous engagement and I can't miss it," Trip said.

He lifted Caleb into his arms.

"Listen to me. We're going home now. It requires my flying us to the portal that joins these two dimensions. Even though you have angel blood, you're still human and the passage might make you feel a little queasy. Don't worry. That's normal. Just hold on to me and you'll be fine. Oh, and please, please, please, don't scream."

"Why would I scream?" Caleb asked.

Then he found out why.

Trip hugged his son close, then opened his wings and took off with Caleb screaming the whole way.

"Shiiiiiiiiit!!!"

Once they leveled off, Trip asked, "You okay?"

Caleb nodded, staring up at him wide-eyed.

"Good. We'll be coming up on the portal soon. You ready?"

"Um, sure, I guess," Caleb answered.

"It'll be better if you close your eyes and hold your breath. It's just a few seconds, but it can really fuck with you. Here we go."

Caleb barely had time to close his eyes. *Hold your breath?* He didn't have a choice as it was practically sucked out of him. Suddenly they were still and everything in his stomach came rushing forth. Trip barely had time to get out of the way as Caleb fell to his knees, retching and heaving.

Then everything went black.

5

Caleb opened his eyes and looked up at Trip standing over him, fanning him with his wings. And what a glorious set of wings they were.

He sat up and croaked, "That sucked."

Trip nodded. "Aye, the first time is the worst."

"Am I gonna have wings like that?" he asked.

Trip threw back his head and laughed. "Oy! Look at you. You just finished puking up your guts and all you want to know is will you have my wings?" He pulled Caleb to his feet and added, "Yes, but you've got to earn them. You good?"

Caleb nodded, then promptly leaned over and started heaving again. Trip patiently waited for him to finish.

"Okay, I'm good now," Caleb said, wiping his mouth with the back of his hand. "By the way, what am I supposed to call you?"

"Whatever you're comfortable with," Trip said. "I'm pretty easy to get along with."

They stood at the edge of a forest, a hazy pink-gray mist surrounding them.

"Come on," Trip said as he started walking.

"Where are we?" Caleb asked.

"What I used to call home. I don't live here anymore, but my parents do. You're going to meet your grandparents. You have the same name as my father. It'll thrill him to no end."

"Do they even know about me?" Caleb asked.

Trip nodded. "I told them. Nobody enjoys being blindsided, even with good news."

"I'm good news?"

"Yes, they always wanted me to settle down and factory out a few offspring."

Caleb laughed. "Factory out? Really, Dad?"

Trip shrugged. "You get the picture."

"Are you married?"

"We don't marry per se. We mate and it's for a preset amount of time."

Caleb frowned. "What do you mean?"

"We have a long life expectancy. It's not realistic to commit yourself to someone for life here. It works where you're from because humans have a short life span. So, what we do is get with the one we want to mate with and predetermine how long we're going to be exclusive. At the end of that term, we revisit the conditions and decide if we want to continue."

"How long is the average term?"

"Forty-nine to seventy years, your time."

"Do folks ever end them early?"

"What, like divorce?"

Caleb nodded.

"Sure," said Trip. "It happens."

"So are you mated?"

Trip smiled. "Yes. Her name is Lylac. She's from Venus. You'll be meeting her too."

"Venus? Since when is Venus inhabited?"

"Again, there are a lot of things that exist outside of your reality. To be fair, though, the Venus you know isn't the same one she's from. You're from a dimension we call Terra-3. She's from Terra-4."

"Is she okay with it?"

"With what?"

"Me."

Trip nodded. "She wanted to come along when I came for you. She was more upset about my missing out on seeing you grow up than the fact that you exist."

"But you didn't know. I mean, what else could you do?"

"We know that, but it doesn't make it any easier."

Caleb was pensive. "So, you really meant what you said?"

"About?"

"If you had known, you would have, you know, been there?"

Trip stopped him. "Look at me."

Caleb did.

Trip placed his hands on either side of his son's face. "Had I known about you? Yes, yes and hell yes, I would have been there. Look at you. You're already an adult. I missed everything, and it tears me up like you wouldn't believe. You're a part of me. I'm responsible for your existence. Are you kidding? There's only one being here that may have a problem with you and you've been sketching her."

"Jade? Why would she have a problem with me?"

"She's my goddaughter. I'm like a second father to her. At least, I'm supposed to be."

"Supposed to be?"

"She has a crush on me. Always has. We thought she'd outgrow it, but—" He shook his head. "—she hasn't. She keeps on insisting that someday she will be my mate. Been saying it since before her first septennium."

"Septennium?"

"When you live as long as we do, you don't count the years. Here, the number seven is sacred. So the first forty-nine years of your life get divided into seven-year increments."

"Seven years of seven years?"

"Exactly."

"So how old is she now?"

"In your time, twenty-seven."

"So she's about to celebrate completing her fourth?"

"Yes. The king is hosting a huge bash to celebrate. Normally, she would have already had her coming-out party, but she wanted to wait for her mother."

"You mean like a debutante ball?"

"Precisely. Traditionally, whenever one of his daughters comes of age, it's the duty of a warrior to, uh, break her in, so to speak."

"Really? You don't save yourselves for your first mate?"

Trip scoffed. "Uh, no. And it's a good thing you didn't save yourself either. I would have been hard-pressed to choose someone for you and the best person I can think of is Lylac."

Caleb stopped. "Wait, a minute. You'd allow your wife… er… mate to fuck me?"

"I didn't say that. I said she's the best, and I'd want the best for you."

Caleb chuckled. "Can I be frank with you?"

"Always."

"You could probably set me up with the worst here, and I'd be okay with it. The end result is still the same."

"True. An unskilled hand or mouth works, just takes a little longer, however, I'm known for being an excellent lover and I'll not have it spread around the kingdom that my son is a lousy lay."

"Wait a minute who said I was—"

"How long does it take for you?"

"Excuse me?"

"When you're with a girl. How long does it take for you to come?"

Caleb shrugged. "I don't know! Why are we even discussing this?"

Trip forged ahead. "You're with her, she drops to her knees to service you. When you're finished, does she come up complaining about her jaw being tired or does she stand up grinning all proud and swallowing?"

"What?!" Caleb sputtered.

"I thought we were being frank. It's a straightforward scenario. Which is it?"

Caleb thought for a moment and grinned. "She comes up smiling and wiping her mouth."

"Ugh! You're too quick. We must work on that."

"What do you mean?"

Trip ignored the question and continued, "Do you eat pussy? Please say yes."

"Of course."

"Cool, are you good at it?"

"I get no complaints. Why is my sex life so important?"

"Sex is very important, son. It allows you to connect with another being on a visceral level. Primitive, even. Not to mention it's an outlet. How cranky are you when it's been a while? Why do you think we're able to masturbate? It's a necessary release. I'll never understand why humans see it as a weird badge of honor to deprive themselves of the pleasure of orgasm. Insanity, I say. Even their bodies know it. If they won't take care of themselves, their brain does it for them while they sleep. By the way, I found your stash."

Caleb wasn't waiting for his father to ask him how often he 'took care of himself'. It was time for a subject change.

"So, Ebony wants you to be her first?" he asked.

Trip nodded. "Kiss, yes. But I can't do it. I'm too close to her. We're thinking about asking a warrior from another realm."

"But it's just a kiss."

"You don't understand. She's crazy about me. She'll want more. Something I can't give her. It would only break her heart. It wouldn't be right, and I would never forgive myself if I hurt her that way."

They reached the other side of the forest and entered a clearing where stood a quaint little cottage. It looked like something from out of a Thomas Kinkade painting.

"This is where you grew up?" Caleb asked.

Trip nodded. "I did. It's been about five hundred years since I played here as a cherub."

Caleb blinked. "Five. Hundred. Years."

"Yes."

Before he could respond, a gorgeous redhead came rushing out the front door. "He's here!" she exclaimed. She ran up and stopped in front of him, tears glistening in her eyes. "You look just like your father did when he was your age. So beautiful. I'm Indira. I'm your grandmother."

Not one gray hair. Not one wrinkle. It floored Caleb. And to think, his father was somewhere in the neighborhood of five hundred. What did that make her? The door burst open again and what had to be his grandfather came out. Same blonde hair and blue eyes as his, with a full beard and a smile so brilliant it could cast shadows. Good looks ran in this family, for sure.

"Oy! Look at you, boy! Looking just like my Pubbins!" His booming voice seemed to carry for miles.

Trip frowned. "Da, watch it, you're gonna deafen him and he hasn't even seen the king yet."

Caleb raised an eyebrow. *Pubbins?* He could barely suppress the grin. The conversation on the way to the kingdom was going to be interesting.

Trip shook his head. "Don't."

Big Caleb snorted. "So what? Who cares what Titus has to say, anyway?"

"I'll let him know you said that," Trip said.

"Oy! Please do! Maybe it'll cause his royal kingly ass to come visit an old friend," Big Caleb retorted.

They laughed.

"Come here, boy! Let's have a look at ya!"

Caleb went to his grandfather, who gathered him up into the strongest bear hug ever. He had often wondered about them and what would they think if they knew about him. One thing was for sure. They loved him. Unconditionally. The beast of an angel was squeezing him and speaking to him in hushed tones in some strange language—and Caleb understood it. *What the fuck?*

"We're so sorry, son. We didn't know about you. We have so much lost time to make up for." The big angel buried his nose in Caleb's hair and inhaled. "You even smell the same as your da' did when he was a wee one." He put him down. "Aye, where's my head? What's your name, son?"

"Caleb, sir."

Indira gasped. "Really? Your ma named you Caleb?"

He nodded. "Yes, ma'am."

His grandfather placed his big beefy hands on Caleb's shoulders. "Well, my son, that is one big strong angel name.

We share it. When you're here visiting, we'll call you Junior or Little Caleb, understood?"

"Or you could just call me Chip. That's what my Nanny calls me back home," he said.

"Chip? Hmmm. Why not? You're certainly a chip off the old block. Chip it is, or until you get another nickname," Big Caleb added with a wink.

Okayyy… Whatever that meant.

They spent the afternoon eating, drinking, and being quite merry. Grandpa Caleb served him up a huge stein of mead alongside the stew his grandmother had made. It was the best freaking stew he'd ever eaten, and the best apple pie he'd ever eaten followed it. Caleb pushed his chair back from the table and looked at his grandfather.

"Do you eat like this every day?" he asked while rubbing his very full belly.

Big Caleb laughed. "Every fuckin' day, son. Indira knows how to keep her mate happy." He leaned into him conspiratorially and said, "After you leave, we'll take this party to the bedroom." He winked, then added, "You're welcome to join us anytime."

Caleb looked at him in shocked surprise. "Um—"

"Oy! He means for meals! What the fuck?" Trip said, smacking the back of his head.

Caleb rubbed the smarting spot. "Hey, I didn't know! Especially after that conversation we were having on the way here!"

Big Caleb looked at the two of them. "What did I miss?" Then he realized. "Oh, you thought the invitation was for—"

Then he was laughing so hard his face almost turned purple.

"No, son. I don't share my mate with anybody. She cooks

in the bedroom even better than she cooks in the kitchen. And she is all mine!"

He reached out and pinched her bottom as she passed him. Indira squealed, then playfully swatted him with the dishrag.

"Behave Papa!" she said.

Caleb was speechless. *Could we not do this in front of the kids? Even if they are adults.*

"Da! Come on! Really? I can't with you two," Trip said.

Caleb frowned at his father. "Oh, like that's any worse than what you were grilling me on?"

"I didn't once bring up your mother," Trip said, frowning at his own father who just smiled back at him. Shameless.

"Yes, and could we please keep it that way?" Caleb retorted.

He watched as Indira continued cleaning up with a small smile on her face. Broken filters appeared to be common in this place, and nobody seemed to give a damn.

Trip stood up. "On that note, why don't we leave you two to your 'next course'."

They gave hugs and kisses. Then they left, stopping once on the way so Trip could show him how to bow properly to the king when first greeting him.

Titus received him as warmly as his grandparents had, with open arms.

"It's a pleasure to meet you, son. Allow me to offer you my deepest condolences for the loss of your mother. She was a sweet lady. Would you excuse your father and me for a moment? Have a seat in the hall. It won't take long."

"Yes, sir. Thank you, sir." Caleb said and stepped out.

"Where is she?" Trip asked.

"The stable. Where else?" Titus answered, grinning like an idiot. "Vanessa's last day as a pegasus."

Trip shook his head. "You do realize that you could have avoided the whole thing—"

Titus pointed at his old friend. "Shut it, Avenger!"

Trip laughed. "So is it safe to say the king's quarters will have a 'Do Not Disturb' sign hanging on the knob?"

Titus nodded. "After twenty-something odd years of celibacy? Damn straight."

Trip snorted. "News flash. Blowjobs and masturbation do not count as celibacy."

"Watch your mouth," Titus said. "I kept up my end."

"Right, whatever you say," Trip teased.

"Fuck you," Titus said, then nodded toward the door. "How's he doing?"

"Got to him just in time. Titus, I had to read him and it was bad."

Titus sat down at his desk. "How bad?"

He listened with rapt attention as Trip relayed what he'd seen.

"Wait, Xavier? The same one that—"

Trip was already nodding. "Yes, the same one that tripped Pippa when she was competing for her wings except he was a Fallen."

Titus whistled and ran a hand through his hair. "And they were going to reanimate him? He was in multiple parts?"

Trip nodded. "I didn't think that was possible."

"Oh, it's possible, but it's against the statutes. Why would Drago risk that? He could lose his kingdom. Technically, the only way he could get away with it is if he had a god on his side. Even then, he could still get thrown under the bus. And Minerva? She's been trying to retrieve those eggs ever since he got hold of them. Was she in the room when they discussed what they planned on doing with Xavier?"

"No. She got that canister and rolled."

"So she may not have known what else he was up to."

"Correct. I don't think she was party to that, but she was all over trading Sienna for Isabel which, to me, is just as disturbing."

"Agreed. It speaks to hard feelings against us for Isabel's consequences. Even her own mother understood that she had made her bed. Isabel knew the risks of siding with her father and he burned her. A shame, really."

"Don't tell me you have regrets. Titus, she was straight-up evil. She got what was coming to her. Don't forget what she did to Julian. He was a mere cherub, practically newborn."

"I know, but I can't help feeling like I could have done more to protect her. I knew full well what my brother was capable of and she was no match for him. He knew all along that he had promised her to Drago. She had no idea. Do you think she would have gone along with him had she known?"

Trip couldn't argue. "Aye. I see what you're saying. A lamb to the slaughter. Maybe, the Master took it into consideration when she met Him."

"I like to think so. I like to think that maybe she's finally found peace and has a better incarnation next time."

They both placed their hands over their hearts, bowed their heads, and said, "If it be so. Amen."

Thus offering a prayer for the fallen angel.

"So what do we do now?" Trip asked.

"Let's get through tonight, then find Xavier. See if he is a Fallen. If not, then we'll know what you saw happened in another reality, not this one. That's not to say it still isn't going on, but at least our young ones are safe."

"Aye, agreed."

"So is that everything?"

"Well, there is one more thing."

"Ok?"

"He got into a fight before we left. His hand is swollen, may even be broken. And, uh um…"

"What is it you're hesitating to say?"

"He's got tattoos."

Titus shrugged as if to say "And?".

"Dragons."

Titus frowned and shook his head. "I'll take care of it. A lot of black, I'm sure."

Trip nodded.

Titus winced. "It's gonna hurt."

"I kinda figured. Can you do it quick? Like ripping off wax?"

Titus suppressed a grin. Only his resident freak would think of hot wax whereas anyone else would've thought Band-Aid.

"Of course," he said, then pointed at the door. "Now, get out. Send in your son. Go see your goddaughter. And Trip?"

"I know. I know. She's going to be livid."

"Maybe not. She may surprise you."

"She point blank asked me, Titus."

"She was five years old. She didn't even know what she was asking you. And if my memory serves me, you never really answered her."

"A technicality," Trip said.

He sighed, then headed to the stable to face the music.

"The king wants to see you," he said as he passed Caleb in the hallway.

When Caleb entered the king's office, Titus was rolling up his sleeves.

"Remove your shirt, please," he said.

Caleb complied. The king stared at his chest and arms, frowning. He twirled his pointer finger, signaling Caleb to turn around. He did. When he faced the king again, Titus was shaking his head.

"This will not do. How much did you spend on that work?" he asked.

Caleb looked down at his arms. "It's over a thousand dollars' worth and a lot of hours."

"Yeah, I was afraid of that. You have a lot of black ink. That had to hurt some."

Caleb shrugged. "Nothing I couldn't handle."

Titus sighed. "Good. This is going to hurt like hell, but it'll be quick. You have dragons tatted down your arm. They have to go. Dragons are Lower Realm dwellers. We don't worship them here. As a human, I get why your species has an obsession with them, but understand something. They ain't all that."

Without warning, Titus raised his hands and opened them. A flash of purple-white light shot out from them and Caleb gasped, then watched in fascinated horror as the black ink lifted from his skin. The tiny dark droplets floated in the air for a moment, then dissipated.

It was one thing to sit for ink work with a triple tip. Hurt like a son of a bitch. But to have all of it undone at one time? It felt like a million razors had just lifted out of his skin, leaving his arm an angry inflamed red. He stood with his eyes and mouth wide open.

"Easy son. Breathe into it. It's over. You're okay. Breathe," the king was saying.

Breathe? Breathe?! Caleb didn't want to breathe. He wanted to scream, but no sound was coming out. The air was flowing the wrong way.

Then Titus took the swollen hand into both of his and closed his eyes for a moment.

"It's not broken. Some ice on it tonight will do the trick.

Same for the arm. Cool compresses tonight. Tomorrow you'll be good as new. Sorry about the ink reversal. They suck balls. I hated to do it, but folks in the kingdom would judge your father for allowing you to sport that. It would be humiliating. I hope you can understand."

Caleb nodded, still too stunned to speak. After all, a million bees were currently stinging his arm. He hissed and watched as the arm continued to redden.

"You a drinker?" Titus asked, opening the top drawer to his filing cabinet.

Caleb nodded.

Titus poured two shots and passed one to him. "Bottoms up. Welcome to the Upper Realms."

6

"Ebony! Wait up!" Stryker called to his friend. She was flying ahead of him, weaving in and out of the upper branches.

"Try and catch me!" she yelled back, laughing. Just as he caught up to her, one of his wings snagged a branch. He cried out, then fell to the ground. Ebony gasped. "Stryker!" He was lying on his back, moaning. "Are you okay? Let me see." She tried to roll him, then he reached out and grabbed her.

"Gotcha!" He exclaimed.

"You asshole! I thought you were hurt!"

"Awww. You really do care." He reached up and tucked a curly lock behind her ear. Then he sat up and leaned in.

She leaned back. "Stryker, come on. You know I don't feel that way about you."

"Sure you do. You're just afraid to admit it," he said with his signature cocky grin.

No question, the guy was hot as hell. With his almost black hair, green eyes, and sun-bronzed skin. When they first met back in secondary school, his hair was a sloppy mop of dark waves that insisted upon hanging in his eyes. Now, he kept it short and sported a goatee. He could have any female he wanted. All he had to do was flash that dazzling smile. But he insisted upon pursuing her, the one that was always saying "no". She suspected that was part of the appeal for him. Enjoying the chase and whatnot. That's not to say he didn't make the rounds, after all, a guy had needs. And there was no shortage of females willing to fulfill them. Still, she was the one he always came back to. The one he liked to hang out with. The one he shared his most private thoughts and dreams with. They were best friends and Ebony wanted it to stay that way. Lord knows, there were plenty of chicks jealous of her for being so close to him. Of course, the assumption was they were sleeping together when they never even so much as kissed. The truth of the matter was she was still a virgin, saving herself for her own unrequited dreamboat, Trip. Never mind the fact that he was her godfather, and she'd known him all her life. She swore up and down that someday she was going to marry the avenging angel and she wanted him to be the only one she would ever give herself to.

She'd been saying it ever since she was a child and still half-human. A series of unfortunate events caused her to have to move to her father's kingdom sooner than she was originally supposed to. Back then she was wingless and her mode of transport became a black pegasus named Vanessa, who housed her mother's soul. That time was soon ending, now that Ebony had earned her own wings. Her mother's soul would be free and her parents would be back together. The thought reminded her she had someplace to be.

"I've got to go. I'll catch up with you later?" She said as she took to the sky.

"Sure. I'll stop in later on," he said, but she was already clearing the trees. He shielded his eyes from the sun with a hand as he watched her go. "Someday, Ebony Jade, someday," he whispered.

Ebony flew into the stable that was home to her mare. Vanessa looked at her and started pawing the ground.

Ebony laughed. "Okay, one more time."

She turned and started running. Five, four, three, two, one... then came the thunder of hooves. Just as the mare caught up to her, Ebony took flight with the horse close behind. They spent the afternoon flying and chasing each other. It was bittersweet. After waiting over twenty years, her mother was finally returning to human form. Ebony knew her father was counting down the days. They had some wonderful memories and some not-so-wonderful, but this would be one of the good ones. A shrill whistle came from down below. Trip! They turned and flew back to the stable. He was wearing jeans and a white t-shirt. That meant one thing. He'd been to Terra-3. She could smell it on him. The horrible air quality there had a way of permeating one's clothes and hair.

"Ugh! Terra-3 today? What's up?" she asked.

"We need to talk," he said. Then he turned to Vanessa. "Milady, would you excuse us?" The horse nodded and strolled out to the adjoining meadow. Trip still saw her as the queen, even in her current form. They all did. They loved her before and her return was eagerly awaited, not just by the king. He sat down on a bale of hay and patted the spot next to him. She sat down and turned to him, doe eyes wide with anticipation.

"What is it, Trip?"

"Why don't you call me uncle anymore? I miss that."

She blushed. "I'm an adult now. I'd like to be seen as equal."

Read: It would be creepy to lust after someone referred to as uncle.

He smiled. "I see. Look at these." He pointed to a smattering of crescent-shaped scars on his forearm. "You remember where they're from?"

She nodded. "You got them the day I was born. You were Mom's coach while Daddy delivered me."

"That's right. They're important to me because they mean something. You are important to me, Ebony. Nobody could ever replace you in my life. Do you understand?"

She nodded, suddenly wary of what he may have to say. He rarely called her Ebony unless she was in trouble, or he had something to tell her that he thought would upset her. Well, she knew she wasn't in trouble, but what could it be? She swallowed, her mouth suddenly dry.

He continued. "Do you remember when we lived on Terra-3? You were pretty small—"

"I remember," she said, quietly.

"Do you remember Miss Llewelyn?" he asked.

She was already gearing up to be pissed. He could feel it. The temperature in the stable seemed to drop ten degrees.

"Yes. I remember her. Is that where you were today?" she asked.

He nodded. "Listen, something happened between me and her back then. We—"

"You had sex with her, didn't you?"

"Yes, I—"

"But you lead me to believe you didn't. That what happened with her was just you making sure she was safe. That's what you said. You said you were making sure she was safe just like you do with me."

"Bean, listen—"

She stood up, glaring at him. "So, you went there today to see about something that happened with her over twenty years ago? How is she?" She said with no attempt to hide the sarcasm.

Trip was tired of being on the defensive. In the grand scheme of things, he really didn't owe her an explanation. This was a fucking courtesy. All those years of handling her with kid gloves when it came to his sex life were taking their toll. He knew how she felt about him and he had told her, repeatedly, that it would never happen. He could never bring himself to look at her in the same light that she saw him in. He had changed her diapers for Chrissake! No way he could even remotely entertain the idea of a sexual relationship with her. As far as she was concerned, he walked on water. The sun rose and set on him in her world. And he knew the only way to change that would be to change her view of him. Was that why he had never done it? He didn't want her to change how she saw him? No, it was because it would require him to break her heart and he couldn't bear the idea of seeing that kind of hurt in her eyes, especially if he caused it. There was no getting around it this time. He steeled himself for the onslaught.

"She's dead, Ebony. Okay?" He spoke the words with a slightly sharp edge. "She died in a plane crash. Feel better now?" he said, giving it right back to her. After all, she was an adult now. Right?

Ebony gasped and clapped a hand over her mouth, shaking her head. Had he really just said it like that? Is that the impression she left him with? No wonder he couldn't be interested in her. She was a stone-cold bitch. Anybody who could wish harm on another couldn't be anything else.

"I… I… I don't know what to say. I'm sorry, Trip. I was so busy being wrapped up in my own feelings I never considered yours. Please forgive me."

Well, shit. "Bean, there's nothing to forgive, but I still have something to tell you."

"Oh, well, what is it?"

He took a deep breath. "Yes, we had sex that night and I haven't seen her since."

"How did you find out she died?"

"How do you think?"

"Blaze?"

"Blaze."

"I see. So you had to go back to attend the funeral of someone you barely knew all those years ago?"

He shook his head. "Not quite."

"I don't understand."

"That's because I haven't gotten to the point yet."

She gave a nervous laugh. "How bad can it be?"

A male voice from behind her spoke. "Hey, Dad. You out here? The king said you'd probably still be here."

Her eyes met his as her mouth fell open. When she spoke, it was barely above a whisper. "She got pregnant?"

He nodded. "Yes."

If he lived to be two thousand years old, he would never forget the look on her face at that moment. It was far beyond heartbreak. And it was his fault.

"A son?" she asked, her voice now shaking. Tears were welling up in her eyes.

"Yes. His name is Caleb." *And right now, I need my sword so I can fall on it.*

He always knew this day would come. The day the pedestal tipped and he would fall from grace. And fall he did.

Ebony couldn't say anything else. She didn't trust herself to do so. Especially since someone had just sent a wrecking ball right through her chest. She felt more than heard the heavy footsteps approaching. Then his voice again.

"Oh, there you are. I... Dad? Are you okay?"

From Caleb's vantage point, he could only see his father, and the look on his face was nothing short of devastation.

"Uh, son, could you give us a minute, please?"

His words were the impetus needed to break the spell. Ebony shook her head and wiped the tears from her face. "No, no, you spend time with your... uh... son. I've got... uh... things... to... uh..."

She turned and stumbled past Caleb, evading any contact. She didn't even look at him. She couldn't. Not yet.

"Ebony, wait!" Trip called to her.

Then she was running. Running as fast as her legs could carry her. Never mind that she could never outrun or out-fly him. She didn't care. She just needed to be anywhere but there. She took off towards the tree-line at the edge of the kingdom. As a cherub, it was the boundary she was told to never cross. Well, she was an adult now, wasn't she? Just as she was about to exit, a dark form flew in front of her, blocking her exit. Vanessa. The black mare hovered in front of her, snorting. Ebony tried to dodge her, but the horse was faster and she wasn't about to let her leave the kingdom.

"Mom, please?" Ebony begged as fresh tears rolled down her cheeks.

The mare wouldn't budge. Ebony dropped to the ground, sobbing. Vanessa followed, then stood licking away her daughter's tears. Funny how things come full circle. The last time this happened Ebony was five, and it was the morning after Trip conceived his son. Ebony had practically accused him of cheating on her. Vanessa had sent her to her room in tears. Now, here they were again dealing with the same situation.

"He lied to me, Mom. He lied to me!"

The mare shook her head.

"Yes, he did! He said he didn't—"

The mare stomped a foot on the ground and shook her head again, but Ebony wouldn't be swayed.

"He did too! I hate him! I hate him! I hate him! I hate him!"

The mare stomped the ground again and neighed, loud.

Ebony looked up at her mother, sobs still hitching her chest.

"It's not fair," she whispered. Defeated.

Vanessa nuzzled her and licked her cheek, patiently waiting for the tantrum to pass. She wished she could tell her daughter to let it all out, that it would get better with time. That what she was feeling would pass and everything would be all right. Most of all, she wished she could wrap her daughter up in a hug and make it all better. Soon enough…

After a while, Ebony stood up and wiped her eyes, then ran a hand through her mother's mane. "I meant to cut a braid for you," she said.

Vanessa lifted her head and struck a ridiculous pose. Ebony snickered. She couldn't help it. It was funny. Then she plaited a braid in that glorious mane. Tearing a strip of fabric from her shirttail, she tied off the end. Vanessa turned toward the kingdom, looked back at her daughter, then signaled her to follow. Ebony did her one better. She climbed on her back and grabbed the mane with both hands. "One last time, Mommy. Let's go home."

The horse neighed her approval, then took to the sky.

They arrived back at the palace to find Trip and his son gone. Ebony carefully cut the braid and tied the other end off.

"I'll present it to you tonight at the party."

The mare nodded her approval.

"Do you think his son will be there?"

Another nod, followed by a snort.

"Do you think I'm overreacting?"

The mare nodded vehemently, then stopped and shook her head.

"Thanks, Mom."

Vanessa nuzzled her and licked her ear.

"I'm gonna go get ready. I love you. I'll see you tonight."

The mare watched as her daughter made her way across the meadow and entered the palace.

"I love you, too, sweetie," she said.

7

Trip didn't know what to say after Ebony took off. For a moment he considered going after her, then decided against it. Better to let her cool off.

"Was that her?" Caleb asked.

Trip nodded. "Yes."

"She seemed awfully pissed off."

"Really? You think?" Trip retorted, irritably.

"Was it because of me?" Caleb asked.

Trip sighed and shook his head. "No. It was because of me."

"I'm at a loss here. Could you bring me up to speed?"

Trip nodded. "Yeah, it's a long story. Let's go somewhere else."

He glanced at Caleb's arm and winced.

"I see Titus took care of that. Sorry, I know it sucked."

Caleb shrugged and said, "Nothing I couldn't handle."

Trip gave him the side-eye. "Oh, really? Then it won't matter how I lift you for flight?"

Caleb frowned at him. "Just don't touch it."

"Thought so," Trip said, slinging Caleb over his shoulders.

They found themselves at The Edge, a small pub on the outskirts of the kingdom. It was owned by the king's eldest son, Darius, but ever since he took over as head of the king's army he rarely had time to run it. The job went to his younger sister, Coral, and her boyfriend, Sed.

Father and son took a booth at the back of the bar. Trip ordered two large steins of mead, then told Caleb the entire story.

It took a while and by the time he finished; Lylac, Pippa, and Blaze had joined them, ready to get their pre-party buzz on.

"So, Uncle Trip, are you going to give our girl her first kiss?" Blaze asked, teasing his old friend.

"Fuck you, Blaze, you know I'm not."

"I don't know. I think the king may have other ideas. You may want to see him first."

Trip rolled his eyes. "Enough already, all right?"

"How'd she take it, Trip?" Pippa asked, nodding towards Caleb.

"As well as you're thinking she did."

She hissed and winced. "Sorry, sweetie. You know, I kinda figured she would have outgrown that whole crush thing by now. Wow."

"Can I make a suggestion?" Caleb asked.

"What's that?" Trip said.

"Why don't you just do it?" Caleb said.

Blaze nodded in agreement. "Yeah, just make it all lousy and sloppy. She'll change her mind then."

"No! I'm not doing it! Can we please talk about something else? It's bad enough she's probably not even speaking to me."

"But—" Blaze began.

"I said no! And the next being that mentions it is getting throat punched! Got it?"

Pippa leaned into Caleb and said. "Betcha never figured your dad to be so damned sensitive, huh?"

Trip's eyes narrowed. "I heard that, Red."

He reached out and plucked a feather from her wing.

"Ouch! Motherfucker!" she hissed at him while vigorously rubbing the tender spot.

"Wanna go for the whole wing?" he challenged.

"Let's not go there, guys, okay?" Lylac interjected. She'd been through just such an ordeal, and it was not pleasant.

"Sorry, babe," Trip said to her, then turned to Pippa. "You know you're not above a throat punch, Guardian."

She turned to Blaze. "Are you gonna let him talk to me like that?"

"Trip, stop. Don't threaten my wife like that," Blaze said, dryly.

"Oh, yeah, that was convincing. You're just as bad as he is," she said to him, then rolled her eyes as Trip gave her mate a fist bump. That lightened the mood considerably, and they ordered another round.

Just as their drinks arrived, Trip felt he was being summoned. He looked at Caleb.

"Hey, this is normal here. So don't freak out, okay? Blaze?"

Blaze nodded. "Got it. See you soon."

Caleb watched in shocked horror as his father disappeared right before his eyes.

"It's okay, bruh," Blaze said, "the king summoned him. He'll be back."

Caleb nodded, then tipped his shot back. *Boy, is this place ever weird.* He couldn't help thinking.

◈

Titus was tightening the strings on his dress leathers when Trip arrived.

"Everything okay?" Trip asked.

"I don't know. You tell me. Is it?"

Trip shrugged. "I guess. I haven't seen her since this afternoon. I think she's avoiding me."

"Can you blame her?" Titus asked.

"Come on, Titus. You too? I already feel like the resident asshole here. Yet, for the life of me, I can't figure out what the hell I did wrong."

"You did nothing wrong. I called you here for a job."

"Oh, what do you need?"

Titus turned to him. "I need you to give her what she wants."

Trip blinked. "What?"

"You heard me. She wants you to be her first kiss, so give it to her." He said it so matter-of-factly, they may as well have been talking about the weather.

"No!"

Titus's eyebrows shot up. "No?"

"Come on, Titus, don't do this to me. I'm begging you. Get Blaze to—"

"She wants you. She's been saying it ever since she could, well, say it. What's the big deal? You gave Coral hers."

"Titus, you know what the big deal is. She's gonna want more."

"Just give her the kiss, Trip, okay?"

"Do I have a choice?"

"No. Not only do you not have a choice, warrior, but you'd better make it good."

The fuck? "Make it good?"

"Yes, make her toes curl. I know you know how."

Trip stared at him, half expecting him to burst into gales of laughter. Hoping. When it didn't happen, he quietly asked, "Why are you doing this to me?"

Titus pinned him with a severe glare. "I'm not doing anything to you. I'm simply giving my princess what she wants. End of discussion. Dismissed."

After Trip disappeared, Titus stood staring at himself in the mirror. He had his suspicions, and he hoped that he was right. For Trip's sake, he prayed that he was right.

"Everything okay?" Caleb asked upon his return.

"It's fine," Trip answered curtly, then flagged the barmaid. "Double shot of triple tequila, please? Make it two."

"Jesus. That bad?" Blaze asked.

"You don't want to know. Hey, it's a celebration, right? Let's get fucking merry!" Trip said.

"Well, what did the king—" Caleb began.

His father shook his head. "Rule number one, I'm a warrior. When a warrior gets an order, he doesn't discuss it. Not even with you. Understood?"

Caleb nodded. "Yeah. Sure. Okay."

"Good," Trip raised his glass. "To princesses."

They all followed suit. "To princesses."

Ebony put the last touches on her make-up and smoothed her leathers. Everyone would be wearing dress leathers. She had received special permission to wear white because she wanted to match with Trip. But after the shock and letdown of the afternoon, the last thing she wanted was to match him. As it was, she couldn't bear the idea of having to deal with him at all, not yet. And what of his son, Caleb? She didn't even know what he looked like since she refused to look at him. She frowned. He probably looked like Miss Llewelyn. Which would mean he was very good looking. Even though she had despised the woman a long time ago, she couldn't deny the fact that she was very attractive. Her best feature was her eyes. They were gray, and she also had a pretty mouth. It never occurred to her as a five-year-old all the things Miss Llewelyn could have possibly done to him with her pretty mouth. Back then the worst crime would have been kissing, but now? Well, she wasn't five anymore, and the thought made her heart hurt. Her nose burned as the tears threatened to well up again. She shook her head and held it up. No. She would not shed another tear over it. He was an adult. Of course, he was going to do adult things. Just because she was saving herself for him didn't mean he was saving himself for her. Well, that was obvious, wasn't it? "Mini Llewelyn" was a testament to that. Yeah, no dress whites for her. It was time she became her own being. She would wear her usual black. Teenage rebellion at its finest, even though she was almost thirty. She didn't care. It was how she felt. And as she looked at herself one last time, her eyes fell upon her necklace. It was half of a heart on a silver chain. A gift from him on her seventh birthday, the first day of her second septennium. He had the other half, and he never took it off. It was the same for her. She had worn it for twenty years straight. She sighed. It was time to let him go. She reached up and removed it, placing it on her nightstand. There. It was done. Now she could truly say she was an adult.

She was leaving behind the childish ideas and notions that it represented to her. Done and done. Now, she needed a good stiff drink. No way she could face him or his son sober. She quickly stuffed the plait from her mother's mane into her pocket, then headed to The Edge.

The place was hopping and in full swing when she arrived. It seemed everybody else had the same idea she did. Get that buzz on before the party. Who knows? There might even be a hook-up party afterward. Who was she kidding? There was always a hook-up party after every major celebration. Why should that night be any different? She was surprised to see Darius tending the bar. A rare thing. She took a seat.

"How come you're here?" She asked.

"Stopped in to relieve Coral and Sed so they could change. You ready for tonight?"

"I'm about to be. Double shot of triple tequila, please," she said.

Darius shook his head. "Uh no."

"Why not? I'm an adult now."

"I said no, Beaner. Pick something else."

A hand slapped the bar, then Stryker said. "She'll have a Himalayan Mudslide."

Darius shook his head. "I thought you were her friend. What are you doing? No!"

"All right, then I'll have one," said Stryker.

Darius nodded, then went off to prepare the concoction. Somewhere at the back of the bar, a group was getting rowdy.

She heard her sister, Pippa, "No way! It's your turn to drink!" Followed by pounding on the table amid the chant. "Chug! Chug! Chug!"

Stryker turned to her. "Now that group is having fun. Let's go!"

Darius arrived with his order, then slid a shot in front of his sister. "You're gonna want to stay here," he said, making eye contact with Ebony. Then his eyes went to her throat. Noticing the necklace was no longer there, he added, "Trust me."

She knew what that meant. Trip was with them.

"It's okay, Darius, really," she said.

"You sure? He's not alone." Oh, so Caleb was with him, too.

She nodded, then tossed back the shot he had given her. She winced and shuddered. "What the fuck was that?"

"What you ordered. Double shot of triple tequila. Feeling all grown up yet?"

She sat up straight and said. "Fine, I'll have another."

"No, no, no, you don't want that," Stryker said. Even he had limits.

She grabbed his glass and tipped it back, almost gagging. "Jesus, Stryker! What's in that?"

He laughed and finished the drink. "Ask your brother. He made it."

Darius shrugged. "A little bit of this, a little bit of that, and a whole hell of a lot of alcohol. You good?"

She nodded. "Of course." *Just don't ask me to walk yet.*

Stryker was way ahead of her as he guided her off the barstool and steadied her. "Just hold on to me, yeah?" He said in her ear. She nodded. Then they were making their way to the back of the bar.

Pippa spotted her first. "Hey! There she is," she said, running up and giving her baby sister a squeeze.

Lylac followed suit. "You okay, sweetie? I know it was a shock. Trust me, nobody was more surprised than he was."

Ebony returned her sister's hug. *I beg to differ*. She thought as she peeked over Lylac's shoulder. Trip and Blaze were sitting together and watching her. Where was Caleb? She had already steeled herself for the introduction. Trip stood up as she approached the table.

"Hey," he said.

"Hey, Uncle Trip," she said, forcing a smile.

Ah, so it's like that, is it? He thought. When he told her he missed her calling him that; this was not what he had in mind. This felt like he was being put at arm's length and he didn't like it. They needed to work this out. "I thought we were wearing white," he said.

She looked down at her black leathers and shrugged. "I changed my mind." She watched as his eyes drifted to her throat.

"I see. Is that all you've changed your mind about? Where's your heart?"

She gave a nervous laugh. "Oh, I must have left it on my nightstand or something. Sorry. Where's your son?"

He ignored her question. "I gave that to you for completing your first septennium. You've never taken it off. Why now?"

Was he angry? So what? She couldn't be concerned with that. She was angry too, and she wasn't about to back down. "It's time for me to put away childish things. Don't you think, Uncle Trip?"

Immediately sensing the tension, everyone else slipped back to the table to leave the two of them to their business. Everyone except for Stryker. He was waiting to see fireworks. Lylac grabbed him by the ear and dragged him away.

"My gift was childish?" Trip asked.

"No, but, I was a child when you gave it to me. A lot of things went on when I was a child, and it's kinda silly of me to still hold on to them. I mean, I—"

He grabbed her by the hand and practically dragged her

out the rear exit door, slamming it behind them. Whoa. This was new. She'd seen him angry before, but not like this and not with her. Maybe she'd taken things a bit too far?

"Uncle Trip—"

"Stop!"

"But—"

"No! It's my turn, now, and you will stand there and you will listen. Do you understand?!"

"You're yelling at me," she said, quietly.

"You're an adult now. You can take it. You wanted my attention? You've got it."

Alas, Princess Ebony was about to get schooled on choosing one's wishes wisely.

8

Caleb had missed all the excitement, human bladder prevailing. He returned to the table and looked around. "Where's my father?"

"King business again. He'll be back." Blaze said.

Caleb took his seat, then noticed a new face at the table staring at him wide-eyed. "Hi," he said, offering his hand.

Lylac said, "Oh, I'm sorry. Caleb, this is Stryker. Stryker, Caleb. He's—"

"Trip has a son?" Stryker asked, making no attempt to shake the hand offered. Instead, he leaned back and crossed his arms. "Huh."

Blaze frowned and kicked him under the table.

Stryker jumped then said, "Oh yeah, right, nice to meet you." He gripped Caleb's hand and squeezed.

Caleb returned it. This game wasn't new to him. In his world, the opponent was usually a jock, mainly football or wrestling. Most of the time not very attractive, but this guy was gorgeous even to him. What was his problem anyway?

"Really, Stryker? A dick measuring contest? Here? Now?" Blaze seethed.

Stryker released Caleb's hand. "Aw c'mon. It's all in fun. Besides, he's Trip's son. He's no pussy, right?"

Caleb nodded. "Right. No harm done." His hand was throbbing, but he would be damned before he'd let this asshole know it.

Stryker looked at Blaze. "See?"

Blaze wanted to punch the smart ass motherfucker right in the mouth. It was obvious Stryker was going to have a problem with Caleb since he had been trying to hook-up with Ebony for as long as he'd known her. Everybody knew it. And now that Trip had a son, there would be competition. Big time. Blaze decided he was going to enjoy watching the young Redeemer strikeout.

"What are you, about three seps?" Stryker asked.

Caleb nodded. "Yeah, give or take."

"So that would mean you came to be at about the time Ebony first moved here." He gasped, "Your mother is the schoolteacher, isn't she?"

Caleb's eyes narrowed. "Why? What would you know about it?"

"I know Ebony's not crazy about your mom."

"Well, Stryker, Ebony doesn't have to worry about my mom. She's dead."

The others were watching the verbal match like tennis spectators. All eyes were on Stryker now, waiting. At least, he had the decency to show contrition. Never mind the waves of pain radiating off of Caleb. They could all feel it.

Stryker said, "Yo, man, I'm sorry. I didn't... I didn't know."

"No, you didn't. But hey, you and Ebony are more than welcome to go celebrate that little nugget of information later," Caleb retorted. He signaled the barmaid, who wasted no time responding.

"What can I get for you, cutie?" Helene asked, coyly tossing her red curls.

He remembered what his father had ordered earlier. "A double of triple strength tequila, please."

"You are definitely your father's son, honey. You got it," she said, then went to fill the order.

"Caleb, that stuff is no joke. Even for us. You may want to rethink that," Blaze suggested.

"Yeah, Caleb, maybe you should rethink that, being human and all," Stryker said, all remorse now gone.

Blaze had had enough. "You know what, Stryker? Why don't you shut the fuck up and put away your dick! Nobody even invited you."

"I don't need an invitation. I'm with the birthday girl," Stryker retorted.

"Uh, no, you're not," Pippa said. "Right now, Trip is with her. So why don't you just go home? We've got this."

"No, I think I'll stick around to make sure my friend is okay. I'm sure this—" he nodded at Caleb, "—came as quite the shock."

Blaze scowled. "You're not sticking around to make sure she's okay, you're here to make sure she doesn't fall for him."

"Fuck you, Blaze!" Stryker said, standing up.

Blaze stood, too. "No, fuck you, Stryker! None of this is any of your goddamn business."

"Yes it is, Ebony—" Stryker began.

Blaze cut him off. "Yeah, Ebony. So if you want to know what's going on or what you missed, you can ask her later."

Stryker's eyes narrowed. "Wait, a minute. She hasn't even met him yet, has she?"

"Again, mind your damn business."

"She is my business, asshole. We're friends. I care about her feelings."

Blaze scoffed. "No. You care about whether or not she has feelings for you. How many times has she told you 'no', Stryker? I'm not an idiot. I'm sure you've tried."

"Now who's digging into someone else's business? Take your own damn advice and mind yours," Stryker retorted.

"Well, there's where we differ, Stryker. I'm family. So if something affects her? It is my business. Trust and believe I will damn well make it so."

"And that's what's really going on here, isn't it? You're all trying to hook her up with him," he said, pointing at Caleb.

The accusation stepped on everyone's toes.

Pippa spoke first. "And what if we were? Like Blaze said, it would be none of your business. You say she's your friend. Well, she's my baby sister and I really care about her feelings with no ulterior motive. From where I stand, your friendship appears to have strings attached. Some wishful thinking on your part, maybe?"

"Exactly," Lylac chimed in. "How much of a friend would you still be if they did hook up? You'd drop her like a hot tomato."

"It's potato," Pippa said to her sister out the side of her mouth.

"Whatever! He knows what I meant."

Caleb waved his arms. "Uh, hello? Could we not talk about the human as if he weren't here?"

Helene returned with his order, and he wasted no time, downing it in one gulp. Everyone froze. Holy shit!

"What?" he asked.

"I think you've got more angel in you than we first thought," Blaze said.

"Why?" Caleb asked.

Stryker said, "Because, human, that shit you just tossed

back is known for putting hair on one's chest—" he glanced at Caleb's lap, "—or balls."

Pippa scoffed. "Wait for it."

They all turned to her.

"What do you mean?" asked Blaze.

"How quickly you forget. I was human, too, when I first came here. And I pulled that same stunt with an Avalanche. It's got a delay."

"I'm fine," Caleb insisted, even though he could already feel the initial effects of the powerful spirit.

"You're gonna be on your ass in less than ten minutes," Pippa informed him.

Stryker stood smirking at him. Damn if he wasn't waiting for it to happen.

Caleb addressed Stryker. "Why don't you join me, 'friend'? You said it yourself. I'm no pussy."

That wiped the smile off his face. Stryker flagged Helene. "Two Avalanches please."

"And another double of triple strength tequila," Caleb added.

She nodded and left.

"Caleb, I don't think that's such a good idea," Lylac said.

"Why not? What's good for the goose. If he's going to challenge me to drink with him, he needs to catch up."

"You ordered that for me?" Stryker sputtered. "I don't drink that shit!"

Caleb leaned back and smirked. "I see. Well then, it looks like I misjudged you. I've already shown that I'm no pussy, but you?" He shrugged. "I don't know."

Stryker knew he was being goaded, but there was no way he was going to allow this human to drink him under the table. Hangover be damned.

"Fine, bring it," he said.

Blaze shook his head. Should he stop this and risk embarrassing Caleb or just let the chips fall where they may? He had to admit, Caleb was hanging in like a champ. No surprise there. His father was one fierce warrior. And therein lay the answer. Trip would let it play out. So be it.

Helene returned in record time and placed the drinks on the table.

"Blaze! Do something!" Pippa demanded, alarmed.

"No."

"But they're going to—"

"No."

"He's going to be—"

He leveled her with a glare. "I said no."

She stood up. "Fine, but I don't have to watch." She gave it one more try. "Don't do this, Caleb. It's not worth it. He's not worth it."

Caleb raised the Avalanche. "Cheers." Then he tipped it back and guzzled.

"Fucking men and their testosterone," Pippa grumbled as she stalked off.

"Yeah, I'm not so sure I want to see this either," Lylac said then followed her sister.

Blaze was on his own on this one. He calmly watched as the two matched each other drink for drink. The pace picked up when they switched to mead. If he was a gambler, his money would be on Stryker simply because of his biology. He had to hand it to Caleb, though. He was hanging in there, but Blaze could tell he wouldn't be able to continue much longer. Something would have to give. It was just a matter of time before his stomach or his bladder would give it up and when that happened Caleb would have no choice but to stand up. One thing was for sure. Caleb would have one hell of a hangover in the morning.

Stryker stood. "Time to drain the lizard. Another round?"

Caleb shook his head. "Nah, man. I'm good."

"Maybe you're right. We could use some food. The bacon cheeseburgers are killer here. You like onions?"

Caleb swallowed. Food was the last thing he wanted. As it was, he already knew he was going to be puking his guts up before the night was over. The question was, when? And Stryker was dead set on rushing it along. No point in backing down now. If he ate, he would at least have something in his stomach besides alcohol.

He nodded. "Sure. Whatever you're having."

"Cool. Helene!" Stryker called to her on his way to the men's room.

"Are you fucking stupid?" Blaze asked him after Stryker left.

"No, but—"

"You do realize he's trying to make you puke, right?"

Caleb nodded. Bad move. He could already feel his gorge rising. He swallowed.

"Yeah, that's your mouth preparing for what's coming," Blaze informed him.

"I'm fine." Caleb insisted and swallowed again.

"Sure you are. I'll wager you won't even get one bite in before it all comes back up."

"I'm fine," Caleb said again, this time with less resolve and more swallowing.

Stryker returned. "I ordered two specials. The bacon cheeseburger with everything and a side of fries. Cool?"

Blaze was staring at him, scrutinizing. His eyes narrowed. Stryker ignored him.

Caleb was also watching. "What gives?" he asked, speech badly slurred.

"You want to tell him, or should I?" Blaze asked.

Before he could answer, the food arrived. A monster-sized burger so big it was held together with a large steak knife protruding from the bun. Now Caleb was deep breathing along with the swallowing.

"What he's not telling you is—" Blaze started to say.

But Caleb didn't get to hear the rest of the sentence as he jumped up and ran out the rear exit door.

"—he already puked." Blaze turned to Stryker, "You're an asshole. You know that?"

"Whatever. I told you guys I don't drink that bullshit triple tequila," he said, then devoured his burger.

9

Ebony stood before her godfather, looking down at her feet, waiting for the well-deserved tongue lashing. She was surprised he hadn't done it sooner. Gods knew she certainly deserved it.

Trip didn't hold back. "You have been treating me like a spurned lover ever since you were five. Which is crazy, since a five-year-old knows very little, if anything, about sex. But you were right. You actually called me on it. You asked me if I slept with her, then you accused me of 'fucking' her. Well, now that you're no longer five and you are now officially an adult, I can tell you the whole story. Do you want every detail or just the abridged version? Doesn't matter to me, I remember everything. What'll it be, Ebony?"

She shook her head. "You don't have to—"

"Oh, but, I do. I really do. I will not allow you to continue treating me like shit because you disapprove of me being an adult male. I have been walking on eggshells for far too long. Carefully analyzing what I say or how I say it so as not to upset you. No more, Miss Jade, no more." He sliced the air with his hands, emphasizing the words. "You wanted to know about Ileana? Well, let me tell you. We started out hanging with her friend Rodger and drinking. Then she got sleepy, so I carried her back to her room."

"Stop! Please, just stop!"

"But we're just getting to the good part. This is the stuff you really wanted to know about, right? Well, I'm giving you what you want. You've waited twenty-two years for this. Now there's living proof of what really went on that night. But, I digress, back to the story. Anyway, I carried her back—"

"Please, Uncle Trip. I don't want to know. Please don't do this! I'm so sorry."

She grabbed his hands and looked up into his eyes. The anger was no longer there, now there was just love, pure love. Not that romantic bullshit that she thought she wanted from him, but the real deal that he had always offered her. She couldn't believe how much of a brat she had been towards him all those years. Even harder to believe was the fact that he had let her. Why didn't he just put his foot down sooner? She wished he had. Preferably on her neck.

She said, "You're right. You're absolutely right. I acted as if you had cheated on me and how can you cheat on somebody you're not committed to? If anybody should be upset, it's Lylac, and she's so sweet and understanding and—"

"Forgiving?" he offered.

She nodded. "Yes, but there isn't anything to forgive, is there?"

He shook his head. "No. We knew where we stood with each other. At the time, we weren't officially committed yet. I had my assignment, and she had hers. We were both very busy, but we didn't want the other waiting around and not enjoying living or loving. Can you understand that?"

She nodded. "Yes. Did you love her, Uncle Trip?"

"No, baby. I barely knew her. It was a one-night stand, and we both knew it. She was fine with it, and so was I. She had a birth control implant. A month after we left her world, she found out hers was part of a bad batch that had been recalled. But it was too late. She was pregnant. And there was no way she was giving him up. The pharmaceutical company paid her enough that she wouldn't have to work, and she focused all her energy on him. She and her friend Rodger even got married so he would have an official father should anything ever happen to her. She never expected to see me again and had she not died in the plane crash, she probably wouldn't have."

Ebony covered her face with her hands. "I am such a bitch! I can't believe all this time I wasted being angry with her." She wiped tears from her cheeks. "I'm so sorry, Uncle Trip. I'm so sorry!" She buried her face in her hands again.

Trip placed his arms around her. "You're forgiven." He gently pulled her hands away from her face, then tilted her chin up. "You know there's something else you've been waiting for."

"What's that?"

"This."

He leaned in and kissed her. Annnd it was so not what she expected. Not only were there no fireworks, but her lunch was threatening to come back up. It felt like kissing her father. She was about to protest when he slid his tongue into her mouth. Ewwwwww! Gross didn't even touch describing it. She pushed him away and placed a hand over her mouth.

"Beaner? Are you okay?"

She shook her head.

"What's wrong?" he asked, alarmed.

That's just great! Titus said to make it good, and now

she's disappointed! Fuck me! The first time had been hard enough, he doubted he could repeat it.

"It was like kissing my dad. Please don't be offended, Uncle Trip, but that was really gross," she said.

"Excuse me?" He couldn't believe his ears. And then he realized. Titus knew! That's why he'd said make it good. He knew it would turn her off. Trip threw back his head and laughed.

"What's so funny?" she asked.

"Something your father said to me. Speaking of which, I could kiss *him* right now."

"Obviously, I missed something and I really don't need to know what. This night just keeps getting weirder and weirder. I think I'm ready to meet Caleb now."

Just as she said the words, Caleb burst through the door and hurled. She went to him and held his hair back until his stomach was empty. He stood up and wiped his mouth.

She held out her hand. "Hi, Caleb. I'm Ebony, it's nice to—"

He slapped it away, hard. "I know who you are. Don't touch me."

"Oy! What the fuck is your problem?" Trip demanded.

"I had an interesting conversation with her 'friend'. They'll be celebrating my mother's passing later on. Enjoy!" He turned to go back inside, muttering. "Royal bitch!"

"Caleb, no! I would never do anything like that. Your mother was a wonderful woman and I'm really sorry for your loss," she said.

He paused and turned back to her, eyes narrowed. "Really?"

She nodded. "Yes, really."

"But Stryker said—"

She rolled her eyes. Of course, Stryker. "Don't listen to him. He's sorely misinformed."

"Are you sure?" he asked.

She nodded. "I'm sure."

He gave a shy grin and offered his hand. "Well, in that case, the pleasure's all mine."

PART II: RETURN OF THE QUEEN

10

The setting sun had the shadows stretching long across the meadow. One could feel the promise of a magical night at hand. Titus inhaled deeply, taking in the sweet aroma of moonflowers, jasmine, and honeysuckle. Yes, it was going to be an enchanting night. He entered the stable and called to her. "Schatzi?" It was his favorite term of endearment for her, ever since she was human.

"I'm here, my love," she answered as she stepped from the shadows, still in horse form.

"So how's this going to go down?" he asked.

She laughed. "Did you bring what I asked for?"

"Of course. One black evening gown with matching stiletto heels. Are you sure that's a good idea? Everyone else is wearing dress leathers."

She purred, "I see that. You're looking good in them there dress leathers, sire."

He shook his head and chuckled. "Don't get used to it. The overcoat gets hot and most of the young ones will have them off before dinner, but, yeah they do look sharp if I do say so myself. Thank you. Barbara did a great job designing them."

"That she did. As for the shoes, walking in stilettos is like riding a bike. Once you've mastered it, you don't forget it."

"Yeah, but—"

"Just leave them, please. I know what I'm doing. There's not much time, you've got to go."

"I can't stay?"

"No, you cannot. This is a private ceremony. Now go. The moon is almost visible and you can't be here."

He sighed. "Fine, I'm going, but how will you get there?"

"Don't you worry about that, baby, I've got a ride."

Titus didn't like being excluded from such an important event, especially in his own kingdom. But he respected The Master, and he trusted her. He did as he was told, disappearing before her eyes.

She glanced up at the sky. The sun and moon were both equally visible. It was time. She made her way inside the stable. Lying down in her favorite spot, she immediately fell asleep.

The stable disappeared and Vanessa found herself standing in The Master's chambers. She kneeled. "My Lord."

"Arise, my child, you've done well."

"Thank you, sir. It was my pleasure to serve you."

He smiled. "You kept up your end. Now, I'm keeping up mine. Titus did well choosing you. Any last requests?"

She smiled. "Just one."

He knew what it was. She and Ebony had matching birthmarks and though it would be a new body, she wanted that birthmark back. "Done," he said, then waved a hand over her face.

. . .

VANESSA AWOKE WITH A START. WHERE WAS SHE? THEN SHE smelled hay and felt straw scratching her skin. She sat up and looked. Yes, she had hands! And feet! And the birthmark was on her hip, just as it was before. It was done. She stood on wobbly legs and slowly made her way to the dress and shoes Titus had laid out. He had even remembered underwear and a bra. And it all fit. She had just finished dressing when a shadow cast across her.

"Milady? Are you here?"

Her chariot was waiting. She ran to him. "I am."

He smiled, then bowed so deeply she thought his face must surely be touching the ground. "Oh, stop that and give me a hug!" she demanded.

Trip stood and gathered her into a crushing bear hug. "I missed you so much!" he said.

She returned the embrace. "It's good to see you too, sweetie." She clung to him enjoying the feeling of being held again. "I'll never take arms for granted again," she said.

He held her at arm's length. "Let me look at you. I can't believe you're back."

She smiled up at him and placed a hand on his cheek. "Right back at ya, babe. Right back at ya." She took his hand. "Let's talk."

"Milady? Is everything alright?"

"You tell me. Please tell me she at least attempted to meet him."

"I'm not sure I follow."

"My daughter, your son."

"You know?"

"Yes, Blaze told me… and so did she."

Trip smiled. "She was not happy with me."

Vanessa laughed. "Oh, I know! Pitched a full-on princess hissy fit."

He laughed too. "Well, she's fine now and yes, she has met him."

"Good, now let's go, so *I* can meet him."

He lifted her and took to the sky. "Wow, I'm impressed. No screaming or clinging this time," he said.

"Pssh. Fear of heights is overrated," she said.

Damn, if that didn't tickle the avenging angel's funny bone the whole way to the banquet hall.

When they arrived, they were greeted outside by Blaze. He bowed just as deeply as Trip had. Again, Vanessa had to make him get up. "Will you two please knock that shit off? I wasn't crazy about it back then, and I'm not too keen on it now."

They looked at each other, then back at her and said, simultaneously, "Yes, ma'am. Duly noted."

She shook her head, knowing full well the king demanded it of them. "Fucking Titus. You won't stop, will you?"

They both gave her that maddeningly beatific, butter-wouldn't-melt-in-my-mouth look and blinked twice. Who knew Blaze could do it just as well as Trip? She wanted to slap them both. Three Stooges style. She tossed down her shoes and stepped into them. "Oh, never mind. Let's go."

They each offered an elbow and proudly escorted their queen into the ball.

Ebony spotted her first. "Mom!"

She ran to her mother and buried her face in her bosom. There was no shortage of tears as mother and daughter were finally, truly reunited. Ebony's perfectly made-up face was now practically running down her chin, which quickly morphed crying into laughter. She pulled back from her mother to look at her.

"It's really you. I remember. I know it's been a long time, but I remember."

Bring on round two of the fountains of tears. This time when they separated Ebony said, "He's been waiting for you. He's actually nervous. Can you believe it?"

Vanessa nodded. "I can. I am too. Where is he?"

Ebony laughed. "Where do you think?"

Vanessa looked around and noticed Trip and Blaze were now missing in action. She shook her head. Out behind the kitchen, smoking. Some things never change. "Should I go?"

Ebony shook her head. "Give him a minute."

Vanessa nodded. "Right. Okay."

She wouldn't have gotten very far anyway as Pippa, Lylac, and Coral descended upon her. Not so many tears this time, but a lot of squealing and giggling.

Vanessa glanced up and spotted Blaze and Trip returning from the kitchen. The two of them exchanged a look and a nod. Trip went and spoke to Joel, who was playing DJ for the night's festivities. Joel nodded, then handed him the mic.

Trip began. "As everyone here is aware. Tonight's party is more than just a debutante ball for a certain little princess who's grown up and blossomed into a lovely young lady. Not that I'm partial or anything."

The crowd laughed as he mouthed the words 'I love you' and blew her a kiss. Ebony practically melted into the floor, despite the early evening's awkward moment.

Caleb snickered as Stryker started grumbling about the king's warriors and their cocky attitudes. Obviously, drama was not exclusive to humans.

Trip continued, "No, tonight, we also celebrate the return of our beloved queen, Vanessa."

The crowd cheered and whistled. Trip waited until they settled down before continuing. "And no one has been more eagerly awaiting her return than our king. This next song sums it up rather nicely. Please clear the floor to allow the king to dance with his queen for the first time in over three septennia."

Vanessa watched as folks started clearing the floor, but there was no sign of Titus. She glanced around, half expecting him to pop in out of thin air. No such luck. Then Blaze joined Trip on stage with his own mic. What were they up to? She was visually sweeping the room again when the kitchen doors swung open. And there he was.

Time. Stood. Still.

His eyes met hers, and he gave her a wink and a smile. That cocky-assed little grin that she loved so much. One hand covered her mouth as the tears started anew. Should she run to him? Hell no. She didn't even trust herself to walk. He started toward her as Trip and Blaze began singing the first bars of "Unchained Melody". Yes, Trip was right. The song was perfect. And who the hell knew those two could sing? Really sing. Harmonizing, even. The crowd parted to allow her unimpeded access to the dance floor.

Pippa leaned into her and whispered. "What are you waiting for? Go to him. You both have been waiting for this."

The words were exactly what Vanessa's knees needed to man up and function. She started toward him, each of them picking up speed as they got closer. By the time they reached the dance floor, she was running then leaping into his open arms. Titus caught his queen and held her, enjoying the moment in silence because there simply were no words. None. There also wasn't a dry eye in the room as he lowered her to the floor and looked into her eyes. Those big beautiful doe eyes that never failed to unravel him and were doing a damn good job of it right then. Even after all that time apart, their bodies just knew. They fell in line with each other, swaying in time as Trip and Blaze continued to serenade them. And damn if Trip didn't hit that high note without wavering once. As the song ended, Titus leaned into her, touching her forehead with his. Then his lips were on hers. And wasn't that what they were really waiting for? Vanessa sighed as his tongue found hers and started tenderly stroking, leaving her breathless. Oh, gods! She'd forgotten how skilled he was with his tongue. It was making her swoon. Were they really expected to stay for the rest of the party? She couldn't imagine him waiting, not after being celibate for so long, or so he said. Vanessa had her reservations about that. Even now, she could feel his hardness through his leathers. He wasn't the only one ready to blow this hotdog stand. The crowd started hooting and cheering. The couple parted and bowed to their audience amidst more cheering. Then Titus took her by the hand and they ran for the kitchen doors.

11

It was like a scene from a movie. The royal couple running through the kitchen to escape. However, every worker stopped to bow as the king passed by. Tonight, he was oblivious. He only had one thing on his mind and he was practically dragging her through the kitchen. It surprised Vanessa that he hadn't just thought them back to his bedroom already. So now, what could he possibly be up to? They burst through the rear doors and one could have knocked her over with a feather.

Behind the banquet hall next to a large vegetable garden was an open field. In the middle of it was a candlelit table set for two along with wait staff at the ready.

"Titus? What—"

He lifted her into his arms. "Rethink those stilettos yet?"

"Had I known about this, I might have reconsidered."

"Leave them here on the porch."

She kicked them off as her king carried her across the threshold. "So what's on the menu?" she asked, coyly.

He raised a brow. "Besides you?"

She laughed. "I knew you wouldn't let me down. But from what I can see from here, there's no room for me on that table."

He gave a low growl. "That's an easy fix."

"And what about the wait staff? Or is this some new thing you wanted to try? Sex with an audience?"

"Uh, no. Another easy fix."

Then she smelled the food. All those years eating nothing but hay, grasses, and apples? Yeah, she was ready for some real food. Sex could wait a little longer. He held her chair for her as she sat down. Vanessa rubbed her hands together, noticing the three large domes on the table. She reached out only to have her fingers playfully smacked.

"Not yet," he said.

"Oh, come on! I can smell seafood. Seafood! Do you know how long it's been? Listen to me, of course, you know how long it's been, but do you know how long it's been?"

He laughed as he took his seat and placed his napkin in his lap.

"We have an hour. They're serving inside now, and we have to be back to dance with our daughter. Then, we are leaving… for good."

"Yeah, about that dance. I want to dance with her first," she said, fully prepared to argue her position.

"You?"

"Yes, I'm her mother and the queen and I think—"

He nodded. "You're right. Of course, you first."

Wow, that was easy. Too easy. Her eyes narrowed. "Who are you and what have done with my husband?"

He laughed. "What do you mean?"

"Titus, now you know, any other time, you would have argued with me just for the sake of arguing, even if you were going to let me have it in the end. You've changed."

"I have," he said. "Vanessa, I'm so, so sorry. Sorry for everything. I was upset and angry when I said what I did and by the time I'd tried to rescind the words, it was too late, and not a day goes by that I don't regret it."

"Titus, I forgave you a long time ago. Don't you think it's time you forgave yourself?"

He shook his head, staring at the flickering flame. "I don't think I can. My words stole something from you, me, and Ebony that we can never, ever, get back and—" He sighed. "—I don't deserve forgiveness."

"Titus, how can you say that? Everybody deserves forgiveness, especially if they're truly sorry."

He looked into her eyes and gave her a weak smile. "Gods, but, I love you, woman. You and that pure heart of yours. You say I've changed. Well, you haven't. Despite everything, you're still you. The woman I fell hopelessly in love with. I, literally, put you through Hell, and here you are still sticking it out with me. Whatever did I do to deserve you?"

"When I married you, I meant what I promised. Through thick and thin, baby, it's gonna take more than a few words spoken in anger to get rid of me." Her stomach growled, loudly.

He laughed. "Sounds like somebody's hungry. This little scenario seems vaguely familiar."

She smiled. "That it does, Mr. Walker. Are you going to seduce me with a peach again?"

"That depends. Are you going to deep throat a banana?"

She gave him an impish grin. "Who needs a banana when they have the real thing?"

That shut him up.

"Now, can we eat? Please?" she asked.

He cleared his throat and nodded. "Of course."

She lifted the first dome and gasped, "Is that a Philly cheesesteak?"

"It is. I remember how much you loved your 'East Coast' cuisine."

"A Nathan's hot dog? With coleslaw?"

He smiled and nodded. "Judging by your facial expression, these were excellent choices, yes?"

She took a bite of the hot dog and closed her eyes. "Mmmmm, this is sooo good! Yes, very good choices. I can't believe you remembered! It even has the mustard with the seeds I love."

"Yes, well, the devil is in the details. I wanted this to be perfect."

"You did good," she said, mouth still full.

He rested his chin on his hands and watched as she finished the dog and took a huge bite of the steak sandwich.

She stopped chewing and asked. "Are you not going to join me?"

"I will. I enjoy watching you eat. You savor every bite. It's almost sexual."

"Now, this *really* feels like deja vu," she said. Halfway through the sandwich.

She laid it down, then lifted the second dome.

"Crab cakes and lobster tail! Oh my god, Titus, you're gonna have to roll me back into the banquet hall."

He laughed. "Don't worry. We'll work it off later. I promise."

He didn't have to say it twice as she dug into the seafood. And he continued to watch. She paused, mouth full, lobster claw in hand.

"Eat with me!" she demanded.

"Okay, okay, calm down. I was waiting for you to get to

dessert. Besides, I want you to eat your fill first. Don't you remember?"

Oh, she remembered alright. He waited for her to be full and then polished off everything else and wash it down with a cup of coffee, which he had shamelessly slurped. And he was still sex on legs. How could she forget? After all that, he had noisily sucked the hell out of a peach in such a way it left her a quivering mass just watching him. Even as she was remembering, he lifted the dome off the third plate. A peach, a banana, and a bowl of strawberries with whipped cream. She squealed with delight.

"I can't believe you did this! You are such an asshole."

He grinned and raised a brow. "Am I now?"

She quickly grabbed the peach with both hands and pursed her lips. *So there.*

He shook his head and tsked. "Ah, Schatzi, didn't you think I'd anticipate that move?" He replaced the dome and lifted it again. There, on the plate, was another peach. He grabbed it and raised it to his nose. "Mmmmm, smells delightful."

"That's so not fair!" she said, pouting.

"What's not?" he asked as he slowly bit into the fruit, slurping the juice as he did.

"That thing you just did. Making a new one appear. I can't do that."

"Oh no? You sure about that?"

She scoffed as she covered the plate, then removed the dome just as he did. This time there were two bananas. "Really?" she asked. "So I'm not allowed to enjoy a peach?"

He moaned as he licked his lips and fingers. "What do you mean? You have a peach. Go ahead, dig in. I want to watch."

She frowned at him. "Are we still talking about fruit?"

He threw back his head and laughed. "Of course we are. What else would we be talking about, Schatzi?"

Two could play this game. And this time she had something going for her she didn't the first time around with him. Confidence and knowledge. The confidence to dive right in and the knowledge of what he liked and how he liked it. She tossed the peach over her shoulder. Then picked up a banana and peeled it. He froze. Yep, that's the response she was after. She dipped the end in the whipped cream, then ran her tongue around the tip a few times, licking the cream off and making sure just a little stayed on her lips. Then she nibbled at the underside. Taking small bites along the full length of it. He was still watching her with his half-eaten peach dribbling over his hand when she paused.

"Aren't you going to finish that?" she teased.

He cleared his throat and swallowed. "You first."

She shrugged. "Okay." She reached in and grabbed two strawberries. Now, he was positively bug-eyed. "Strawberries and bananas go so well together. Don't you think?" she asked.

He nodded, slack-jawed.

She lovingly licked the two berries then sucked them into her mouth one at a time, then they were in her hand again and she was licking away.

"What are you doing?" he asked, amused.

"Oh, I'm just making sure I get all the cream. Gotta be gentle, though. You don't want to bruise the fruit, you know."

He smiled. That cocky little grin showing off his dimples. "No, you wouldn't want to bruise the fruit. Our time is almost up. We should finish—"

Suddenly, she popped both berries in her mouth and

chewed them up, making him wince. The banana quickly followed. She closed her eyes and smiled as she slowly chewed the fruit and swallowed.

"Mmmmmm. That was delicious."

The small bit of cream she'd left on her lips was still there, and she wiped it with a thumb and sucked it into her mouth, then ran her tongue around her lips.

"Your turn," she said.

"So it is," he agreed, then sucked the remaining fruit from the pit.

She pushed her chair back from the table. "That was a delicious meal. Thank you."

"It was my pleasure, believe me," he said, tossing the pit over his shoulder.

She smiled and nodded. "I do, but don't think I didn't notice the only thing you ate was a peach."

He stood and wiped his mouth, then his eyes were taking in the length of her body before making their way back up to meet hers.

His lids were hooded as he said, "Tonight, it's all I'll need. Now, let's go dance with our daughter because I've got plans for you."

"Really? What if I'm too tired?" she asked.

"Too bad."

She laughed as they clasped hands and started back to the hall. "About tonight, there's something I think you should know beforehand," she said.

He stopped. "Oh? What's that?"

"This body is not exactly the same as it was before."

"What do you mean?"

"I mean that, well, it's never been used. It's like new."

"Like new?"

She nodded, patiently waiting for understanding to set in.

"I still don't follow," he said.

"Titus, this is a new incarnation. The last time I was human was another incarnation. It's not the same. So, know that this isn't the same body that gave birth to Ebony. That's long gone. This is a whole new me."

He looked at her hip. "Is the birthmark gone?"

She laughed and shook her head. "No, I specifically requested to keep it. Especially since you made sure Ebony had the same one."

"Okay, so what's different?"

"Well, since we were having such a good time with it, let's stick to fruit. Think cherries."

"Cherries?"

She watched his face as understanding finally set in.

"Oh cherries!" he said, then lowered his voice. "You're a virgin?"

She nodded. "Yes."

He took her hand and started walking again. Silent.

"Titus?"

"Yes?"

"Are you upset?"

"Upset? Of course, not. Why would I be?"

"Well, you're not saying anything."

"I don't know what to say."

"What? You? Speechless? Do you have a problem with me being a virgin?"

"Not at all. I'm honored to be the first."

She smiled. "Really?"

"Really. And just so you know—"

"What's that?"

"It's been a long time for me too. So it's gonna be kinda like Christmas for both of us."

She stepped into her shoes, ready to dance with her daughter and eager to rediscover her husband.

"Christmas, huh? I like that," she said.

"Me too," he said.

They went inside.

12

After Titus and Vanessa left, the wait staff came through ushering everyone to their tables. The king's daughters and warriors were the first ones seated, followed by the guests. The menu consisted of an entrée of lobster tail or filet mignon accompanied by asparagus or green beans amandine and rice pilaf.

Caleb had the privilege of being seated at the head table between Lylac and Ebony, much to the chagrin of Stryker, who sat next to Blaze's daughter, Sienna. Lucky for him, the poor girl had a massive crush on him and had invited him to be her guest. He had promised her a dance in exchange. It was the least he could do to offer his gratitude. Although she was just as drop-dead gorgeous as her mother and there was no shortage of males interested in her, none of them dared speak to her for fear of her father or brother's wrath. Even now, Julian, her twin, sat on the other side of her glaring at Stryker, who was completely oblivious. His focus was on Ebony and her interaction with Caleb. Blaze's eyes narrowed. *This motherfucker!* He bristled. He didn't like the idea of anybody looking at his daughter as of yet. Hell, maybe never, but Sienna had graciously invited Stryker to the table and he couldn't even acknowledge her presence? Don't think so. And to make it worse, Sienna was making all kinds of googly eyes at the asshole. Pippa patted his hand, which he now realized was balled into a tight fist.

"Easy papa bear," she whispered. "She's fine."

He scowled. "No, she's not. He's totally disrespecting her."

"Oh, and you've never ignored a young girl fawning over you? I somehow doubt that."

"I don't have young girls fawning over me," he said.

Pippa laughed. "Are you kidding me, right now? The first time I met you and Trip, you had an entourage of giggling fans. And you were both ignoring them."

He scoffed. "What giggling fans?"

Pippa pursed her lips and raised a brow. "Need I say more?"

"Of course, I wouldn't have noticed any giggling fans as I was too busy dealing with a big-mouthed redhead."

Trip and Lylac were within earshot, and both were watching and waiting for her response. She didn't disappoint.

"Oh, really, now? Well, at least you won't have to deal with one tonight. This big mouth and these long legs are now closed—for the night." She turned to her daughter. "Sienna, offer your guest the bread basket before your father, here, has a stroke."

Sienna was more than happy to do as her mother asked. It gave her an excuse to touch him. She tapped his shoulder. He continued to watch Caleb and Ebony, ignoring her.

"I'm about to thump his ass," Blaze warned through clenched teeth.

"And embarrass your daughter? Think first, warrior," Pippa said.

"I have a daughter. I don't have to think when it comes to dealing with knuckleheads," he said.

"Would you rather he be pawing at her?"

Blaze frowned at her. "Fuck no! If I had my way, she'd be wearing a chastity belt, but nooo. That's outdated and barbaric," he said, speaking the last words in a mocking tone. "There's something to be said about the Elizabethan era."

Pippa waved him off. "Oh, stop it!"

Trip chimed in. "Just let me know, brah, I've got one."

Pippa turned to him. "Jesus, Trip, don't encourage him, and why the hell would you have a chastity belt?"

Trip leaned in, looked right into her eyes, and asked, "Do you really want to know?"

Pippa thought for a moment and decided against it. With Trip being known as the resident freak, the answer could easily haunt her for days. "No, thanks."

Trip and Blaze exchanged a look. "We'll talk later," Blaze said.

Trip nodded. And as usual, Pippa just rolled her eyes.

Caleb watched the exchange between his father and his friend. Four hundred years—at least. He couldn't imagine having a friend for that long a time. The bond between them had to be stronger than any marriage. They kind of even acted like an old married couple. The familiarity between the two of them as they finished each other's sentences and somehow just seemed to know what the other was thinking. A look, a slight gesture, even the clearing of a throat. It was like the two of them had their own language. Caleb couldn't help wondering, was he going to find someone here like that? His father had told him all he had to do was earn his wings. Would he be an angel then? And if so, what would his life expectancy be? Would he be able to visit his human friends and family from time to time? He was already missing Rodger. For him, Rodger would always be Dad.

"Hey, are you okay?" Ebony asked him.

He shook his head, clearing the thoughts. "Uh, yeah, fine."

"You looked sad for a second."

"Is everybody here so observant?"

She smiled. "Yes. Angels are very sensitive to the feelings and emotions of others. You're missing them, aren't you?"

Caleb nodded. "Yeah, I am. I just lost my mother and now —" He ran a hand through his hair and took a sip, nay, a large gulp of his water.

"Again, I'm so sorry for your loss," she said. "I mean that."

"Thanks, I appreciate it," he said. They ate in silence for a moment, then he asked, "So what's the deal with you and Stryker?"

"We're friends. We grew up together."

"I get the feeling he's desperately trying to make his way out of the 'friend zone'."

She laughed. "See? You've got angel blood too."

"So I'm right?"

She nodded. "Yes. He likes me, but I don't feel that way towards him. Just friends and I'd like to keep it that way."

"You know he's been staring at us ever since we sat down."

She nodded. "I know. I can feel it."

"The girl next to him has been staring at him the whole time."

Ebony laughed. "Sienna. She's my niece."

"What's wrong with him? She's beautiful. Her eyes are amazing."

"She is, they are, but, have you noticed who her father is?"

He nodded. "Yeah, the eyes kinda give it away. I'm surprised she doesn't have somebody staring at her."

"Trust me. Nothing with male equipment comes within ten feet of her without Dad or Julian around."

He winced. "I feel sorry for her."

Ebony laughed. "Don't. Her mother will make sure she's good when the time comes. She knows how to deal with Uncle Blaze."

"Uncle? I thought he was your brother-in-law?"

"Yes, but I was a little girl when I first came here. It just stuck."

"I see. So did you have to earn your wings too?"

She nodded. "I did. It surprised me that flying came easier than I thought it would."

"That's good to know. So what do I have to do to earn mine?"

"Well, let's see. If my math is correct, you're twenty-two years old, right?"

He nodded.

"You just missed it. So you'll have to wait until your next septennium starts."

"Next septennium? Isn't that like six years away? How am I supposed to get around?"

"Well, I—"

"That can't be right. Are you sure?"

"Yes, I—"

"But they were already coming in. According to my father, that's why the urgency to bring me here. What the fuck?"

"I'm sorry, Caleb, I didn't mean to upset you. I was just telling you what I know."

A large hand rested on Caleb's shoulder. "What's the problem, son?"

Caleb looked up into the king's smiling face. Was he supposed to bow? How should he address him? He was trying to remember everything his father told him.

"I was just asking Ebony, here, what I need to do to earn my wings, and she says I have to wait another six years, uh, your majesty."

Titus chuckled. "Well, she's right, mostly. But just like everything else. There are ways around it. And ease up, son. You don't need to be so formal."

"Uh, yes, sir."

"That'll do."

"So what can I do to um—"

"Expedite the process?" Titus asked.

Caleb nodded. "Yes, sir."

Titus shrugged and said, "Die."

Caleb stared at the king, dumbfounded. Was he kidding?

"Daddy! Don't tell him that!" Ebony exclaimed.

Titus reached over his daughter's shoulder and snagged a lump of lobster meat from her plate. "Why not? It's the truth. Albeit there are rules, and extenuating circumstances prevail, but it's a shortcut. That's how Pippa got hers."

Caleb looked down the table at Pippa, who still appeared to be bickering with her husband. "She died? Really?"

Titus nodded. "She did. But listen, son. Don't go getting any ideas about rushing it along. There's a reason it's the way it is. And there are consequences for deliberately fast-tracking it."

He frowned. "Consequences?"

The king nodded. "Yes."

"What consequences?" Caleb asked.

"Well, you're forcing your wings so another part of your body has to go. You know, in exchange."

"I don't follow."

Titus sighed. "Look, Caleb. Let me be frank with you. The going exchange rate for a male set of angel wings is a set of testicles. Tit for tat. No pun intended."

The words came as a shock. Caleb sputtered, "What?!! Are you—"

He was interrupted by his father and Blaze howling with laughter and pointing at him.

Titus winked. "Gotcha. Welcome to my kingdom."

13

Okay, yes, it was cool that the king was a jokester. And, yes, everybody was being extra nice to him, but Caleb couldn't imagine hanging out there for the next six years with no way to get around except by hitching a ride with someone with wings. It was undignified. Would his father understand? Who knew? All he knew is that he wanted to go home. At the very least, he expected an argument. The worst? Trip would simply say "no". And what could he do about that? Absolutely nothing. He looked over at his father and lo-and-behold, he was already staring back at him. *Deep breath, Caleb. May as well get this over with.*

"Can we talk?" he asked.

Trip nodded. "Come on, let's step outside. I have to be back for the dance, though."

Caleb nodded.

Trip led his son through the kitchen and out the back door. The king's table had long since been cleared and the field now stood empty, moonlight shining over it almost as bright as day. "What's up?" Trip asked, already suspecting.

"If my wings aren't coming in for another six years, I want to go home."

Trip nodded. "I see. You know we were just joking in there."

Caleb shook his head. "It's not that. That was actually funny. Your king is pretty cool."

"*Our* king, Caleb, and this is home."

"Not for me. I'm not from here and I—" he paused to compose himself. "—I miss my family already. JJ would love this. Can't I, at least, bring him here? So I'm not alone?"

"No, son, you can't. It's out of the question."

"Then take me home. Now."

Dealing with a tantrum was not new to Trip. Titus pitched them all the time. As did Ebony. Was his son *demanding* that he take him home? Trip gave him the benefit of the doubt. "I beg your pardon?" he said.

"You heard me. Take me home. Right now. I don't belong here. Not yet." *Maybe never?* "This was a mistake."

Trip took a deep breath. No point in him getting pissed off too—yet. "Caleb, there's something you're not understanding here. My blood flows through your veins. That means, yes, you are from here and this is your home. I understand how you feel about your family. I really do, but Caleb, they were nothing more than—"

"Don't—"

"—surrogates."

"Fuck you, man! How can you even say that? *You* weren't there! *They* were! I don't even know you. You're practically a stranger to me. And you come into my life and scare me into coming here with you based upon some bad dreams I had and some weird anxiety symptoms."

Even as he spoke, the back itch was flaring up. He gritted his teeth against it.

Before Trip could respond, they could hear silverware on glass multiplied by everyone in the room. It was time for his dance with Ebony. He ran a hand through his hair. "Everything I said to you was true. We don't lie, especially not to each other. Just think about it, please?"

Caleb sighed with resignation, then nodded. "Fine."

Trip wasted no time when they returned. He guided Ebony to the floor and swept her off her feet. "You look beautiful tonight, Beanie. Even though you changed your mind about the color scheme," he teased.

She rolled her eyes and said, "Ugh! Don't remind me. Can you forgive me for my horrid behavior all those years? I'm so sorry."

He smiled at her. "There's nothing to apologize for. The heart wants what the heart wants, and who's to say? A different time and under different circumstances, things could have been different."

She nodded. "We'll never know. Speaking of hearts, I think your son is interested in somebody here."

Trip nodded. "Yes, he is. Are you okay with it?" Maybe if she returned his interest, Caleb would forget about leaving. One could only hope.

She nodded. "Of course. He's a great catch. Son of a warrior and just as good looking. A definite 'yes'!"

Trip smiled. "That's a relief. I wasn't sure how you'd feel about it."

"It's great. I don't know about tonight, though. You may want to help him find someone for tonight."

Trip nodded. "Understood. No need to rush things, right?"

"Exactly. I'm not sure how 'Daddy' would handle it. May need to ease him into the idea." She glanced over at Blaze, who sat frowning at Stryker. *Yeah, definitely ease him into the idea.*

"Good point," Trip agreed. He looked over at Titus standing with his queen, both of them beaming. Then they disappeared. *Won't be hearing from them for the rest of the night.* Trip thought with a grin.

"Maybe you could help lay the groundwork? Especially since you're so close. He listens to you," Ebony suggested.

Trip scoffed. "I don't know. We're talking about his little girl and a male. Close or not, he may not be ready to hear it. Never mind her age."

Ebony nodded. "That's true. Let's just see how things go."

"Agreed," Trip said. "Now, allow me to take my leave as you are going to be busy for a while." He nodded toward a line of males waiting to dance with her. He bowed and kissed her hand. "Princess."

With that, he went back to the head table and took Ebony's seat next to Caleb. "You must have said something good. She's receptive," he said.

Caleb shook his head. "I'm not so sure. I got mixed signals."

"Still in a hurry to go back?"

Caleb nodded. "Yes, but—" He frowned, thinking.

"But what?" Trip asked.

"How about if I go home until it's time to earn my wings. I just can't see hanging out here for the next six years with no way to get around. It's kind of undignified."

Trip sighed. How could he make Caleb understand the danger he was in if he returned to Terra-3? He couldn't. Not without scaring the bejesus out of him. So, even if it meant he and Lylac going back with him for his protection, he would honor his son's wishes. Reluctantly, he nodded.

"If it's what you really want. I can't make you stay. Are

you sure there's nothing I can say to change your mind? You know, I think Ebony is interested in you."

Caleb gave him a wan smile and shook his head. "I thought this was what I wanted, but, I'm not so sure I'm ready for this life. It's a lot to take in."

He watched as Stryker took his turn dancing with the princess. The familiarity between the two couldn't be ignored, but as Stryker turned his back to him, she peeked over his shoulder and winked. Caleb winked back.

Maybe his father was right. It couldn't hurt to give it a shot.

Vanessa had forgotten how disorienting thought travel could be. They had stayed just long enough to watch Ebony dance with her lifelong crush, grateful that things had worked out well.

"You did good, Papa. She turned out wonderfully," Vanessa said to him.

"No, *we* did well. You were here too. Now, we have our own business to take care of. Twenty-two years isn't a very long time when you're upwards of a thousand, but without sex? I'm ready."

"Me too," she said.

His bedroom was a grand spectacle. The focal point being a massive four-poster bed with a canopy of drapes. Intricately carved wood furnishings abounded, complete with an immense ornate mirror. Vanessa froze, staring at herself. It had been so long. She had the same face, the same hair, the same body, yet it wasn't the same at all. This body felt stronger, and she didn't have "the craving" gnawing at her as she had before since this body had never known drug addiction. Titus stood behind her, admiring their reflection. He slid one strap off of her shoulder and kissed her neck. She closed her eyes and sighed. It felt so good. Better than she'd remembered. He slid the other strap down and gave a low moan as he slid his arms around her waist and buried his face in her hair.

"I missed you so much," he whispered.

"I missed you too," she said, her voice trembling.

The memories came flooding back as she turned to him and they began tearing each other's clothes off. This was more like it. This was how it was before. Sex with Titus was nothing short of passionate, and they had ruined many a shirt in their quest to devour one another. Vanessa smiled as she remembered how she used to find shirt buttons in random locations throughout their bedroom in the days that followed an especially rambunctious session. She couldn't help herself and started laughing. He stopped.

"What?" he asked.

"You remember how your buttons would end up flying around the room?"

He laughed. "I'd forgotten about that. We'd be finding them—"

"—everywhere!" she said with him.

He nodded. "Yes."

She stood before him, open, ready, untouched, and eager to accept him. He stroked her face. "My love, I've waited so long for this. I love you so much."

She placed her hands over his. "I love you too, Titus."

Then his lips were at her neck again, aggressively this time. She sighed. Enjoying the sensation of his mustache and beard tickling her as he made his way to her ear. She whimpered softly. Damn, he was so good at seduction. She could

SON OF THE AVENGER

almost hear him saying, *"There's a reason it's called necking."*. He stopped and looked into her eyes.

"We'll go slow. Okay?" he said.

Slow? What? Why? Then she remembered. "Oh, yeah, that."

"Yeah, 'that'. But trust me, even if 'that' wasn't there, we'd still be taking it slow. Twenty-odd years? Yeah."

"I don't know, Titus. Do you think cherries grow back over time?"

He laughed. "Vanessa, we are not having this conversation right now."

She shrugged. "I was just wondering."

"If I didn't know any better, I'd say you were stalling. Are you stalling?"

"No! Of course not. I want this just as much as you do. Maybe more even."

He chuckled. "I highly doubt that. But…"

"But?"

"Remember that peach?"

She raised an eyebrow. "How could I forget? After that shameless display of yours, I couldn't even look at a peach without shuddering in anticipation."

He gave a low growl. The sexy motherfucker.

"I like that. I'll make sure they're everywhere from now on," he said.

"I believe you," she said.

"And well you should. Speaking of peaches…" He picked her up and carried her to his bed.

It was luxurious! Duh, of course, it was. It was the king's bed. And now it was her bed too. No straw here. You've come a long way, baby and all that. She stretched out and closed her eyes. Oh yes! He was grinning down at her.

"You like?" he asked.

"Like it? I love it!"

"Good." He kissed her shoulder. "I'm glad you approve."

Then, he started making his way down the length of her body, leaving a trail of soft kisses. Teasing... teasing... he reached her left hip and paused.

"Told you. It's there," she said.

"Yes, I see," he said. Cutest birthmark ever. "You kept it. For her?"

"And you."

"Me?"

"Of course. You always stopped at it on your way to... uh... the peach."

"Really? Are you saying I'm predictable?"

"Predictable? You? Never."

He chuckled. "If you say so."

"Oh, I say—"

She gasped and sighed as he found his "peach" and began savoring it—with fervor. He'd been waiting so long for this, and he was damn sure going to enjoy the hell out of it. He couldn't help grinning as her fingers found their way to his hair and her nails started raking his scalp. Oh yeah, just like old times. And just like old times, he teased her as he laved her silken folds. A few long slow licks followed by some direct attention to "the man in the boat". Then back to all the surrounding flesh, avoiding that turgid bundle of nerves. He could tell when she was close and would back off, leaving her panting, wanting. It was just a matter of time before she would grip his hair in her fists and start pulling. He was waiting for it. Who was really the predictable one, here? Certainly not his queen as her new body experienced its first orgasm. She cried out as her thighs squeezed his head in a vice-like grip. And if that wasn't confirmation of a job well done, well, what the hell was? He smiled, gently kissing her thigh as she slowly recuperated, staring up at the ceiling breathlessly repeating, "Omigod, omigod, omigod" over and over. Titus grinned up at her, making a lewd display of licking and smacking his lips.

"Mmmmm. I love peaches. Especially this one." He made an exaggerated slurping sound. "Nectar of the gods."

She shook her head and tsked. "Still shameless."

"Damn right," he said, giving her hip bone a playful nip. She squirmed and giggled as he continued to make his way up to her lips, licking, sucking, and kissing the whole way. Then his lips were on hers, aggressively as he gently parted her thighs. In their previous life, he would already be fully sheathed inside her. Now, he was slowly rubbing his hardness against her core, making her shudder and moan. She stole a glance down at him. Whoa! And to think, there was a time when she had playfully called it "the kracken". He tilted her chin up.

"We'll go slow. I promise. But I'm not going to lie to you, Schatzi. This is probably going to be uncomfortable for you."

"Titus, since when do you sugar coat anything? It's going to hurt. I know it and you know it. But I'm okay with it. Just try not to be… brutal."

"Brutal?"

"Aggressive. You know how we used to get. I wasn't always gentle with you either."

He growled. "Yes, I remember well. I liked it like that."

She nodded. "So did I. We're just gonna have to work our way up to it again."

"Agreed. Besides, you know I can help afterward."

"Not a chance. This moment is ours. And I want to remember it. All of it. It's not like you're going to kill me, you know. And like you said, we'll go slow."

He nodded. "Yes, slow."

He started by kissing her neck and earlobes, her sighs and moans urging him on. Then he had a mouthful of nipple, greedily sucking and teasing it to hardness with his teeth. *Can't have the other one feeling left out now, can we?* He thought as he turned his attention to it. It had been a long time for them, but he remembered well all her most sensitive zones and he was taking full advantage of that knowledge. He wanted to make sure she was good and ready. However, she thought he was dragging it out, unnecessarily.

"Titus?" she whispered.

"Yes?"

"Now."

"Now?"

"Yes. Now."

"Okay."

He lifted up and guided himself to her entrance. Oh, gods! She was so warm and wet, and he hadn't even entered her. He looked down to watch as he slowly disappeared inside her. She looked so small compared to him. He'd never noticed that before. She gasped and stiffened. He stopped, waiting for her. Her eyes were closed, and she was wincing.

"Don't stop," she pleaded. "Not now."

He did as she asked.

It wasn't like she was his first virgin. She wasn't. But his normal sexual prowess was a little too lively for a virgin body. He preferred to leave the business of deflowering to his warriors. There was no shortage of females looking for those kinds of bragging rights, anyway. But she specifically wanted to share this moment with him, and he wasn't about to disappoint her. He had promised to take things slow, but going too slow could be just as uncomfortable as going all out. He eased back ever so slightly, then thrust forward. Vanessa gasped and cried out as her flesh gave way allowing him unfettered albeit strained access. She was tight. He took his time, gently easing his way. When he was finally in as far as he could go, he stopped and looked into her eyes. It was a relief to find no tears, but the pain was there.

"You okay?" he asked.

She nodded. "Yeah, I am."

He leaned in to kiss her. Then Titus and his queen made love for the first time in twenty-two years, and it was everything they both thought it would be. She lay in his arms afterward, tears streaming down her face. He wiped them away with a thumb.

"I'm so sorry, my love."

"Don't be, I'm not."

"But I made you cry."

She shook her head. "Oh, no, baby. I'm not crying because of that. It's just that we've waited so long for this. And now that we're here. I... there are no words."

"Your cup runneth over?"

She nodded. "Yes, exactly. My heart is full."

"Mine too," he said.

She yawned.

He shook his head and laughed. "Just like old times. This time, I'll let you sleep afterward, but don't go thinking that it's gonna become a habit."

She laughed. "Oh, I remember. We don't sleep until you've had your fill."

He smirked, giving her that cocky grin that she'd fallen so hopelessly in love with all those years ago.

"What can I say? It's good to be the king."

He looked at her expectantly, already knowing what was coming. She didn't disappoint as she smiled then snuggled in closer to say it.

"Yes, but it's even better to be the queen."

14

Sienna sighed as she watched Stryker dance with her aunt. Ebony was so lucky. Stryker followed her around like a lovesick puppy. And if Sienna could, *she* would follow *him* around like a lovesick puppy. Having a father and a brother that hovered like wasps killed any prospects of that. On many an occasion, she had begged her mother to intervene and get them to back off. That didn't work. Her mother took their side. "They're just watching out for you, baby girl, that's all," she would say. It so wasn't fair. Julian wasn't a virgin anymore. And nobody said "boo" about that. Why was it different for males? Even Stryker got around. She knew she wasn't the only one in the kingdom interested in him. As soon as the princess dance was over, there was going to be a mad scramble of females wanting to dance with him. Even later that night, there was a hook-up party being planned and Julian had plans to go. Not Sienna. Not fair. If only her parents would decide to have more cherubs, maybe there'd be less of a need to dote over her and she could actually get some breathing space. She looked over at them. Now that Stryker was no longer at the table, her mother was the focal point of her father's attention. Most likely, trying to rectify what he'd said earlier, lining up his own hook-up. The look on her mother's face said it all. He wasn't getting any tonight. Good. It served him right.

"Daddy?"

"Yes, baby?"

"About later on."

"Later on?"

"Yes, the hook-up party."

He frowned. "What about it?"

"Well, you know how Aunt Ebony never hooks up. What if I went along with her and stayed with her the entire time? Would that be okay?"

"No. You're not going."

"But Julian is. Why can't I?"

"Sienna, we've discussed this before. Julian is a male. There are certain things he should be skilled at. After he completes his warrior training, there are going to be females from other realms seeking him out for their own first dalliances. It would not do for him to be inexperienced."

"And what about me, Daddy? Don't you think I should be skilled too?"

"Hell no! Not just that. You're the daughter of a warrior. Only a warrior should ever touch you."

Pippa watched the exchange between father and daughter, knowing full well Sienna would not win it. Right about now is usually when she would back down and drop it. Ugh! Why hadn't her daughter gotten her backbone? She knew exactly what she would say to him next if it was her. And damn, if her daughter didn't surprise her by choosing that moment to grow said spine.

Sienna looked her father straight in the eye and declared, "Stryker is the son of a warrior, Daddy."

Everybody within earshot froze, waiting to see what he was going to say. Pippa tried to suppress the grin that was playing at the corners of her mouth. *Good girl.* Nobody knew better than she did that Blaze could be a bastard of epic proportions when he wanted to be. As far as she was concerned? Knowing how to handle a warrior during an argument was a skill her daughter would definitely need. She sat back and crossed her arms. *Rock on sister. Show him what you've got.*

Blaze hadn't expected the comeback. "Excuse me?"

"You said it yourself. Only a warrior for me. Well, you know how I feel about him. So why not tonight?"

Blaze, furious and shouting, was one thing to deal with. Blaze quietly regrouping? Whole new level. Pippa could already see what was coming. He was going to play the "I am your father and what I say goes" card, which trumps anything else Sienna could come up with. *Oh well, sorry baby girl, you tried. Let's hope he doesn't make too much of a scene and embarrass you to tears here.*

"I'll tell you why not tonight," Blaze said through clenched teeth. "Because I said so. As your father, I don't owe you an explanation for any decisions I make regarding your well-being. My years of experience give me the knowledge and my position as 'daddy' gives me the right. You don't have to agree with it and you don't have to like it, but you damn sure have to respect it. This conversation is over."

Sienna stood up. "It wasn't like I was asking to fuck him. I just wanted a kiss. I don't think that's too much to ask!" She stormed off before he could respond.

Julian stood to follow her, but Pippa stopped him.

"Let her go. She needs to cool off and your status tonight ain't gonna cut it."

"What do you mean?" he asked his mother.

"I mean, part of her issue is that you get to do things she doesn't. I'm guessing you're one of the last people she wants to see right now."

"Maybe I could talk to her," Caleb suggested.

Blaze's eyes narrowed.

Caleb put up both hands. "Just talk. I promise."

Reluctantly, Blaze nodded.

From the dance floor, Ebony saw Blaze nod, then watched as Caleb stood up and followed Sienna. Hmm. Maybe they would be okay with it after all. Nice. Now to see if Sienna would be receptive. If so, maybe a certain princess could convince Uncle Blaze to allow Sienna to hang out with her later. She could see Sienna's face now. She'd be the best aunt ever.

"What are you looking at?" Stryker asked.

"Family drama. No big deal. I think Caleb likes Sienna."

"Caleb? Trip's son? Sienna?" Stryker asked, incredulously.

"Well, yeah, why is that so hard to believe? He was just saying how pretty her eyes are."

"There's no question. Sienna is very attractive. But between her father and brother, the poor girl will die an old maid. No guy in his right mind will ever go near her. Not if they like their balls."

"Stop. It's not that bad."

He scoffed. "Oh, but it is. Do you think I couldn't feel Blaze and Julian glaring at me the whole time I was sitting there? I even ignored her on purpose so as not to give them a reason. As it is, I promised her a dance tonight. I'm sure they'll both be out on the floor, too."

Ebony couldn't help picturing Blaze and Julian dancing together just to keep an eye on Sienna. The visual was ludicrous as hell. She started laughing.

They'd been friends for so long that Stryker didn't even have to ask. He knew what she was thinking. "Your ass is stupid!" he said, joining her "I didn't mean together! I'm gonna get some air while you finish your royal duty. May as well go get her while I'm at it."

※

SIENNA'S HEART RACED AS SHE MADE HER WAY THROUGH THE kitchen, expecting to feel her father's heavy hand on her shoulder any minute, demanding an apology for her behavior. But it never came. She stepped out into the cool night air and leaned her back against the railing on the stoop. The door opened and Caleb stepped out. Her friends would be sure to grill her the next time they saw her. He was just as hot as his father... and available. Another one who would probably get lucky later. Trip would make sure of it.

"What do you want?" she asked, removing her overcoat and draping it over the railing.

"To talk," he said.

"Did my father send you?"

He shook his head. "No."

"Good."

She surprised him by reaching into her pocket and pulling out a pack of cigarettes. At least, he thought they were cigarettes. They were black with a gold band at the filter. She lit up and inhaled deeply. That was not tobacco. Whatever it was, it was primo.

"May I?" he asked.

She nodded and passed it to him. He inhaled deeply of the pungent stoge. Oh yeah, this shit was smooth and strong. Wicked strong. It made his lungs burn, his eyes water, and his head swim.

"Whoa! What is this?" he said, coughing.

"Do you always ask to partake of something you're not sure of?" she asked, taking it back from him.

He shrugged. "I'm willing to try anything once. Why not?"

"Fair enough. It's a blend of wild herbs, tobaccos, and grasses. My allfather designed it himself. You can only get it here."

"I see. Allfather?"

She smiled. "The king." She paused. "You like her too, don't you?"

"What? Who?"

"Ebony."

"Funny, I came to ask you about Stryker."

"What about him?"

"It's obvious how you feel about him. Have you told him?"

"No. He still thinks me a cherub," she said, flopping down on the stoop.

Caleb scoffed. "How?"

The light on the porch was just enough he could see her blush. "He's a whole septennium ahead of me," she said.

"And that matters, why? There doesn't seem to be any real barriers in this world."

She shrugged. "Your third sept is a big deal. I've only hit my second."

"So you're only fourteen?" he asked, incredulously.

"Don't say it like that! You make it sound like I'm a child! I'm not a child! And no, I'm only a year shy of it. Try twenty!" she said, then sat down on the stoop, stretching out her legs.

"Ohh. I see. Where I'm from, turning twenty-one is a rite of passage. It's the legal drinking age in my country. I mean, you're considered an adult at eighteen, but twenty-one? You're what my cousin would call grown-grown. They don't recognize that here?"

"Adulthood is based upon sexual maturity here." She pointed at the hair growth on his chin. "That's a sign of adulthood. That and hair below." She nodded toward his crotch as she spoke the words.

He shrugged. "Makes sense."

"So, when did you get your first one?"

She asked it so matter-of-factly; it left Caleb flabbergasted. "Does everyone here have broken filters?"

"Broken filters? What's that mean?"

Asked and answered.

He shook his head. "Your question is inappropriate, but I'll bite. Honestly? I don't remember. It's been too long. Do you remember yours?" he asked sarcastically, hoping to make her see how inappropriate her question was. Yeah, that didn't happen.

She nodded, beaming. "Of course. I got my first one just after my first septennium."

What in the actual fuck? Who openly shares such information with a stranger? Caleb stared at her with his mouth hanging open as the realization sunk in. Sienna didn't suffer from a broken filter, she simply never had one. And who has pubes at what, seven? And now all he could think about was what she must look like nude. Stop. That. Now!

She stood up, shook out her hair, and leaned against the rail. Not helping. She was tall, statuesque even, like her mother. She had the same gorgeous red hair her mother did and soft feminine features. She was busty, with a tiny waist that accentuated the flair of her hips. And her legs? Those jokers went on for days. Her brick red leathers, almost the same shade as her hair, exposed her midriff from just below her halter to the waistline of her pants, which rested on those hips just at the hairline. A single teardrop diamond sparkled below her pierced navel. Very sexy. She had her father's ruddy complexion, and of course, his eyes. On a scale of one to ten, she was easily a thirteen, but she still wasn't Ebony. Not to say that under the right circumstances he wouldn't hit that. He totally would, and more than once. Yeah, she wouldn't stand a chance where he was from, brother and father be damned. She'd be able to choose whoever she wanted. The guys would love her and the girls would hate her. He could easily see where her father was coming from. Was Stryker blind? How could he not notice her? He knew the answer. As alluring as Sienna was, again, she wasn't Ebony. Hers wasn't the face Caleb saw every night when he closed his eyes. Did Stryker think of Ebony the same way he did? He decided that he didn't want to know. As if on cue, the door burst open, and Stryker stepped outside.

"You owe me a dance," he said to Sienna.

She nervously bit her lower lip and nodded. "Yes, I do. Some hostess I am. Sorry."

"Don't be. Would I be wrong if I said you were out here because your father and brother are in there?"

She frowned and nodded. Wow. That was her father's facial expression through and through. And it didn't detract from her looks one iota. They were all about to head in when a woman appeared in their midst. She had dark hair tied up with a sash. And she was wearing robes, similar to ones seen on goddesses in museums. She smiled. "Well, well, look who we have here."

Sienna and Stryker bowed. "Minerva. Good evening."

Caleb just stared at her. She looked at him and squinted. "You're not Trip, but you look enough like him for me to guess you're his son?"

"Yes ma'am," he said, then bowed, following their cues.

Sienna said, "Allfather has retired for the evening. Would you like me to pass on a message?"

Minerva smiled. "No, dear. You won't be here to give it."

Sienna looked confused. "I'm sorry?"

"You're not who I want to hear that from," she said, dryly. "Shall we?"

They disappeared.

Inside the hall, Blaze looked around and frowned. Sienna hadn't returned and hadn't he just seen Stryker go through those double doors? Fuck that.

"Julian, go check on your sister, please," he said.

Julian arrived at the rear door to find Minerva standing on the stoop holding overcoats. He bowed. "Good evening, Minerva, have you seen my sister? She—"

Minerva smiled. "I did. I saw her, Stryker, and Trip's son. They're all awaiting their fate right now as we speak. Tell your allfather that quid pro quo. He took my granddaughter so I've taken his. And since Banger played a part in it, I took Stryker too. And the other one, Trip's son, well, he will serve as a witness to their fates. He'll be able to give a full report, if he returns. Run along, dear. Make sure you pass on every word."

Then she disappeared.

Titus and Vanessa had just dozed off when Pippa and Ebony burst into their bedroom.

"Daddy! Wake up! Oh gods! She took them!" Pippa exclaimed, frantic.

Titus sat up, ready to be pissed off at the intrusion. "What?"

"Minerva! She took Sienna, Stryker, and Caleb. Daddy, she's going to hurt my baby. Please! Do something!"

"Meet me in my office," he said, jumping up and hastily dressing.

Vanessa rolled over. "What's going on?"

"I don't know yet, but I'll fill you in later. Sleep now, Schatzi."

She rolled over and was back to sleep before he left the room.

It looked like the party had reconvened in his office. Pippa and Blaze stood pacing while everyone else sat on chairs lining the wall.

Banger stood up. "Ahh, Titus, I knew this shite would come back to bite us in the arse. She's just as off as your brother was! No offense."

Titus put up a hand. "None taken and I agree. It was just a matter of time, but I wasn't expecting this."

"None of us were," Connie said with his gravelly voice.

Titus sat down at his desk, brow furrowed. "Any ideas where she may have taken them?"

Blaze, Constantine, and Banger spoke simultaneously, "The Lower Realms."

Titus nodded. That would make sense. It's where it all started. Was Drago involved? "We need to go see Drago, guys."

Connie and Banger nodded in agreement. Then the three disappeared.

Pippa looked at Blaze. "What the fuck? Now what?"

"We wait," he said.

In her panic and worry for her daughter, Pippa had forgotten about the others. She noticed Trip sitting alone, a stoic expression on his face. Christ! He'd just found his son. This had to be a shock. She placed a hand on his shoulder and asked, "How are you holding up, warrior?"

He looked up at her. "He's human, Pippa. If she thought him to Hell, he's sick and confused right now. I just hope she didn't separate them. On his own? Right now? He wouldn't survive the night, contingent upon where she dropped him." He took a deep breath and started rubbing his hands on his thighs.

She'd only seen him in this state one other time. And it was not pleasant. She leaned down to look into his eyes. "We'll find them, Trip. Don't worry. We'll find them. And if we don't?" Her voice faltered. "We'll make her pay. I promise you."

She watched as his eyes frosted over, becoming a steely blue-grey; cold as gunmetal. "There's where you're wrong," he said, icily. "She's going to pay either way."

PART III: MULAWOGS, GROUNDSWEEPERS AND DRAGONS, OH MY!

15

Thought travel differed greatly from passing through a portal. Caleb blacked out the moment he landed. The first thing to come back to him was his sense of hearing. Birds chirping. He was outside. The ground beneath him was hard and cold, causing him to shiver. What happened? One minute he was behind the banquet hall chilling with Sienna and Stryker, and the next minute some woman shows up. And... and what? She transported them somewhere else, that's what. He took a deep breath and opened his eyes. Oh lovely, he had puked. Something for Stryker to break his balls over. He sat up and looked around. He was in a forest, at least it looked like one. He looked up. Holy shit! The trees had to be ten stories high. All of them. And there were no lower branches. Someone or something had broken them off. The birds went quiet, causing the hairs on the back of his neck to stand on end. Something shrieked. An inhuman, animalistic, primal scream. He looked around, trying to pinpoint where the sound was coming from. Nothing. It came again, closer this time. He stood up, ready to run. Yeah... run. To where?

There was nowhere to hide and with no lower branches, nowhere to run to for safety. He looked at the trees. Had that been deliberate? Had whatever removed the lower branches done so to keep its prey from being able to get away? *Fuck me running! I'm gonna die here!* Whatever the godforsaken place was, it was going to be the last thing he saw in this life. The landscape shifted and what appeared to be a dark cloud was suddenly rolling along the ground toward him. Caleb froze. As it got closer, he could see glowing red eyes and rows of sharp teeth. Oh God, lots and lots of teeth! His legs finally responded to the command his brain had been giving him ever since the hairs stood up. *Run, motherfucker, run!* He ran.

The creature let out another screech, and soon he could feel the warmth of its breath as it gained on him. He realized he may never see his father again. Either of them. Something inside him felt like this was all wrong. If he was going to die, he was going to die facing whatever the fuck that thing was, head on. He stopped and turned just in time to see that dark maw open wide enough to swallow him whole. Bloody chunks of flesh and skin hung from those horrible fangs, and the putrid stench of rotting meat and death was overwhelming. The creature reached out to grab him with a pair of claws that looked so long, sharp, and terrifying he was sure they would shred him to ribbons. Well, so fucking be it. If he were lucky, it would be quick. Something gripped his shoulders, then he was airborne.

He looked down upon the thing that had just tried to eat him as it looked up, shrieking in protest. "Ugly fuckers, aren't they?" Sienna asked from above him.

Caleb breathed a sigh of relief. "You have no idea how happy I am to see you."

"Same here," she said, lifting higher.

He took one last look down and watched in disgust as the creature ate his vomit. "That's gross!" he said.

"It is," she answered.

"What the fuck was that thing, anyway?"

"A groundsweeper and why weren't you running?"

"I knew I couldn't outrun it. And I wasn't about to let it get the best of me."

"Your bravery should serve us well here. Have you seen Stryker?"

"No, I just woke up."

"You're lucky. It would have eaten you. So how much more of that bravery stuff do you have?"

He smiled. "I like to think it's unlimited. Why?"

"Because you're gonna need it. Groundsweepers are the least of our worries. We need to get as far as possible before night falls."

"Why?"

"Just trust me on this. We'll discuss it after I find us a safe place to hide for the night. First thing in the morning, we'll search for Stryker."

If he isn't already dead. She thought with dread.

―◈―

STRYKER PEERED OUT FROM HIS VANTAGE POINT, SILENTLY thanking his father for all those hours spent sitting in a cramped, uncomfortable position, surveilling. At the time, he was pretty sure it was just his father's way of getting rid of him for a few hours, and maybe it was, but boy was it ever paying off now, in spades. He wasn't alone. He had been watching the creature pace lazily back and forth for what felt like hours. Since arriving, he had already dodged three black rolling cloud thingies, two flying dragon looking jobbers, and now was trying his best to not be eaten by something that looked like a giant, white, hairless bear with very loose skin. Where the fuck had Minerva dropped them? And where were the other two? If he had to guess, Caleb was already dead. No way a human could survive there. Flight skills were a true necessity. You needed wings to get high enough to clear the rolling black clouds, and you needed skills to out fly the dragons. It didn't keep them from spitting on you, though. And that shit burned like a motherfucker. He glanced down at his thigh where a dragon had hawked a rather large, caustic loogie. It had burned right through his leathers and was a son-of-a-bitch to wipe off. The shit was sticky as fuck and you couldn't touch it with your bare hands. He had used his vest to remove it. Still, it was going to leave a scar. It was taking too long to heal. Truthfully, there was no telling what all that saliva contained, and he hadn't gotten the chance to tend to the wound properly. The best he could hope for at that point was to survive long enough for the bear to leave. Then maybe find some untainted water because if that wound got infected? It would be curtains for him too. Poor Sienna would be out here all alone, and that would be a most unfortunate outcome.

The bear grunted, then made a farting noise. Hairless bears fart? The stench that followed answered that question. It also gave him a clue as to the creature's diet. Vegetarian. He parted the leaves, barricading the small crevice he had slept in the previous night. The movement startled the creature, causing it to cry out and run... and stumble. The damn thing was clumsy. Stryker was about to crawl out when a dragon swooped down and grabbed the bear by its shoulder, then another one flew in and grabbed the foot. The two beasts fought over their meal for a moment until the bear's body gave way, leaving each with half. The first dragon flew ahead of the second one, and Stryker watched, stunned, as a burst of flames shot from its ass, burning the second one to a crisp. The charred dragon fell, landing a few feet in front of him in a cloud of ashes. It smelled like barbecued meat. Stryker's stomach grumbled despite having eaten shortly before arriving. Another trick his father had taught him was how to go without eating for an extended amount of time. It was a mind game, but right now his body wasn't aware of any such game and it wanted to be fed. Was dragon meat poisonous? It didn't smell like it. And the extra protein would help heal that burn. He hissed as he peeled back the strip of leather and looked. It was a nasty, angry red, and weeping with pus. Not good. Definite signs that an infection was brewing. By tomorrow it would stink and be oozing with thick green drainage of some sort as the infection took hold. Eat the meat. He carefully made his way to the carcass, hoping he had a few minutes before the smell attracted more dangerous critters. Unsheathing his knife, he sliced off a piece close to where the wings had been. The thin bat-like appendages had been vaporized. Lucky for him, the flames had also taken care of the skin and its underlying fat layer. The meat was salty and delicious. *Please don't be poisonous*, he prayed as he greedily ate his fill. He still had a piece of leather left from his vest. He sliced off extra meat and wrapped it up to take along. If he ran into Sienna, she would be hungry. He inhaled, sniffing the air for any signs of water. None. But there had to be some. All life forms needed water for sustenance. Even the dragons were getting theirs from the bear thing, which was a vegetarian, placing it near the bottom of the food chain. Yes, the bear was the key. Water couldn't be too far since the bear got around on foot. A large beetle skittered across the stones and crawled atop the dragon carcass. Another followed, then another, and soon a swarm of them had it covered. They made loud chittering noises as they devoured the burned parts from the body. They didn't seem to be too interested in the underlying tissue and departed as quickly as they'd shown up, leaving plenty of flesh for the taking. Stryker glanced around, not sure he wanted to be there for whatever else may show up to finish the job. A high-pitched screech followed by an odd clicking sound was enough to tell him he did not. He lifted off to go in search of water and Sienna.

※

Sienna and Caleb were also searching for water. Water, food, and shelter. They were going to need someplace safe to sleep. Sienna was relentless, but Caleb knew she was getting tired. It had to be a lot for her to fly and carry him too.

"Hey, why don't we rest for a bit. You must be exhausted," he said.

"I'm fine, though I'm beginning to wonder whether Stryker is even here," she said.

"Me too," he said.

Neither was willing to admit their actual fear. What if Stryker was dead?

They flew in silence for a little longer, then Sienna spotted what appeared to be a small crevasse on the side of a rocky ridge.

"I'm sorry we found nothing to eat or drink," she said as they landed. "You're right. I do need a little rest."

"You know, you're pretty strong for—" he began and stopped.

The look she gave him caused him to rethink the completion of the sentence. *Do you like your balls where they are, mister?*

He backpedaled. "—someone your size."

Her eyes narrowed. "Someone? Or a female?"

"Look, I meant nothing by it. It's just that I know I weigh over two-hundred pounds. That's even heavy for me to carry, much less fly with. I meant no offense."

She sighed. "I know. It's okay. I guess I'm just a little on edge. I'm really worried about Stryker."

"So am I, but the sun will be setting soon and we need to bed down for the night," he said.

"We do. Guess we'd better check out this spot and make sure it's empty."

Caleb reached down, grabbed a handful of pebbles, and tossed them into the opening. Nothing happened.

"You still have your lighter?" he asked.

She nodded and fished it out of her pocket.

The opening was oblong and low. Caleb had to crouch down to his hands and knees to enter. He didn't hesitate as he crawled inside with the lighter held out in front of him. Suddenly, he jerked and cried out. Sienna screamed and grabbed him by the leg, dragging him out. He rolled over and started laughing.

"You asshole!" she screeched. "That's not funny! I thought something got you!"

He started laughing even harder. "You should see your face! Oh, my god!"

She turned her back on him and he watched as her shoulders shook. Was she crying? She had her hands over her face. He hadn't meant to scare her that badly.

He leaped to his feet and placed a hand on her shoulder. "Hey, I'm sorry I just thought we could use a little comic relief. I didn't mean to scare you all like that."

She lowered her hands and grinned. "Really? Now, whose face looks comical?"

"You got me. I guess I deserved that."

"Damn right, you did! I could still kick you in your ass for it," she said with feigned indignity.

"Sorry. The space is fine. We could both fit if we huddle together. At least, it'll protect us from the elements. I'm not crazy about it, but it's all we've got for now." He rubbed his arms. "I wish I had kept the coat on now," he said.

She nodded in agreement. "Me too. The temperature is going to drop faster once the sun sets. Guess we should settle in. You first."

"Uh, no. I need to be guarding the opening."

Sienna opened her mouth to argue, then stopped herself. *It's a male thing. Let him be the male.* "Okay, if you insist," she said, then crawled into the small space.

Caleb crawled in behind her. They lay within the cramped space facing each other. The last rays of the sun's light were reflecting off her face, but it was dimming fast.

"You realize that if anything were to attack us here, we're cornered," he said.

"Yes, but it's this or we sleep up in a tree. And the trees here aren't conducive to that."

"Yeah, I noticed. So what else is out there?"

"Dragons. Many varieties, all poisonous."

"Dragons? As in the mythical fire breathing kind?"

She shook her head. "They don't breathe fire. They spit acid and blow fire out the other end. It's a defense mechanism to allow them to get away."

"Get away? From what?"

"Bigger dragons."

"Oh." They were quiet for a moment, then he said, "You know, I think you were right."

"About?"

"I wouldn't survive the night here alone."

"No, and the only reason you survived last night is

because you were passed out. Dragons hunt based on movement, not smell. Imagine having acidic snot. It would be hard to maintain a sharp sense of smell or even taste."

"Yes, and they fart fire. One can only imagine what their digestive tract must be like."

Sienna giggled. "Technically, they don't fart fire. They have a gland at the base of the tail that secretes a highly flammable liquid and then, yes, they pass hot air to ignite it."

Caleb laughed as he imagined how many school-age boys would love to have that skill. "You're pretty smart. How do you know so much if you've never been here?"

She shrugged. "I read."

"Read? What kinds of books have information on this place? And what is this place?"

"The king's library has detailed chronicles and diaries of every realm ever visited. And this place is in the Lower Realms somewhere between Hedon and Purgatory."

"Hedon? Purgatory?" he scoffed. "And I suppose Hell is just around the corner, right?"

"Yes, but not that close. You'd smell it if we were that close," she said, casually.

"Right," Caleb said, wondering if she was having a joke at his expense. But she wasn't laughing. Not even a twitch of her mouth. "You're serious, aren't you?"

"Well, yes, why would I lie?"

"So, Hell? As in Lucifer, the Devil, Satan?"

She shook her head. "Those are all human concepts of a place no human has ever visited and lived to tell about. Pure speculation," she said.

"Oh, boy. They would burn you at the stake for stating such where I come from."

She nodded. "Your chronicles have the sulfur smell

correct, but that's about it. Hell isn't hot. It's actually freezing, bitter cold. And I'm well aware of how fiercely loyal humans are to their beliefs. I have no desire to visit Terra-3 Earth, ever. They can keep their burning stakes and judgments."

"Terra-3? That's what it's called?"

"Yes. You'd be surprised at how much information there is in our library about it. I come from a family of Reapers. And Terra-3 is so busy it has its own team assigned to it. My Uncle Jared leads it."

"Reapers? As in the Grim Reaper? Angel of death kind of deal?"

"Something like that."

Night fell quickly, as did the temperature. Caleb's teeth chattered.

"We need to huddle," she said. "Your body temperature needs maintaining."

"What about yours?" he asked.

"Barring infection, my body maintains its temperature regardless of external reads. Trade me places." She rolled over him, then wrapped her arms, legs, and wings over him. "Is that better?" she asked, her breath whispering softly in his ear.

It was much better. "Yeah, it is. Thanks."

"You're welcome," she said, shifting her weight and pressing in closer.

Her breasts were now pressed against his chest and she smelled nice. So very, very nice. His body fired up in response. *Not now, not now!* His silent, desperate request went unheeded as the blood continued to flow south and engorge. He shifted his hips away from hers, only to have her tighten her grip on his legs and pull him back in. His full-on erection was lined up right at her center. And if they were naked? He was trying not to think about that. The shudder in his breath was not just from the cold.

"Caleb?"

He swallowed. "Yes?"

"It's okay. It's a physiological response. I know it's not about me."

He nodded. "Okay, but promise you won't tell your brother or your dad? I'm kind of attached to my junk."

She laughed. "I promise."

"Talk to me about something else. Anything else."

"Okay. Like what?"

"Do you know anything about earning one's wings without competing?"

"Oh, sure. You have to die."

"Why?"

"You must forsake your humanity, either physically, spiritually, or mentally. In competition, you do it by proving your worthiness. But when you die, you automatically give up your humanity. By default."

Her words struck a familiar chord, but he couldn't imagine where he'd heard them before. How was that even possible? This place was causing his imagination to run rampant. That's all.

"So what keeps people from committing suicide to get them?" he asked.

"Nothing, but that's risky. Everything is about intent. If your intent is just to get those wings, well, the very act of suicide proves you're not worthy. But if something happens beyond your control, as it did for my mother. You not only get the wings, but you can get promoted too. It just depends."

"On what?"

"On what The Master reads within your heart."

"Interesting," he said.

"Yes. The Book of Rules is one of my favorites. I've read it more than once."

"You weren't kidding, were you? You do read a lot."

"As much as I can."

"Nerd."

"Excuse me?"

He laughed. "I'll bet you think guys aren't interested in you because of your dad and brother. But it's not just that. They're intimidated by your intelligence. You're a nerd. A beautiful one, but still a nerd."

"Are beauty and intelligence mutually exclusive where you're from?" she asked.

Spoken like a true nerd. He couldn't help thinking and laughed. "No. I know plenty of pretty girls that dumb themselves down for the sake of some idiot."

"Why would they do that? If a male isn't smart enough to be in your company and appreciate you, then you don't need his company."

He leaned back to look at her. His eyes had grown accustomed to the dark and he could still see her eyes. "That's exactly right and don't you ever forget it."

She smiled. "I won't. You know when we get back, you should tell Ebony how you feel about her."

"What do you mean?"

"Now who's pretending to be stupid? I saw how you looked at her while she was dancing with Stryker."

"Oh, really? I'm surprised you saw anything else besides him. What's good for the goose."

"What do you mean?"

"I mean when we find him. You should tell him how you feel."

"He knows. Everybody knows. He's like you. He only has eyes for her. They've been friends for a long time."

"Yes, and he is stuck in a holding pattern we humans like to call 'the friend zone'. Very hard for a guy to break out of that particular hell."

"So it's easier for a girl?" She sounded hopeful.

Caleb realized she saw herself in that position with Stryker. "It's much easier for a girl, Sienna, because for guys that zone doesn't exist." *Read: All pussy is fair game.* No way he was telling her that.

"Because females are more highly desired for sex by males than the other way around. Did I say that right?"

He chuckled, "Yes, exactly." *Nerd.*

"Okay."

He could hear the relief in her voice. The hope. "Don't give up, Sienna. Just give him a chance to see you as a woman."

"Do you?"

"Me?"

"Yes."

"Of course, I do. Why do you think this huddle is so uncomfortable for me?"

"Ah, got it."

They lay in silence as it was now completely dark and they didn't want to give their position away with sound.

Caleb was dozing when he heard her whisper his name. "Caleb?"

"Mm? Yeah?" he said, groggily.

"Thank you."

"Don't mention it."

They slept.

16

Caleb awoke to a horrible screeching sound. He recognized that one. A groundsweeper. He opened his eyes to Sienna's gold ones staring back at him, grimacing.

"What's happening?" he whispered.

"I'm protecting you. It can't get you. I won't let it."

Her body was oddly shaking, and Caleb realized, with horror, that it was attacking her.

"Sienna!"

"Shh. It's okay. I won't let it hurt you. I promise."

"But—"

"Don't worry. It'll leave soon," she said, tears streaking down her face.

There was a horrible crunching sound, and Sienna screamed. Then they were no longer covered. The creature had torn off her wings and, by the sound of it, was now devouring them. Caleb never felt so helpless in his life. He didn't know what he could do, but he damn sure would not allow her to continue covering him while the thing tore at her back. He felt her arms go limp and her eyes were now closed.

"No! No! Sienna?" He was sure she was dead. No way was he ever going back without her. He'd die first. With superhuman strength he pulled her in and switched places with her, coming face to face with a mouth full of teeth, chewing. His stomach rolled over as he saw her beautiful feathers disappear down the creature's throat. He was defenseless. Or was he? He reached out for the creature's eyes. It shrieked and tried to back away. *Fuck. You. For real!* He dug his fingers deeper and pulled. The creature went to claw at his arm when there was a flash of light and suddenly that deadly claw was lying on the ground. Besides the screams of the creature, there was another sound, but he couldn't identify it over the deafening roar of his own heartbeat. Then there was another flash of light and he realized he was seeing light reflecting off of metal as a knife came down and cut off the other claw. The creature howled in agony as its ink-like blood poured over him, but he still had hold of its eyes and with one mighty jerk he removed both orbs from their sockets. The creature retreated, shrieking the entire way, disappearing into thin air.

Stryker leaned into the small cave. "Holy shit! You're alive?"

Caleb just stared back at the angel, wide-eyed, still gripping the groundsweeper's eyes. Stryker reached in to pull him out. Then Caleb was fighting him tooth and nail. On some level, he knew who it was, but it was as if his body hadn't yet received the memo. Fortunately, Stryker was much stronger and snatched him out of the cave then sat on him pinning his arms down.

"Caleb! Stop! It's me! Stop fighting. You're okay now. Easy."

Slowly Caleb calmed down, then he was scrambling back to the cave. "Sienna! We have to help her!"

The blood drained from Stryker's face. "Sienna's with you? She was in there too?"

Caleb nodded. "Stryker, it took her wings. She was protecting me and it took her wings."

"Damn. Let's see how much damage it did."

He carefully pulled her from the cave and turned her over. He checked her pulse. She was alive but unconscious. Her wings looked horrible. At least it hadn't pulled them from her body. It had bitten them off. Blood flowed freely down her sides and back. Stryker frantically looked around for something to bind the stumps with. Caleb was already removing his vest. Together, they carefully bound her wounds. Then the realization sunk in. With Sienna wingless, they were screwed. Caleb felt utterly useless. At least, Stryker had a knife, and he definitely knew how to wield it.

"You can rip out their eyeballs," Stryker said. "That's something, right?"

The two of them looked at each other, then they were both laughing, hysterically.

Caleb nodded toward Stryker's thigh. "What happened?"

"Dragon spit on me."

"At least it didn't fart on you."

Stryker nodded. "Aye. There's that. Oh, wait. You hungry?"

"Fucking starved."

Stryker took out the meat he'd scavenged and shared a piece with Caleb.

"I must be really hungry, because this shit fucking bangs!" Caleb said between bites.

Stryker nodded in agreement as he licked his fingers. "It does. It surprised me."

On the ground beside them, Sienna stirred and tried to roll over. She cried out as she accidentally rolled onto one of her wing stumps. They rushed to her side, leaning over her. "Don't move, baby. Stay there," Stryker said.

"Is Caleb okay? I wouldn't let it get him," she said.

"He's fine. You did good."

She sat up and closed her eyes, waiting for the wave of pain to pass. "We've got to get moving."

"What are you talking about? You're in no condition to —" Stryker began.

"No, you don't understand. There are things here far worse than groundsweepers. We have to go now."

"Groundsweepers? That's what those things are?"

She nodded. "We need to go, Stryker. Now!" She looked at him. "What's wrong with you?"

He shook his head. "Nothing, you're right. Let's go."

She reached out, touching his forehead. "Stryker, you're burning up. What happened?"

"A dragon spat on him," Caleb said.

"Where?" she asked.

"On my leg," he said, then recounted to her what had transpired since he arrived. Sienna's face lit up. "Wait. The beetles only ate the scorched parts of the dragon?"

He nodded.

"Do you know where the nest is?"

"No, I mean, I guess I could show you which direction they came from. Why?"

"They're scorch bugs. If we can get one, we could use it to debride your wound and maybe stop the infection."

Stryker shook his head and laughed. "Leave it to you to have all the information on this place."

Caleb exchanged a look with her, then said. "Told you. Nerd."

"Oh, shut up," she retorted. "Let's go."

They made their way back to find the only thing left of

the dragon was its skeleton. The bones polished clean. "This is great!" Stryker exclaimed, wiping sweat from his brow and rubbing his forehead.

"What's great?" Caleb asked.

"The bones," Stryker answered. "We can make weapons out of them. The ribs can be sharpened and the jawbone with those teeth? Hell yeah," he said, wincing.

"Let's see your leg, Stryker." Sienna said.

"No."

"Why not? Just pull your leathers down to the wound."

"No."

She rolled her eyes. "Please don't say it's because you're shy. I've seen my brother's junk on more occasions than I'd like to recall. Unless you've got an extra penis, I promise not to be shocked."

He rolled his eyes. "Fine."

Reluctantly, he pulled down his leathers. Sienna's heart sank as she saw what she was hoping not to. The wound was ugly. The veins leading away from it dark and pronounced. It was bad. But if they could get that beetle soon enough, maybe they could halt the spread, giving his body a chance to heal itself. He looked at her, already knowing.

"It's bad, isn't it?" he asked.

She nodded. "We need that beetle."

The nest turned out to be closer than expected. The hard part was catching the blasted thing. After being reassured by Sienna that they were harmless unless you happened to be burned with dead tissue, Caleb raided the nest and successfully retrieved two beetles. It took a little coaxing, but once they realized there were some good eats on Stryker's thigh, the critters were on board. It took both Caleb and Sienna to hold him down once the beetles started getting close to the underlying healthy tissue. He was screaming. "Fuck! Make 'em stop! Make 'em stop!"

"They'll stop on their own, Stryker, trust me. It's almost over. Just a little while longer." Sienna pleaded with him. Her own back was on fire and she wasn't sure how much longer she could hold him down.

And damn if they didn't stop and amble off back to the nest as soon as she said the words. Stryker was lying on the ground, shivering, sweating, and exhausted. But they couldn't stay there. They still needed a safe place for him and Sienna to rest and heal. They eventually found a cave large enough for the three of them. After piling brush and twigs to cover the opening, they left Caleb standing watch with a sharpened rib and the lower jawbone of the dragon. There was no choice now, but to wait.

17

Despite the beetles work on the wound, the infection continued to spread. Caleb frowned as he saw the dark veins were now extending up across Stryker's abdomen and down to his knee. He cut a fresh strip from his vest and changed the dressing. Stryker was now delirious with fever, rambling on in some strange language. Every once in a while he'd cry out and thrash about fighting off some imaginary predator. It got so bad Caleb had to hide his knife from him, fearing he may lash out at him while he was tending the wound. Sienna wasn't doing much better. She appeared to be sleeping, but attempts to wake her were unsuccessful, as if she was in a state of suspended animation. Her mangled wings were already growing back in, but they looked strange and misshapen. Before his delirium set in, Stryker told him her wings needed to be bound while they healed, but there was nothing big enough to do that with. In a perfect world it would be done with a linen sheet, cocooning her while they grew back in. This place was as far from perfect as it got. The only redeeming factor was nothing had disturbed them in their current haven, but Caleb was in trouble. They still hadn't found a supply of water. The lack of it wasn't affecting the angels yet, but he was becoming severely dehydrated. It was day three of their stay in this strange realm, and he knew it was just a matter of time before his own body would shut down. Maybe that was a good thing. Maybe if he died, he could get his wings and do more to help. They needed a break. Something had to give. He checked on his charges one more time, then took his position at the cave opening again. He was able to stay awake most of the night stealing snatches of sleep here and there, but the hyper-vigilance soon took its toll and he fell asleep.

A few hours later, Caleb awoke to find himself face to face with a pair of green eyes crazed with fever, a knife at his throat.

"Who are you?!" Stryker shouted.

Caleb raised his hands, defensively. "Stryker, it's me, Caleb."

Stryker looked confused. "Caleb? I don't know any Caleb."

Caleb nodded. "Yes, you do. We arrived here—"

"Don't tell me I know you, asshole! Who are you? What have you done to Sienna's wings?" he demanded, still shouting. The knife was now touching Caleb's throat.

Caleb swallowed what felt like a mouthful of sand. "Stryker, you need to calm down and be quiet."

"Don't tell me what to do, asshole! Answer me! I swear if you did anything to her… did you touch her? Well, did you?!"

Caleb shook his head. "No, I didn't. A groundsweeper attacked her. Don't you remember?"

Stryker's eyes narrowed, then he looked down at himself, noticing that his pants were open. "Oh, I see how it is. You didn't touch her, you touched me!"

Caleb backed up, shaking his head. "No, no! I just changed the dressing on your wound. I swear it."

He was trying his best to remain calm so as not to give Stryker cause to escalate. He nervously glanced at the cave opening, hoping there was nothing out there listening.

"You've got three seconds to tell me who you really are or I swear I'm opening you up ear to ear. Now talk!" Stryker demanded.

Caleb was panic-stricken. He had no idea what to say. But if Stryker didn't stop this, they were all going to be dinner for some unimaginable creature. He balled his hands into fists, prepared to cold-cock the crazed angel and hoping he could do so successfully. He tried one last time.

"Trip's my father, remember? You know him."

Stryker sat back, still confused. "Trip?" he asked, a semblance of recognition finally setting in. "Oh, Trip. Well, damn, dude, why didn't you just say so?" The knife clattered to the cave floor. Then Stryker crawled back to his spot and fell into a fitful sleep. Just like that.

Caleb heaved a sigh of relief and ran a hand through his now very greasy hair. The knife. He needed to hide that thing better. He was about to reach for it when there was a low rumble outside. Thunder? A flash of light confirmed what he was thinking. Rain? Yes! He scrambled to the cave opening and peeked out just in time for the rain to begin. He didn't care anymore about creatures hunting them down. He needed water. He ran out and turned his face up to the heavens, thanking the gods for such a much needed break. He cupped his hands and took a sip. The water was cool, refreshing, and just wonderful.

After drinking his fill he went back inside searching for something he could use to hold water besides his hands. The only thing left was Sienna's halter. He had to be quick as there was no telling how long the rain would last. He quickly and carefully removed it from her, then wrapped his vest around her again, covering her breasts. The halter did the trick. Who knew being busty would come in so handy? And just in time, as the rain stopped as quickly as it started.

"Where were you?" Sienna asked, startling him as he returned to the cave. She sat up and winced.

"How are you feeling?" He asked.

She looked down at herself. "Um, a little exposed?"

"Sorry, I needed something to catch and hold water."

"Water? We have water?"

He nodded. "And we saved you piece of meat too."

Her stomach rumbled, loudly. "Food?"

He couldn't help smiling at her. "Yes, food."

She had fallen into that weird coma before they could feed her. He figured she had to be famished. He unwrapped the last piece of meat and sniffed. It was questionable. She didn't give him the chance to think about it, snatching it from his hand and wolfing it down. Every bit. Well, obviously, she was feeling better.

She sat licking her fingers and chewing. "Oh my god, that was fucking delicious! Where did you get it? Is there more?"

"Don't you remember? Stryker lucked out with a farted dragon."

She nodded. "Yes, that's right, but I had just lost my wings and he was so sick."

"Yeah, you went down yourself after he settled. Gave me quite the scare. I couldn't wake you up."

She was still licking her fingers and lips with such gusto one would think she'd just eaten a rack of ribs. Caleb watched as she savored the last remnants of her meal. The cutest thing ever. He always did like to see a chick with a healthy appetite. The whole starving oneself to satisfy some knucklehead's unrealistic idea of perfection was just another version of dumbing oneself down. If you had to do it, he wasn't worthy. She sat back and loudly belched like a champ. In that moment, he couldn't help thinking how much every one of his human friends would love her. He could just imagine her hanging out with them, wearing his old football jersey, eating hot wings and drinking beer. Yeah, nerd or not, she would have many male friends.

"So where's the water?" she asked.

"I'm sorry for using your halter," he said as she practically buried her face in the water and drank deeply.

She shook her head and waved him off. "No, it's fine. That's why Allfather has us wear leathers, especially in battle. It comes in handy. As you can see, it's good for more than just holding boobs. And the pouch inside the male's leathers can also be used as a canteen. It's removable and has a drawstring. We can use Stryker's next time."

"Ohh, I was wondering about that. I didn't wear mine. I wasn't sure how it worked," Caleb said, not relishing the idea of drinking water from Stryker's "canteen" at all.

She caught his face expression and laughed. "Trust me, after three days without water, one does not care where their only source comes from. Besides, you turn it inside out first."

"Still a little too close. I'll pass."

"Suit yourself, but as soon as we find a water source, we will be removing it and filling it. We should pack up."

"Pack up?"

"Yes, we need to keep moving. We got lucky with the rain, but we're going to need an ongoing source of water and food. If I could figure out how to make a dragon do that whole thing all over again, we'd be eating good tonight. How's Stryker doing?"

Caleb shook his head. They went back in the cave to

check on him. At least, now he was resting quietly. Maybe that was a good sign? No. They didn't have to pull down his leathers to check the progress of the infection. It was now past his abdomen and making its way up his chest. Sienna tilted his neck to see if it had climbed that far. Not yet. She looked up at Caleb, worry in her eyes.

"What is it?" he asked.

Her lip trembled. "He's dying."

This situation was grave. The only one of them able to fly was dying from a nasty infection. And even though the groundsweeper hadn't removed her wings at the base, the damage was still enough to incapacitate her. She tried. But those gnarled up, feather-covered bonsai were no good. She also knew that once they returned, her wings would need to be shorn off and started afresh. Not looking forward to that. And Caleb, though he was healthy, he was the most vulnerable. She sat down next to Stryker and started stroking his hair.

Caleb watched her, unable to imagine her heartbreak. The closest he could come was the loss of his mother. They sat in silence.

A few moments later, she broke it. "Caleb?"

"Yeah?"

"How long was I out?"

He shrugged. "Half a day, maybe. Why?"

"So this would be day three of our stay here, right?"

He nodded. "Right."

"Right," she sighed.

"Sienna, what is it?"

"Do you know what menstruation is?"

He scoffed and nodded. "Oh, yeah."

"We don't menstruate in our realm. Allfather has complete control over reproduction."

"Well, that's a relief. The last thing we need is some creature with a sharp nose coming after us."

She looked at him, shaking her head, eyes filling with tears. "As I said, 'in our realm'. We are no longer in our realm."

"Oh. Oh! Did it? Are you?"

She hastily wiped her face and shook her head. "Not yet, but I'm going to say we have about a day and a half, maybe two. And yes, there are beasts here that are attracted to blood. We've been lucky so far, but—"

"This is different."

"Yes. The strongest drive among living creatures is reproduction."

"It's not even about the blood. It's about the hormones that come along with it, right?"

She nodded. "I'm sorry, Caleb. I'm so sorry."

"Don't be. It's not your fault, but it changes things. Big time."

"I know. When it happens, I won't be able to stay here. Whatever shows up will see you as competition and—"

"What do you mean whatever shows up?"

She explained. "Dragons are opportunistic with reproduction. They can mate with any female if she's in heat. The male will show up, deposit his seed, and move on. If the act doesn't kill the recipient, she will carry it's young to term, at which time it will claw its way out of her and she will become its first meal."

Caleb stared at her in abject horror, shaking his head. "But if they can't smell, how would they find you?"

"It's different with hormones and pheromones. Certain species have other sensors that can pick it up. Not to mention, the scent of blood attracts other creatures too. The dragons simply follow them to steal their food."

"You mean, like the groundsweepers?"

She nodded.

"And what happens if more than one male shows up?"

"They'll fight to the death and the winner gets laid."

"No. I can't let that happen to you. I won't," he said, shaking his head adamantly.

"There's nothing you can do about it, Caleb. But there is something you can do for me."

"What?"

She gently lowered Stryker's head and crawled over to him on her hands and knees. "Kiss me."

"What?"

She leaned in to him. Her delicate breath was soft against his mouth.

"I've never been kissed and as you can see, the one I… well, he's incapacitated right now. You understand."

He wanted to say "no". He wanted to tell her it would be all right. He wanted to do anything he could within his power to stop this from happening. Now he knew what she meant when she said there were worse things than groundsweepers. Now, he understood why she insisted on them moving and moving and moving. She wanted to be sure they were away from dragons. But there really wasn't any safe place in this odd realm, was there? Once it started, there would be nowhere for them to hide. So, he would do the only thing he could do. He would give her what she wanted.

Caleb placed a hand behind her neck, gently pulling her in. Then his lips were on hers and his tongue was licking her teeth. She opened her mouth, allowing him full access as his other hand found its way into her hair, pulling her closer. She tentatively touched his tongue with hers and sighed. Kissing was everything her friends had bragged about it to be and more. Her friend Layka had told her Julian was the best kisser ever. *I don't think so, Layka.* She thought.

He paused. "It's okay if you want to, you know, pretend it's him. It won't offend me."

She shook her head. "No, I would never disrespect you like that. You've been nothing but sweet and kind and patient and I love you for it."

He smiled at her. "I'm in the 'friend zone' aren't I?"

She nodded. "I'm sorry."

"Don't be. It's his loss."

He pulled her in again, and this time his arms went around her waist as hers slid around his neck. He kissed her long and deep and with all the passion he could muster because, dammit; she deserved it. When they finally pulled apart, they were both weeping.

"It's not fair," he said. "You're the sweetest girl I've ever met and you don't deserve this."

"It's okay, Caleb. If you get back, tell my daddy I'm sorry for talking to him the way I did. And tell him, tell him—"

Caleb tilted her chin up. "Trust me, he knows. They all do." He wiped her eyes. "Now, there's something I need you to do for me."

She nodded. "Anything."

He looked into her eyes and said, "Kill me."

18

Sienna stared at him as if he'd just lost his mind. "What?"

He took her hands in his. "Hear me out. You said it yourself if I die I forfeit the human side automatically."

"But Caleb, there's no guarantee you'll be back."

"How did it happen for your mother?"

She told him the story exactly as her mother had told it to her.

"So, He gave your mother the choice to return or not? Ok, so I'll choose to come back. What if your father comes to escort me?"

She shook her head. "He doesn't do it anymore. Maybe you'll get my Uncle Jared. If you do, you could tell him where we are, but what if you don't? There are too many variables, Caleb. I don't like this idea."

"You've got a better one?"

"I don't know if I can."

"You have to."

"Caleb—"

"Dammit, Sienna! Just get the knife," he said with more anger than he intended to.

She backed away from him. Her feelings hurt. He reached out and took her hands in his, then looked into her eyes, pleading. Reluctantly, she nodded.

With the two of them going back and forth, they hadn't noticed Stryker was awake, still in his feverish state, and creeping toward them with the knife between his teeth.

This motherfucker! Stryker thought. Who the hell did he think he was touching Sienna? And now yelling at her? He stood up, the knife now in hand. "Don't you talk to her that way!"

Caleb and Sienna turned to him, surprised, mouths agape. Grabbing Sienna, Stryker shoved her out of the way.

"You said you didn't touch her! You lied! You lied! I saw you!"

With that, he brought the knife down, burying it in Caleb's chest. Even in that weakened state, Stryker was still stronger and Caleb never stood a chance. His eyes were wide as he stared back into Stryker's bloodshot, red-rimmed, crazed ones. Stryker pulled the knife and plunged it in again and again. The first stab hurt like hell, but Caleb didn't feel any of the ones that followed. And Stryker didn't notice when his eyes glazed over. Satisfied that Caleb would not fight back, he dropped his knife, then crawled to his spot and went back to sleep. Sienna sat there in shock, unable to even scream. She pulled her knees up and rested her chin on them. Then watched, unseeing, as the blood poured from Caleb's body and out the cave opening. Her stomach hurt and somewhere in the back of her mind, she wondered if the dragon meat had been spoiled. She sat like that for what seemed hours. Not noticing Stryker muttering, tossing and turning in his sleep. Not hearing the piercing shriek as a groundsweeper found their lair. Not noticing as the creature grabbed Caleb by the arm and dragged his body out of the cave opening. Not even when it noisily devoured him, leaving nothing but a few shreds of clothing. And as the pain in her belly increased, she didn't notice the sticky warmth now pooling in her leathers.

Sometime in the night, Stryker's fever broke. His body was finally getting ahead of the infection. He awoke the next morning to find Sienna curled up and asleep. A large pool of blood was at the cave opening. He could only guess. Something had gotten Caleb in the night. He shook his head. "Damn." He turned to Sienna and shook her awake. She cried out, backing away from him.

"Hey, hey, it's okay, baby. It's me. I didn't mean to startle you. We've got to get out of here. Something got Caleb. I'm sorry, but he's gone."

She stared back at him, incredulous. "You don't remember?"

"Remember what?"

Should she tell him? How would that make him feel? She didn't know.

"Where's my knife?" he asked, looking around. "Oh, there it is," he said as he found it a few feet away from where he had been sleeping. But that wasn't right. He always kept his knife on his person. How did it get over there and why was there blood on it? "What happened here, Sienna?" he demanded.

No point in keeping it from him now. So she told him. Everything.

THE DEATH ANGEL THAT CAME TO ESCORT CALEB WAS A female. Smokin' hot, of course. *Damn! Maybe I should die more often,* he thought.

She smiled at him. "Thanks, you're cute too."

"You can read my mind?" he asked.

She shook her head. "No, your face."

"So what's your name?"

She threw back her head and laughed. "You are definitely your father's son."

"You know my father?"

"Honey, everybody knows your father."

"Is that a good thing or a bad thing?"

She shrugged. "It is what it is. Well, here we are."

Caleb looked up and sure enough, they were standing in front of the biggest double doors he had ever seen. They opened as the two of them approached.

She nodded toward the adjoining room. "He's waiting for you. Good luck, little Trip. It was nice meeting you."

"Wait. I still didn't get your name—"

But she was already gone.

Caleb paused, took a deep breath, then entered The Master's chambers.

"Be not afraid, son. We've been expecting you," a voice said, cordially.

We? Caleb thought with some trepidation. He approached two figures sitting at a small table set with tea for two. *Wow, Alice In Wonderland, much?*

The Master chuckled. "I can see why you'd feel that way. Interesting literary work, though, I must say." He motioned to an empty seat. "Please, join us."

Caleb took the empty seat and turned to see that the other figure was his mother. She had her hands over her mouth and was crying.

"Mom?" he said, his voice breaking. He fell to his knees before her and rested his head on her lap. Then he openly and shamelessly wept.

"I missed you so much," he said.

Ileana stroked her son's head. "Shhh, it's okay. Don't cry. I just wanted to see you one last time. You met your father?"

"Yes, ma'am. He came for me after you—" A round of fresh tears.

"Listen to me, Caleb. Your father's a good guy. You can trust him. I know he would have been there if he had known. Give him a chance. Promise me?"

"Okay, but where are you going?"

She smiled and started to fade.

Caleb panicked. "Mom! Mom! No! Don't leave! Please don't leave! Why can't we just stay here?"

She became brighter and solid again. "We can, sweetheart, but I didn't think that would be your choice."

"Choice?" he asked.

Now The Master spoke. "Yes, son, you must make a choice. Right here, right now. You can stay here with your mother or you can go back to your friends and the new life your father has invited you to enjoy. It's up to you."

Caleb couldn't believe it. He'd actually forgotten about them. And now, he could clearly see the aim of this test. If he stays with his mother, then the human side wins. Go back and be with his father and the angel side wins. Thus proving himself worthy of his wings. He looked at his mother. "What should I do?"

She smiled at him and shook her head. "I can't make that decision for you, my love. The choice is yours and yours alone."

He knew what he needed to do, and on some level, he knew he had already decided. He wrapped his arms around her and squeezed. "You were the best mother a guy could ever ask for, but I have to go back."

She smiled and nodded. "I know, and I'm so very proud of you. Always have been, always will be." This time when she faded, it was for good.

He stood for a moment, reeling from the pain of losing her a second time. At least, he got to say goodbye. He turned to The Master. "What happens now, sir?"

The Master smiled at him. "You decide what kind of angel you'd like to be."

He didn't hesitate. "I want to be just like my father."

The Master nodded. "Excellent choice, son, excellent choice."

19

Stryker couldn't believe what he was hearing. He killed Caleb?! They had their differences, but he never wanted him dead. He shook his head. "I didn't mean it. You have to believe me!"

"Of course, you didn't, but it's going to be okay. It was what he wanted. Truth be told, you saved me from having to do it and I'm not so sure I could have," Sienna said, hoping to ease his concerns.

"But what if he doesn't come back?" Stryker asked.

Before she could answer, they heard a strange warbling sound off in the distance. Sienna's eyes grew wide as she backed up against the cave wall. "Stryker, you've got to go. Now."

He frowned. "What? Why?"

"It's coming for me and if it finds you, here, it'll see you as competition. Go. Make sure you tell my parents and Julian how much I love them. Okay? Promise me."

He was shaking his head. "No. Whatever it is, we face it together. Why would it be coming for you?"

The creature outside was growing anxious as it drew

nearer, its cries more urgent and shrill. She quickly explained to him what was happening. "So you see? You can't be here when it gets here."

Stryker grabbed the sharpened rib and the jawbone. "Well, I've got news for you and that thing. I *am* competition and anything coming up in here thinking it's going to mate with you will have to go through me. So we stand together or we die together, but I'm not going anywhere, Sienna. Do you hear me? I won't leave you here to face a dragon alone. What kind of warrior would I be if I did that?"

"Stryker, I can't be responsible for—"

He placed a hand on either side of her face. "Now, you listen to me. You are not responsible for any of this. Minerva is. No matter what happens here. I blame her for all of this. But she'll get hers. Just you wait. Now, let's kick some dragon ass so we can get the fuck up out of here."

She nodded. The beast was now just outside the entrance. Sienna swallowed. "Stryker?" she whispered.

"Yes?" he whispered in return.

"I'm scared."

"It's okay. I won't let—"

"If you see that we're losing, will you—"

"Yes, and I'll make it quick."

"You promise? Will you be able to do it?"

"Absolutely, no way will I let you go out like that. I swear it."

"So what's the plan?"

The leaves and branches they had at the entrance were being cleared away.

Stryker remembered Caleb fighting the groundsweeper on his own and succeeding. "Let it come to us and go for the eyes first. Okay?"

She nodded. As if on cue, a bright yellow eye peeked in

between the remaining shrubbery. With one sweep of a horrific talon, it cleared the remaining brush. Then the beast stood in the cave opening. It took one look at Sienna and made a cooing sound.

Stryker chuckled. "I'll be damned. It's wooing you."

She nodded. "Yes. And as long as you keep your distance and don't move, it won't feel threatened."

"Let's fix that now," Stryker said and advanced upon the creature.

The dragon turned its attention to him and growled.

Stryker nodded. "That's right, big boy. You've got competition. Shall we fight for the maiden?"

Without warning, he lifted the rib bone and chucked it like a spear at the beast. It landed exactly where he wanted, right through the eye. The beast released a large ball of flame from under its tail, then fell to the cave floor, dead.

Sienna looked at him. "Well, that was effective. How did you know?"

"I didn't."

"Was that the same kind of dragon that spat on you?"

He nodded. "Yeah, but smaller. Much smaller. This thing is a baby compared to what that was."

Her shoulders slumped. "I was afraid of that."

"You think others may follow?"

"I know it. As long as I'm bleeding, they're gonna keep coming."

"There is a way we can stop it."

She shook her head. "Oh, no! No thank you! Let's just take our chances for the next day or two. Besides, it's too late for that. It's already started."

He shrugged. "It was just a suggestion."

"Oh, yeah. Picture it, Stryker. Us getting rescued and me

being pregnant—to you! You thought my father and Julian were bad before? They'd beat both our asses."

"Okay." He turned away from her, relieved. He wasn't so slow that he didn't notice she was growing on him. She was. And under the right circumstances, he'd be okay with being her first. Not like this. She deserved better.

"Stryker?"

"Yeah?"

"Thanks for the offer."

"Sure thing. And now—" He took his knife and carved a piece of flesh from the beast. "—we eat."

The ball of flame had ignited some twigs. They gathered enough to build a proper fire. Then cooked chunks of meat over the open flame. It was risky, but they needed to eat. Accelerated healing burned a lot of calories. After their meal, Stryker assessed himself, gauging the advancement of the infection. The dark veins were noticeably receding, and he felt much stronger. He took flight, testing his wing strength. He was going to have to carry her. Sienna gave him the last of the water, then retreated to a corner to put her halter back on. While she did that, Stryker cleared the area as best he could and dragged the carcass out into the open. Sienna came out from the cave and froze, staring at him.

"You ready?" he asked.

She shook her head slightly and said, "Don't move."

He frowned at her. "What?"

"Stay very still," she said, now looking past him.

He was about to protest when an enormous shadow fell over him. Then there was a low growl followed by a roar. *Oh shit.* Stryker held his breath. The beast stepped around him and paused, staring at Sienna. It looked nothing like the one that had shown up earlier. It was ugly with dark blue scales and red eyes.

Two nubs covered with tufts of white hair protruded from the top of its head. Stryker could see the hairs waving frantically. Who needs a nose when you can smell with whatever the fuck they were? *Yeah, you found what you were looking for, dude.*

Sienna's eyes were wide with fear, and she was visibly trembling. The first one had almost been cute, trying to woo her, but this one? This one was enormous and obviously an alpha male. There would be no wooing nor cooing. There would only be taking, and a rib bone to the eye would not cut it. Stryker eyeballed the distance between them. They were going to have to make a run for it. He only hoped he was strong enough to fly and carry her. It was time to find out. He met her gaze and gave a slight nod. Tears were streaking down her face now as she blinked twice. She understood. She couldn't have been more than five steps away, but damn if it didn't feel like five miles once he started sprinting. The dragon was so focused on her it didn't notice him until he scooped her into his arms took off.

Pissed. It. Off!

It let out a roar of outrage as it took flight in hot pursuit.

Stryker thanked the gods that the reduction in her wings made a difference in her weight. Though he had a size advantage over the creature, dodging in and out of the upper branches of the surrounding trees. The dragon was relentless in its pursuit. Stryker braced himself for the first spitball, but it never came.

"Why isn't it spitting?" he asked her.

"If I had to guess, I'd say it's not willing to risk injuring me."

"Oh, you're that hot of a commodity?"

"Think about it. All dragons are males. That's why they reproduce the way they do. How many females do you think there are here? How long do you think there's been one? He probably hasn't gotten any in a very long time. What would you do?"

"Point taken."

The beast behind them roared, then another joined it.

"Oh look, now it's a party," Stryker said, sarcastically.

"No, actually this is in our favor. They'll fight to the death. It'll buy us some time. Let's get out of here."

The sound of flaming air followed by a loud thud as the loser hit the ground told them all they needed to know.

Stryker said, "You were saying?"

A spitball whizzed past Stryker's head and hit a nearby tree. He looked back, and the creature was right there. Close enough to bite him if it wanted to. Then it was next to him and in a surprising move, the beast head-butted him, hard. The move stunned him, and he started spiraling downward. Just before they landed, Sienna leaped from his arms and landed on the ground, rolling. Stryker did the same, tucking and rolling at the last second. They sat up and looked at each other, both surprised and relieved that they were still in one piece.

The dragon swooped down and pinned Sienna to the ground with two mighty talons. She screamed and struggled, but the beast was much bigger and stronger. It planted itself between her legs and started humping. She continued to struggle, trying in vain to crawl from under it. Luckily, the beast had no concept of clothing and what purpose it served and continued humping her through her leathers. Sienna looked down in stark horror at the size of its phallus. No way that thing was going to fit inside her body, but the beast didn't seem to care that it wasn't hitting its mark. It continued to hump her until it suddenly shuddered and roared. Sienna's face was now a mask of disgust as the creature ejaculated across her leathers, her belly, and part of her halter. *Eww,*

eww, EWW! As quickly as it started, it was over. The beast took flight with semen still dripping from its extended organ. Wham, bam, thank you ma'am, for real. It took everything he had for Stryker not to say the words.

Sienna couldn't move. It was bad enough she had to deal with her own blood ruining her leathers. She now had the dragon's DNA soaking into them as well. She gagged as her breakfast threatened to make its way back up.

"Sienna?" Stryker said, offering a hand to pull her up.

She looked up at him and damn if the corner of his mouth didn't just twitch. He thought this was funny? Her eyes narrowed. "Not one word."

He coughed and cleared his throat, masking the snicker. Truth was, he was just so relieved that she was all right, he could have fallen out on the ground laughing.

"It's not funny, Stryker!" she seethed.

"I'm not laughing."

"Yes, you are!"

"No, I… wait. Did you hear that?"

"Don't change the subject."

"Shhh. Listen."

She did, and then she heard it too. Running water. It had to be a river or a waterfall, but it was close enough for them to hear it. Reluctantly, she grabbed his hand, allowing him to pull her up. Then they made their way through the forest toward the water source.

20

Caleb woke to the sound of rushing water and birds chirping. He could feel the sun shining on his face. It felt good. He lay on the ground with his eyes closed, basking in its warmth. This time there was no cold ground underneath. A cloud must have passed over the sun as his light went shady. Then there was a large, wet tongue sliding lazily across his head. Caleb cried out as he crab-walked away from whatever it was. It turned out to be a pale, loose-skinned, hairless bear cub. Hadn't Stryker seen such a creature get eaten by dragons? What were the odds that the former was possibly a parent of this one? If his memory served him correctly, Stryker also said the animal was a vegetarian. At least, he didn't have to worry about it trying to eat him. The creature ambled toward him clumsily. Yes, Stryker said that too. It was one doppy-assed critter. It fell forward, tripping over its own feet, then rolled head over heels the rest of the way. Caleb laughed, despite himself. It was actually kind of cute, but he wasn't here to play with bears, he needed to find his friends. He stood up to look around and promptly fell on his back. Whoa. Wings. He forgot about them. They were much heavier than he thought they'd be. He tried to get up again. Yeah, not happening. He lay there struggling for a good ten minutes before he gave up in frustration and exhaustion. Damn wings. He wanted them so desperately, but it never occurred to him he would need to learn how to use them. At least, they were properly tucked and they weren't being damaged.

He looked up at the bear, which was staring at him with its head cocked to the side.

"I guess there's no chance these bad boys come with user instructions, huh?" he said.

In response, the bear looked off into the distance, then suddenly started nudging him with its nose.

"Dude, what is it?" Caleb said.

A high pitched inhuman shriek echoed from where the bear was staring. Caleb looked, but he couldn't see anything. Not yet. The bear started nudging him again. Pushing him toward the river. Caleb tried to stand again and failed. Now he could see the groundsweeper coming at them. This time the bear was out and out, rolling him toward the water. Once Caleb got the idea and started rolling on his own, the bear dropped beside him and followed suit. The creature may have been clumsy on its feet, but lying down and rolling? It was a little champ, arriving at the water's edge long before Caleb, then rolling right in with a small splash. It stood in the water, frantically splashing. Caleb wondered if it wasn't drowning until he saw the groundsweeper was really closing in on him. He watched in horror as he rolled; groundsweeper, sky, bear, ground; groundsweeper closer now, sky, bear, ground; groundsweeper mouth opened and reaching, sky… water. As soon as he hit the water, the bear grabbed him and pulled him away from the shore. He glanced back, seeing the groundsweeper rolling back and forth and shrieking until it finally gave up and faded away. Caleb didn't get the chance to celebrate the small victory as the weight of his wet wings began to pull him under. The bear seemed to sense what was happening and dove beneath him, coming up with Caleb on its back. The creature got them to the opposite shore in no time. Who knew pale hairless bear was an aquatic critter? It deposited him face down on the ground, then shook itself off in a blur of skin and water.

"Caleb? Is that you?" Sienna asked.

He rolled over and looked up. She and Stryker were standing over him, dripping wet, annnd naked. Caleb's eyebrows shot up. *Whoa.*

"Yeah, it's me. Ummm, did I miss something here?" he asked.

Sienna blushed so deeply Caleb was sure that even her toes had to be red. But, he wouldn't know, he was too busy trying to keep his eyes above her neck. Fail. Peripheral vision was taking in everything else just fine. Everything *but* her toes. Now, there was a memo he wouldn't want to be the one sending:

DEAR BLAZE AND JULIAN,

I regret to inform you that your daughter/sister is no longer a child. She is definitely a woman. Get over it.
Sincerely,
Caleb

STRYKER STEPPED INTO HIS LINE OF VISION AS HE SAT UP, strategically positioning himself in front of her. "You can put your eyes back in your head now," he said.

Caleb frowned up at him. "News flash, I've seen it

already. How do you think her halter cups got filled with water? Get over yourself, Stryker. Thanks for the homecoming. Feels good to be back."

It's kind of hard to pull off sarcasm when you're not standing face to face. Maybe they won't notice.

Stryker ran a hand through his hair and sighed. "You're right. I'm sorry. It's just that I've been trying to protect her from all the males in this place for the past three days. I guess I'm still on edge."

"Three days? That's how long I was gone?" Caleb asked.

Stryker nodded. "Yeah. One caught her that first day and—"

"One caught her?" Caleb asked, eyes wide.

"Yeah, but luckily it didn't know what clothes were." He went on to explain what happened.

"It what?" Caleb exclaimed. "You mean to tell me after all that aggression it still didn't get the business right?" Then he did exactly what Stryker had wanted to do. He fell back on the ground laughing.

"You too?" Sienna said. "It wasn't funny, Caleb!"

She picked up a softball-sized rock and lobbed it. Caleb barely had the chance to roll out of the way. The act didn't sit well with the bear and it squatted. Then it was lobbing fresh scat at her—accurately. The first clawful landed on her chest in the middle of her halter. She turned to dodge the second one, leaving it to land in her hair.

"What's it doing?" she asked as she pulled it from her hair. Then realizing what it was she exclaimed. "It's throwing shit at me? Caleb, make it stop!"

Caleb was too busy laughing again, as was Stryker. He reached over and placed a hand on the bear, stroking it. "Easy, Brutus, she means no harm. Even though it could have killed me if her aim was better."

"Fuck you, Caleb! If I wanted to hit you, I would have! Now I have to wash this all over again!" she said as she stormed off toward the river, removing her halter.

"I'm sorry, honey, you're right. It wasn't funny," Caleb said, trying not to snicker.

Stryker said, "Caleb, listen. Sienna told me what happened and I'm really sorry. I didn't mean it. Accept my apology?" He offered his hand.

The bear gave a low growl. Caleb patted its head. "It's okay, Brutus." The bear settled.

Stryker rolled his eyes. "As I was saying before your new pet spoke, I'm really sorry for killing you and it would be great if you would accept my sincerest apology."

Caleb looked up at him. "Can I be brutally honest?"

Stryker looked crestfallen, but he nodded. "Sure, dude, I'm sure I deserve it."

"It's really hard for me to take anything you're saying seriously, right now, with your junk inches away from my head. Could we have this conversation after you have your clothes back on?"

Stryker laughed and nodded. "Sure, man, I was just waiting for them to dry. They're over here. C'mon." He signaled Caleb to follow him.

"I'll be right there," Caleb said, not moving.

Sienna stepped out of the water, wrung out her hair, then wrung the halter. She glanced at Caleb still sitting on the ground and suppressed a grin. She grew up with her wings, but she could easily recognize an angel with new ones. They sat on the ground... a lot... at first. Adjusting to that new center of gravity was challenging, never mind the fact that his were also wet. Obviously, he hadn't figured out how to tuck them.

"What's wrong, Caleb?" she couldn't resist taunting, paybacks being the bitch they are.

"Nothing. I'm good. Just waiting for my hair and feathers to dry. That's all."

Stryker looked back at him as understanding set in. "You don't know how to use them yet and now they're wet."

Caleb nodded and sighed. "Yeah. A little help?"

Stryker smiled. "Yeah, we can do that."

Stryker and Sienna spent the rest of the day and part of the evening helping Caleb adjust to his new center of gravity and teaching him how to tuck them away properly. Even Brutus helped by announcing the presence of groundsweepers whenever they showed up. Stryker and Sienna would go up a tree and Caleb and Brutus went to the water until the threat passed, then they were at it again. Before they retired for the night, Caleb could lift off and fly short distances. Stryker promised him that high lessons would be on tap first thing in the morning.

21

Minerva couldn't be more pleased with herself. Exacting vengeance on Titus and his cronies felt good. It was going far better than she expected. She had been plotting it ever since that dreadful day when she had gone down to the Lower Realms to kill Isabel. The poor girl had gotten the short end of the stick one time too often, and the situation needed to be rectified. She had been so focused on delivering the head to Titus that she neglected to properly dispose of the rest of the body. Drago being the disgusting pig he was, quickly mated with the body before the eggs could die. The thought made her shudder. She should have known better. She was horrified to find that he had successfully fertilized sixty eggs. Sixty! She didn't want to imagine even one offspring of his sharing her bloodline, much less sixty. She pleaded with him to give them to her, but he would not be dissuaded. Not until she offered to deliver Titus's granddaughter in exchange.

Drago specifically instructed her on how to do it. Deliver the girl and a warrior to the wastelands outside of Hedon.

Sons that were born with lizard-like features got banished there to live out their lives. Sienna had to be at least two septennia and mature enough to ovulate once she was outside of Titus's realm. Within three to five days she would have her first bleed. Drago didn't want that. He wanted her for the second one. According to the ugly dragon, it was richer. Whatever that meant. Minerva took him at his word. He said he wouldn't allow any of his sons to impregnate her. He needed her in one piece. "I'm not saying they won't have their fun," he said, grinning. Minerva didn't want to know what that meant either. Males were so disgusting. Why did everything have to revolve around that ridiculous appendage between their legs? What's to keep the dragon from killing her? Well, that was where the warrior came in. He was there to make sure she survived the month. And what was to keep said warrior from impregnating her himself? In the original plan it was to be Julian, a guarantee against just that. But Stryker had been there instead. All the better for Minerva since Banger was also on her shit list. After all was said and done, Stryker would be fed to the dragon that marked her and the female genitalia floating in that horrible canister in Drago's lab will have red hairs, not black. She tried to talk him into handing it over while the plan was being laid out, but Drago would not hear of it. She couldn't have the rest of Isabel until she delivered Sienna. And to ensure that he didn't make any side deals with Titus, she made him agree to give her temporary dominion over the wastelands, which he reluctantly did. She wasted no time sealing the portal after dropping them off. No one in, no one out. And what of Trip's human son? Unfortunately, he was collateral damage. Drago assured her that there was no way a human would survive more than one night.

"And what about when Titus comes looking for them?" She had asked.

"You leave Titus to me," he said.

He didn't have to say it twice. As soon as that portal was closed, she had fled.

As expected, the entire crew showed up. All three barging into Drago's office demanding to know if he'd seen Minerva and what all did he know about the kidnapping. Drago feigned shocked surprise.

"Who knows what's going on in that crazy head of hers, Titus. Have you forgotten how she came down here to cheat me out of the bride your brother promised me?"

Titus sighed. "Yeah, I remember. Do me a favor? Let me know if she shows up. We suspect she may have hidden them somewhere in your domain."

Drago nodded. "Will do. Give me a few days to see what I can find out, yeah?"

"Sure. We'll be in touch."

The moment they were back in his office Banger said, "That son of a bitch is lyin', Titus. 'e knows more than 'e's lettin' on."

Titus nodded. "I know, but he wasn't about to tell and if we tried to force it, he'd just dig his heels in. Give him the few days, then we'll go back and if need be, we'll use force."

"Why not now?" Constantine demanded.

"Because this is Drago we're talking about. Whatever is going down, has to behoove him. Remember, it's happening on his turf so, ultimately, he's the one in control. Give him the few days he's asking for so we can see what he really wants. Once we have that information, it'll be easier to negotiate with him."

"Who's gonna tell Blaze and Pippa?" Constantine asked.

"I know my son. He's going to lose his ever-loving mind. And no matter what you say, he ain't gonna just sit by and wait."

Titus met the Death Angel's eyes. "That's exactly what I'm counting on, Connie."

Titus was right. Neither Blaze nor Trip were going to stand idly by.

"My daughter is stranded gods know where with Stryker?" Blaze said.

Banger spoke up. "What's your point, Reaper? My boy ain't a good enough warrior to protect your daughter? If my memory serves, it was your daughter who was all over him at the banquet, not the other way around."

"That's exactly my point! She was nice enough to invite him to our table, and he fucking ignored her the entire time! I swear to the gods, right here and now if anything happens to her because of his neglect, I'll—"

"You'll what, Reaper? I'm telling ya now, if you put your hands on me boy, you and I will have a problem. I promise ya!"

"Oh? Like we don't have problems now, Redeemer? Had you just let me take Isabel's head in the first place, we wouldn't be here!"

"He's got a point, Banger," Constantine drawled.

"You shut the fuck up, Connie! It ain't like you weren't there too."

"And what of my boy?" Trip said, quietly. "He's an innocent. I had very little to do with any of this, but somehow my son got caught up in it too. Did it ever occur to any of you that maybe she'd been calculating this whole thing from the get-go? Stop and think. What's her endgame? What's always been her endgame?"

Titus said, "The purity of her bloodline. She doesn't want to see it merged with his."

Trip nodded. "Right, so what could she possibly offer him in exchange for Isabel's eggs?"

The blood drained from Blaze's face. "She's trying to trade my daughter for Isabel's... but that would mean—"

He didn't have to finish the sentence as the realization sunk in for all of them.

Trip continued. "For this plan to work, Sienna had to be of age."

"Which means she really has been planning this for quite some time," Titus said, "and Drago would have to be on board with it."

"I told ya that bastard was lyin'," said Banger.

"I say we go down there right now and get that ugly motherfucker to talk!" Blaze said.

Titus shook his head. "No."

"What do you mean 'no'?" Blaze demanded.

"I meant we will wait and see what he comes up with."

"You can wait. I'm not. I wasn't exactly asking for your permission."

Titus slammed a fist down on his desk and stood up. "I'm going to give you the benefit of the doubt here because right now you're a distraught parent, but if you don't stand down, right now, warrior, I will throw your ass in jail until this is over. Got it?"

Blaze's mouth was working, but no sound was coming out. Rare, very rare. Trip stood and placed an arm around his friend.

"He understands," he said, speaking for Blaze. "C'mon, brother, let's go get some air."

Blaze was too stunned to respond as Trip led him out of the king's office.

"What do you think he's gonna do?" Banger asked.

"I think he's going to do exactly what I told him not to," Titus answered.

22

Blaze was grateful for Trip's intervention. He didn't trust himself to not get thrown in jail. Never in his life had he wanted so badly to tell Titus to go fuck himself. On some level, in his heart of hearts, he knew Titus was right. The warrior in him knew his king was right, but the father in him was being rent asunder by his own imagination, picturing all the horrible things Drago could do to his little girl. His little girl. She wasn't so little anymore, was she? The fact that she wasn't was exactly what made the plan so doable. Sienna had grown up on him and he wasn't ready for it. He didn't think he ever would be. And since when did that ever matter to the universe? How could he go back and tell Pippa the best they can do is wait for the dragon to decide what information he wanted to give up? He couldn't. He wouldn't. He shook Trip's arm off.

"I'm good. I'm good. I think I'm just gonna go clear my head."

"No, you're not," Trip said.

"Yeah, I am. I—"

"Who the fuck do you think you're talking to?" Trip

asked, frowning. "We've been through too much together. I know you. You're going down there. And if you're going? So am I."

"You heard him, Trip. I may end up in jail."

"*We* may end up in jail. So be it. At least, there's a chance Sienna is okay. They need her. But Caleb?" he shook his head, then rubbed his eyes. "He doesn't stand a chance, and he has no role in this scenario. He's collateral damage. He just happened to be there. I only hope he didn't suffer. You know?"

Blaze nodded. "I do and I'm so sorry, buddy. I really am."

Trip wiped his eyes again. "Let's do this."

"Guess I should tell Pippa what's up," Blaze said.

Trip shook his head. "Plausible deniability. The less she knows, the better. We'll explain after it's all said and done."

"We?"

"Yup. If we're gonna go down, it may as well be in a blaze of glory, right? I won't let you face that redheaded firing squad alone."

Blaze chuckled. "You know I have to tell her you called her that, right?"

"It would disappoint me if you didn't," Trip said as they took to the air.

※

THEY SURPRISED DRAGO WHEN THEY SHOWED UP IN HIS office.

"Blaze, it's been a while. How's the hand?" he asked, referring to a bite he had given the dark angel upon releasing him as an inmate.

"Healed," Blaze answered.

"I see it left a nice scar. You come back for a matching set?" Drago asked.

Blaze scowled. "No. I came back for my daughter."

"I already told your king I don't know what Minerva did with your daughter. Now, if you'll excuse me. I have some research to do on it."

Blaze was about to snatch the dragon up by the throat when Trip said. "Listen, Drago, you're a parent. You must see where we're coming from. She's obviously unstable and who knows what she's capable of, but I'm begging you as a parent. If you know anything, please tell us."

Drago shook his head. "As I said, I don't know. And yeah, I see where you're coming from. Especially you. He's half-human, right?"

Trip nodded. "Yes, he is. He wouldn't stand a chance down here. We all know that. Please. If you hear anything at all. Their names are—"

Drago was growing impatient. "Yes, yes, I know. Sienna, Stryker, and Caleb. I've got it. Now, will you give me the chance to do my own digging? Or do I need to call your king down here to retrieve you?"

"No, sir. We're going," Trip said. "Sorry to have bothered you."

They flew home in silence. Blaze, sullen and pissed off because he still wanted to wring the beast's neck. And Trip sick with worry, knowing with each minute that passed Caleb's chance for survival decreased. It got worse when they arrived home. The king summoned them as soon as they cleared the portal.

"I specifically told you not to go down there!" Titus bellowed.

"It was my fault," Blaze said, "Trip was just looking out for me. I—"

"Shut up! I don't want to hear anything out of you, right now." He turned to Trip, "What did he say to you?"

"That he was working on finding out what he could."

Titus shook his head. "No. Word for word. What did he say to you?"

Trip recounted the conversation verbatim. A grin slowly spread across the king's face as he listened.

"Was it something I said?" Trip asked.

Titus nodded. "We got him."

This time when Titus showed up in his realm, Drago was ready. He knew he slipped up. On their initial visit, Titus had deliberately omitted Trip's son from the information. Then when Trip showed up, and he knew his name? Yeah, the gig was up.

"Titus, come on, you've got to understand my position," Drago said.

"I don't have to understand a damn thing!" Titus raged. "Where are they?"

"The wastelands."

Titus's mouth fell open. "You let her take a human down there?"

"I didn't know she had a human until after the fact. By then, it was too late."

Titus frowned. "What do you mean, too late?"

"I'd already given her temporary dominion."

"Jesus, Drago! Why?"

"She was still after me for her granddaughter's eggs. She offered a trade," he shrugged. "I wasn't gonna say no. You're *the* king of the Upper Realms. Your blood trumps hers in my book. Sorry." *Not sorry...*

"How long does she have dominion?" Titus asked, already dreading the answer.

"A month. Long enough for the girl to get her second bleed."

Titus pinned him with a glare. "'The girl' is my granddaughter. Have enough respect to say her name."

"Fine, Sienna."

Titus shook his head. "Where's Minerva now?"

Drago shrugged. "That's just it. I haven't heard from her since she dropped them off."

"Fuck. She's in hiding. And she won't come out until it's time to cash in. I swear to you, Drago, if anything happens to any of them, I will consider it a declaration of war and I'll be coming for you. I'll mount that ugly head of yours on my office wall! Think I won't?"

There was no doubt in Drago's mind that Titus was telling the truth. After all, he wasn't known as Titus the Terrible for nothing.

"But what about the human… er Caleb? I didn't even know about him."

Titus's eyes narrowed. "Especially him. He's vulnerable and you know it. You should have done something about that the moment you found out, but no, you were too busy enjoying the drama you knew she was about to stir up."

Drago couldn't deny it. He had even thought it funny. The truth of the matter was, he hadn't really expected her to do it. He didn't think she would have the nerve to go into Titus's kingdom and steal his granddaughter. For a female that hated manly parts so much, she sure displayed the biggest pair of balls he'd ever seen.

"What if I were to help you get back at her?" he asked.

Titus shook his head and pointed at him. "I don't need your help to get back at her. Believe me, I've got that shit on lockdown. And you have one month before your head is mine."

23

It only took Caleb a few days to get the hang of flying and once he had it, he was unstoppable. He wanted to fly everywhere and see everything. Even dodging dragons became a game. The three of them learned to hunt and kill to eat. That rib bone saw many an eye before dinnertime. With Brutus's help, they could discern poisonous plants from edibles. If Brutus didn't eat it, neither did they. It kept them alive in the weeks that followed.

"Why can't we just fly out of here?" Caleb asked Stryker.

Stryker shook his head. "I tried. She's closed the portal. No one gets in, no one gets out. Have you been paying attention to the moon phases? Didn't Sienna say that bleeding thing would happen again in about a month?"

Caleb nodded. "Yes, she's right."

"Too bad we can't pinpoint it more accurately. It would be nice to have some sort of warning."

Caleb stared at him like he'd sprouted an extra head. "You're joking, right?"

Stryker shook his head. "No, why would I kid about that?"

Caleb laughed, enjoying the moment. There was actually something he knew about that Stryker didn't. "Trust me, there's plenty of warning," he said.

Stryker frowned. "Like what?"

"It's called PMS. Her leathers will fit tight and she'll be bitchy about it. She'll be bitchy about everything. You watch. Oh, and her boobs will get sore. She'll be—"

"—bitching about it?" Stryker added.

Caleb nodded. "Exactly. Oh, and she may get weepy."

"Weepy?"

"Yeah, stupid things will make her cry. Just watch, you'll see."

"How do you know so much about it?"

"It's a regular thing where I'm from. Had to deal with it every freaking month."

"From who?"

Caleb grew quiet. "My mom."

"Oh, sorry, dude. I didn't mean to—"

Caleb waved him off. "Don't worry about it. At least I got to see her again. I should probably thank you for that. Thank you."

"Anytime," Stryker said.

They fist-bumped.

Sienna was gathering small sticks and twigs for their nightly fire. She dropped her armload and said, "Aren't you two going to help? Why do I have to do everything?"

Stryker cocked an eyebrow and glanced at Caleb, who nodded. *Yep, it's coming.*

Sienna knew it was coming too. She could feel the changes. From the tender boobs to the moodiness. She knew she was being overly sensitive, but she couldn't help it. Everything the two of them did seemed to irritate her. Brutus was the only one not on her shit list. He just seemed to know.

He would crawl over to her to lay his big, hairless head in her lap and sigh as she stroked it and talked to him in soothing tones.

Stryker said to Caleb. "I wonder if that would work for us. You know, just snuggle up to her and place your head in her lap. Think it would work?"

"I think I'm willing to pay top dollar to watch you try," Caleb said. He paused, then added. "You know, Stryker. You should say something to her."

"About what?"

"You like her now. You should tell her."

"She's a cute cherub. Nothing more."

"Really, brah? Is that the best you can do? Calling her a cherub? Reducing her to child status? She's put up with so much more than us since we arrived here. And she's done so with the grace of a lady. If that's not the definition of a woman, then I don't know what is. Even if she was still of a child-like mind when we arrived, that innocence is long gone. Give her some credit."

Stryker thought for a moment then said, "What about you?"

"What about me?"

"I see how you look at her."

"Jealous, are we?"

"Fuck you."

Caleb shook his head and laughed. "No, she's only got eyes for you, man. Go for it."

"Friend zone, huh?"

"Something like that, but it wouldn't change anything. As you said, she's cute but… no."

"It's Ebony, isn't it?" Stryker asked, not dreading the answer as much as he thought he would.

Caleb stood up and said, "We'd better help her before she yells at us again."

"Yeah, I thought so. You know what's funny?" Stryker said.

"What's that?"

"Ebony thinks you like Sienna."

Caleb frowned. "Why would she think that?"

"Maybe you oughta take your own advice," Stryker said. Then they went to help Sienna start dinner.

THE NEXT MORNING IT WAS LIKE SOMEONE HAD THROWN A switch. She woke up singing to herself as she and Brutus gathered berries for breakfast. Stryker looked at Caleb. "Is it over?"

Caleb looked worried. "No, it means the bleeding has started."

As if on cue, a loud shriek pierced the air. That was no groundsweeper. The shadow that passed overhead confirmed their fears. Stryker would swear it was the same one that caught her the month before.

"It very well may be," Caleb said. "If what you said was true, it basically marked her with its scent."

Stryker nodded. "That's what she said. She actually wore those stained leathers for the duration of it without washing them, and it worked. It kept others away."

"I'm not willing to take the chance on it not tearing her leathers off, this time. Are you?"

Stryker shook his head. "No, I'm not."

They both reached for their rib bone spears just as Sienna and Brutus returned.

"I think it's after me," she said, eyes wide with fear.

"Come stand between us. We won't let it have you."

"You have little choice in that," Minerva said as she appeared. The look on her face belied the fact that she wasn't expecting to see Caleb. "Well, well, well, it looks like you really are the son of a warrior, human." She clapped her hands. "Bravo."

The dragon circled in and landed right in front of Minerva, its focus entirely on Sienna. The three of them backed up as the beast roared.

Minerva laughed. "I don't think he likes you two being there with her. The portal is open. You're free to go."

Stryker reached for Sienna. "Not her," Minerva said. "She stays. You can thank your father and allfather for that, young lady."

"Oh, fuck that," Caleb said. "We're not going anywhere without her."

The dragon advanced upon them. Sienna stepped back and tripped over a rock. Caleb and Stryker had her back on her feet in a flash. The beast stood, moving its head from side to side as it continued forward. The movement was almost hypnotic. All the while, Minerva stood behind it, laughing and jeering.

"Oh, this is going to be fun to watch," she said.

"Sienna!" a voice called from their left. They turned to see Blaze, Trip, Titus, and Banger approaching. Monitoring the portal, daily, had paid off.

"Stay back!" Sienna called to them. "It wants me. It won't hurt me."

Against everything the warriors stood for, they listened to her and stopped.

"How do you like it, Titus?" Minerva hissed at him. "So close to being able to save her, yet powerless. Powerless!"

Caleb said, "Sienna, remember when you threw that rock

at me? You said you could have hit me if you wanted to. Did you mean that?"

"Yes," she answered.

"Good, pick up that rock you just tripped over."

She did.

He continued, "Stryker, you get the left eye and I'll get the right. Sienna, right smack in the middle of the forehead. On three, we all throw together."

"Its left or my left?" Stryker asked.

"Dammit, Stryker, the one that's on your side!" Caleb said, exasperated.

"Got it."

Minerva continued to stand behind the creature, taunting Titus. Oblivious.

Caleb whispered. "One…"

The three of them stopped.

"Two…"

They raised their weapons.

"Three!"

Sienna whipped that rock with all her might and knocked the creature smack dab in the middle of its forehead just as a rib bone pierced each eye. Titus and his cohorts watched in shocked horror as the creature released a huge gaseous ball of fire from beneath its tail, instantly incinerating Minerva. Then the beast fell forward, dead.

"What the fuck did we just witness?" Blaze asked.

Titus smiled and said, "Poetic justice."

Drago appeared amidst them. "Look, he lives!" he declared, pointing at Caleb. "Looks like I get to keep my head, eh, Titus?"

Titus nodded. "For now, Drago, for now."

Drago chuckled. "And the eggs too?"

"Looks that way," Titus said.

Trip ran to his son and threw his arms around him. "I thought you were dead. I thought for sure you were a goner. Forgive me."

Caleb wriggled out of his father's grip to look at him. "Dad, there's something I need to tell you."

"What is it, son?"

Caleb stepped back and opened his wings, causing everybody to stop what they were doing.

Titus's eyes narrowed as he turned to Drago. "There's only one way that could have happened here."

Drago took a step back, then pointed to the dead dragon. "Let's call it even Stevens. At least you got yours back."

Then he was gone.

Titus looked around. "It's been some time since I've been here. Nothing's changed. I see you've made friends with a mulawog." He nodded toward Brutus.

"A what?" Sienna asked.

"A mulawog." Titus scratched Brutus under his chin, causing the creature to smile and sigh.

"Brutus? We thought he was some sort of hairless bear," Caleb said.

Titus chuckled and nodded. "I can see that. Lucky for you, they're pretty low on the food chain here. They know how to get around. You learn anything from him?"

Sienna nodded. "Yes, we followed him and ate the same plants he did. He actually saved me from eating something poisonous. Slapped it out of my hand then barked at me."

"They're very smart. Anybody piss him off? That's always a special thing to see."

Sienna blushed, while Caleb and Stryker started laughing and pointing at her.

Blaze looked at his daughter, then at the creature. "Why? What's it do when it's pissed off?"

"It throws its shit," Stryker said, gasping for breath.

Sienna pouted. "It wasn't funny! Just like when the dragon—" She stopped, realizing her father was listening intently.

Blaze frowned. "When the dragon what?"

She waved him off. "Nothing. Can we go now?"

"No. We're not going anywhere until you tell me about this dragon. What happened?" Blaze demanded.

All three of them looked uncomfortable, suddenly finding their feet to be very interesting.

Titus figured it out and said, "Have you even hugged your daughter yet, warrior?"

"Of course I did. What's that got to do with anything?"

"Do it again."

Sienna's eyes widened as her father pulled her into his arms, squeezed, and sniffed, then froze. "What the fuck is all over your leathers?" He exclaimed.

Trip leaned in and took a whiff. "Um, if I were to guess…"

"Shut up!" Blaze said to him through clenched teeth. "I wasn't asking you." He set her down and made a beeline for Stryker. "You let this happen to her? What kind of warrior are you? And then you laughed about it?"

Stryker was speechless, then Blaze charged him. To everyone's shocked surprise, Caleb stepped in the way, blocking him. "I can't let you do this, sir."

"Get your boy, Trip," Blaze warned.

"Daddy, no!" Sienna shouted. "It's not his fault! Stop!"

Caleb didn't know how to fight hand to hand with a highly seasoned warrior. All he knew was he couldn't let Stryker get beat down for something that was beyond his control. And yes, he would take the beating himself, if need be. Then Sienna started talking.

"Daddy, I love you, but if you lay one finger on him, I will never speak to you again. Ever!"

Blaze paused and turned to her. "Sienna, I realize you think you have feelings for him, but—"

"No, Daddy, this isn't about that. This is about the fact that we somehow survived a month in this horrible place. We did what we had to do to live. We landed here without weapons, without food, without water, and without shelter. All fine and good for me and Stryker, but Caleb was completely vulnerable. And he didn't make it." She was now crying. "And I'm so sorry, Uncle Trip. I couldn't do it. I couldn't, but Stryker, he was sick, and he wasn't in his right mind and… and it was an accident, but he came back. He came back to be with us and he didn't have to do that, but he did."

Sienna knew she was rambling, and she knew she wasn't making any sense, but she needed to get it out. To purge herself, mentally and emotionally, of the burden she'd been carrying from the first day they arrived. In those first few hours spent alone when she had nothing but her own thoughts for company, she had figured out what Minerva's plan was. It was the only thing that made sense. She figured out that Caleb had been in the wrong place at the wrong time. And she had sworn to herself she would do everything in her power to make sure he made it back to his father. She had even sacrificed her wings for him.

When she finished, Blaze looked at his daughter and said. "We'll talk about it when we get home."

She shook her head. "No, Daddy, we won't. I'm finished with this place. When we leave here, I'm never going to mention it again, so please don't ask me to. Understood?"

Much to everyone's surprise, he nodded. "Understood."

A high-pitched shriek pierced the air. A groundsweeper.

Caleb, Sienna, and Stryker were about to head for the nearest tree, when Titus asked, "What are you doing?"

"We need to get to higher ground," Sienna explained.

"Or water," Caleb added.

Titus was shaking his head. "You have a mulawog with you. You don't need to do anything."

"What do you mean?" Sienna asked.

Titus said, "You mean to tell me you've been chilling with Brutus here for almost a month and you've never seen him take on a groundsweeper?"

They all shook their heads.

Titus grinned. "Well, you're in for a treat. Watch this."

The groundsweeper was now visible as it rolled along the ground toward them at full speed. Brutus growled, then dropped to the ground and started rolling straight for it. Sienna clapped a hand over her mouth as the groundsweeper opened its mouth in anticipation of its meal. Brutus kept rolling. Right into the creature's mouth. Then the groundsweeper was shrieking in exasperation as it lost the ability to close its mouth. Brutus was still forcing his way against its teeth, forcing its jaws to open wider and wider. Then Brutus closed his mouth and eyes and blew. Suddenly he was five times his size. Now, all that loose skin made perfect sense. The groundsweeper was trying to retreat, but Brutus kept rolling until the creature's upper jaw dislocated and snapped. With a roar, the groundsweeper disappeared into the surrounding landscape again. Brutus stood up and ambled away, unrecognizable in his current inflated state.

"So how does he go back to normal?" Sienna asked.

Stryker smiled, remembering the first one he'd run into. "The same way all living creatures get rid of excess gas," he said as Brutus let out a loud belch followed by an equally loud fart.

Titus rubbed his hands together. "On that note, we ready?"

Sienna shook her head. "But what about Brutus? Can he come too?"

Titus shook his head. "I'm afraid not, sweetie. He belongs here. He'll be fine."

Tears streamed down her face as she said goodbye to the mulawog. Then Caleb and Stryker said their goodbyes as well. Brutus seemed to sense what was going on. He turned and slowly made his way into the forest. They watched until they could no longer see him. Then each parent embraced their young and Titus thought them all home.

PART IV: OF FATHERS AND DAUGHTERS

24

Since Sienna had already told her story, Titus excused her from the debriefing. She refused.

"I may not be speaking, but I'm going to be there, for them. Please, Alldaddy?"

Titus nodded. "Sure, you can. And if something else comes to mind, speak up. Okay?"

"Yes, sir. I will."

"Don't you want to get cleaned up and showered first?" Blaze asked.

"No, Daddy, I'm fine." Sienna said, irritably.

"But, your clothes—" he started.

"Alldaddy, does he have to be here?" Sienna asked.

"Sienna!" Blaze said, unable to believe what he was hearing. Why would she not want him there?

"Yes, Sienna, he does. If that's going to be a problem, you can take a seat in the hall until we're finished," said Titus.

She gave a heavy sigh. "No, sir. It'll be fine."

Titus used his conference room for the debriefing. In attendance were his son's Darius and Joel; Constantine and his son, Jared; Banger and his sons, Tegan and Ruger; and since they were his top warriors, Trip and Blaze were there too.

Blaze cornered Banger. "I don't know what your son did to my daughter, Redeemer, but when this is over, you'd better believe I'll be finding out."

"You threatenin' me boy again, Reaper? Warrior or no, I still have no problem stepping in to assist him. You should thank him. Your daughter came back in one piece."

"Thank him? Half the shit that happened to her should never have occurred!"

From there, it just escalated.

Stryker was standing with his brothers, who were now getting in on the verbal match, when he glanced up and spotted her. To think, all of this started because she wanted a kiss from him. Caleb told him what she said to her father before storming out back. He looked at the group of warriors yelling back and forth, then he looked at her, sitting all by herself waiting for this to be over so she could finally go home. Caleb was right. She had taken all of it with the grace of a lady. And still continued to do so. He crossed the room to her.

Sienna sat on a chair lining the wall, looking on helplessly as her father continued bickering with Banger. The whole thing was ridiculous. Especially since neither of them had been there. She knew there was no reasoning with her father as she buried her face in her hands and sighed. Her head and her stomach hurt. She took in a cleansing breath, then realized somebody was standing over her. Ugh! Now what? She looked up into Stryker's piercing green eyes. She'd had a crush on him ever since she first laid eyes on him. Back then, he had that crazy mop that kept flopping into his eyes. Somewhere along the way, he started cutting it short, and even though he was still hot, she had always liked the longer hair.

And now, here he stood before her, hair past his shoulders and a beard he had semi-manscaped with his knife. Hot. As. Hell.

"How are you holding up?" he asked.

"As well as could be expected," she said. She looked over at her father and shook her head.

"Don't be too hard on him, babe. He loves you. He's just looking out for his beautiful daughter. It's not like I don't have a track record."

She smiled. "Are you saying he's right to be trying to protect me from you?"

"Damn straight," he answered.

The look he was giving her was one that had always been reserved for Ebony. Sienna was sure she had to be hallucinating until he grabbed her hand and pulled her to her feet. Whereas Caleb's kiss had been sweet and tender. Stryker's was more aggressive. He pulled her in with a hand behind her neck as his other hand slid around her waist. Then his lips were on hers and his tongue was in her mouth. Sienna couldn't believe it was really happening. And it was everything she imagined it to be and more. Wait'll she saw Layka! Her headache and bellyache were suddenly not so bad. She couldn't even hear the arguing anymore. Right there, in that moment, it was only her and Stryker and his take-charge style of kissing. And she was okay with that. Yeah, he was welcome to take charge of her any day, thank you very much.

Caleb cleared his throat and coughed into his fist.

They stopped, but her only focus was still him.

He said, "Whenever you're ready. You let me know. I'll wait for you."

She smiled up at him. "Really?"

"Really. Okay?"

She nodded. "They're all staring at us right now, aren't they?"

He smiled and nodded. "Yep, and not one fuck is given. Now, listen to me."

"What?"

"I want you to go home, get a shower, and get some sleep. Some real sleep."

"But—"

"No buts. We'll be fine. I'll stop in and check on you later."

She nodded. "Okay."

"Oh, and Sienna?"

"Yes?"

"Burn those damn leathers as soon as they come off."

"Will do," she said, then she left, leaving her father with one chapped ass.

"What the fuck just happened?" Blaze asked. "How is it that when I try to send her home to shower and change, I'm an asshole, but when he says it, it's gospel?"

Titus shook his head. "No sympathy here, warrior, I have too many daughters to remember when I found out I was no longer *the* male in their lives. Suck it up. And may I make a suggestion?"

"What's that?"

"You and Banger need to call a truce of some sort. Remember, Romeo and Juliet ended in tragedy. Now, let's get down to business. I'm sure Stryker and Caleb are more than ready to burn their leathers too."

He was right. And they would.

Minerva wasn't dead. Not yet, anyway. She couldn't believe what happened. Had the little monsters done that deliberately? Had they calculated just the right moment to slay the dragon, thus torching her in the process? She couldn't be sure. What she knew was she was in horrific pain and she needed to get home to heal, but she could not think herself out of there. Drago must have closed the portal after Titus left. Just her damn luck. He probably thought she was dead. She was sure they all did. The only thing she could move were her eyes. She looked around at her surroundings. It was quiet. Even the birds were silent. Usually, that was not a good sign. Was there some sort of predator in the vicinity? A high-pitched shriek answered that question. Something was rolling along the ground toward her. Whatever it was, it sure did kick up a lot of black dust. Then, as it got closer, she could make out eyes and teeth. This was it. She was a goner, for sure. The creature rolled along the ground, bypassing her entirely. It was after the dragon corpse. She let out a small sigh of relief. That was a close call. A clicking noise by her ear caught her attention. A beetle of some sort. Oh fuck. She hated bugs. The little creepy crawler reared up on its hind legs and made a chittering sound. Another answered it, then joined it. Minerva's eyes widened as the two insects advanced upon her and started eating. No, this can't be right. She had survived the dragon's ass napalm and the horrible black cloud with teeth only to be eaten by insects? It was totally undignified. She closed her eyes, grateful she still had lids that worked. *Okay. Think, Minerva. How to get out of this?* She could attempt to think herself to another location in the forest, but who knew what was lurking and waiting? No. She didn't have the strength yet for thought transport. She needed to regenerate a little more flesh and a lot more skin. She was going to be there for a while. The two beetles were joined by two more, then from out of nowhere a whole swarm of them were coming at her. Minerva wanted to scream and run, but her body was far too damaged and all she could do was watch in horror as the scorch bugs ate away her burned flesh. At first, there was no pain, then as they got closer to the healthy tissue it hurt, bad. And there she was, unable to do anything. Not even to scream. The beetles surprised her by leaving her once the eschar was gone. But now she was a mass of raw, exposed nerves. Who knew anything could hurt this much? She needed to heal and now. In some ways, the beetles had aided the process by removing the dead tissue. It gave her a head start. She willed herself to shut down, allowing her body to finish its work. What's the worse thing that could happen? She could be eaten, but at least she wouldn't feel it.

25

It felt good to be home, but Sienna wasn't sure if she was ready to face Julian after the way her father behaved. Besides, she didn't feel like walking. She decided to wait for her father.

Blaze was surprised to find her still there after the debriefing. *Oh, right. Stryker.* He thought as he rolled his eyes. He was sure that kiss would have been enough for her to float home on cloud nine. She stood up when she saw him.

"Ready, Daddy?"

He looked around as if to say, "Who me?" Now it was her turn to roll eyes. Blaze couldn't help himself as he gave Stryker a smug grin. Maybe he was still *the* male in her life after all. She groaned as he lifted her into his arms, then they headed home.

"What's wrong, baby?" he asked.

"My stomach hurts."

He frowned. "No doubt from whatever horrible bullshit you were forced to eat. We'll get you straight. Now, about those wings—"

"They're going to have to be shorn off and started over. I know."

He nodded, sadly. "Yes, I'm so sorry."

"Is it going to hurt? It really hurt when it happened. I think I fainted, Daddy."

And if that didn't just break his heart. He remembered well, having his own brutally hacked off at the base by Drago's son. And, yes, he too had fainted as the bastards cauterized them.

He swallowed the lump in his throat and said, "I won't let it hurt, baby, I promise."

"Can you promise me something else?"

He braced himself. "That depends on what it is." *Gods, please don't let it be about that damned Redeemer,* he thought.

"Can you please stop with whatever problem you have with Stryker? I really like him, Daddy. And I think he finally likes me." She scoffed. "And to think, it only took being stranded alone with him for a month for him to notice I even exist."

"I think he noticed you before that. It's just that—"

"It's just that I have an overbearing father and younger brother to contend with. Makes me wonder how many others you two have driven off."

"It's not like that, Sienna. We don't actively go out seeking males who may be interested in you, just to scare them off."

"You don't have to. Your presence is enough. You're the king's top warrior and Julian is the son of the king's top warrior and you both hover over me like bees."

Blaze couldn't help thinking if Trip was having this conversation, he would lighten it up a bit. Maybe respond with something like, "What kind of bees? You know it's all in the stinger. I'd be a wasp just so I could sting a motherfucker over and over." But Blaze was not Trip. And Blaze was nobody's candy maker. He wasn't about to sugarcoat it, not even for his daughter.

"Sienna, I'm your father. I have every right to vet any male who comes sniffing around you, and I won't apologize for that. I will always have your best interest at heart. Yes, I'm well aware that your best friend is already out there, but I'm not *her* father. I'm *your* father. You don't have to like it, but this is the hand you've been dealt. You are the daughter of the king's top warrior and I will have a say about who lays claim to your virginity. It's a big deal."

"Wait! Don't I get a say? That very same friend of mine is doing your son. And that's okay?"

"Yes. It's different. He's the male. She gets bragging rights for fucking a warrior. You said it yourself. He's the son of the king's top warrior. Did it ever occur to you that maybe that's the reason she's your friend in the first place?"

Ouch. Talk about a bee sting. "Are you saying that the only reason I have friends is that they're all after Julian?" she asked.

Or me, he thought. It wasn't unheard of for a young female to wait out an older male's mating contract. The list of females waiting for Titus was easily as long as Blaze's arm. He answered, "No, Sienna, I'm simply asking, are you sure?" He sighed, then said, "Listen, it's easy for you to decide who you want to sleep with. Looks, attitude, personality, all of those things are easy to see and relate to, but from where I stand? It's about character too. A male can say anything to you to get what he wants, only for you to find out he has a shitty character later on. And then where are you? With some asshole out there bragging about bedding the daughter of a top warrior? Not for your first. And I'll be damned if it's going to be a slacker of a warrior from Banger's camp."

Ahhh. So this was about Stryker. *Well, Daddy, you're not the only one with a stinger.*

She said. "Based on what you just said, the only ones worthy would be you or Julian. Is that where this is headed?"

Blaze was so shocked he stopped moving his wings, almost sending them into a nosedive. After quickly recovering, he said. "I'm going to pretend like you didn't just say that. I'm going to assume you're pissed off and were just going for the easy jab. I'll let you have it. This time. And, yes, by those standards Julian and I are the only ones qualified, however, for obvious reasons we will never be candidates. Never accuse me of anything like that again. By the way, there is an excellent candidate available."

"Who?"

Blaze couldn't believe it wasn't obvious to her. Was her head so far up Stryker's ass she hadn't seen it? Who better to deflower the daughter of the top warrior than the son of the second top warrior?

"Caleb," he answered. "What's wrong with him? You spent just as much time there with him and you're gonna tell me he didn't grow on you?"

"Well, in that case, you'll be happy to know that Caleb gave me my first kiss. Feel better now?"

Jesus, where was all this attitude coming from? She was so sweet before she left, but now, she was challenging him on everything. Was this how it was going to be from now on?

His eyes narrowed. "No, I do not. What were the circumstances?"

She just stared back at him, not speaking. Oh, now she shuts up? Don't think so, chica. Blaze was never one to drop a subject, and he wasn't about to start now.

"Well?" he demanded.

"We thought we were going to die," she said, quietly. "And he did."

"I'm sorry. I didn't mean to take you back there. I ask you again, what's wrong with him? Why can't you want to be with him?"

"Are you really that blind by your hatred, Daddy? Caleb is not interested in me. The second warrior's son has his sights set a little higher than the top warrior's daughter. No, check that, a lot higher."

"What?"

"He likes Ebony, Daddy. No matter how much you would like it to be me, it's not. Can't say I blame him. After all, she's the king's daughter and I'm just a warrior's daughter. So, looks like you're going to have to lower your standards for me or I get to die an old maid."

"Understand this, Sienna, I'll never lower my standards for you, ever. And Stryker will never be good enough. He's going to be waiting a very long time."

"You can't be everywhere all the time, you know."

To Blaze, that sounded a lot like a threat and it did not sit well.

"Make no mistake, Sienna. You have no idea where I can and can't be at any given time. I accept your challenge."

It wasn't how she meant it, and she wasn't trying to lose this argument. It was important that she get the last word.

"You weren't in Hell when I needed you to be. Anything could have happened there and you'll never know."

The look on his face was one of deep hurt. She couldn't believe it. She had actually hurt his feelings. She hadn't thought it possible, and it was nowhere near as satisfying as it should have been. She instantly regretted it.

"Daddy, I—"

"You're right, baby, I wasn't, and it's something I'm going to have to learn to live with," he said, quietly.

They flew the rest of the way in silence.

Pippa knew something was wrong as soon as they walked in. That didn't stop her from squeezing her daughter and covering her face with mama kisses. Then Julian was hugging her and frowning.

"Why do you smell like someone dumped a bucket of—"

"Hey!" Blaze shouted, cutting him off. Julian looked at his father, questioningly. Blaze shook his head and mouthed the word, *Don't*.

"I'm glad you're home, Sissy," Julian said.

She shoved him away. "Whatever."

Then she went to her room and slammed the door.

Pippa regarded Blaze with narrowed eyes. "What did you do?"

"I did nothing. She came home like that. She's been cranky and irritable the whole time, and it baffles me. Since when does our sweet daughter even have a bitch mode setting?"

He stomped off to the kitchen and put the kettle on.

"What are you doing?" she asked, following him.

"She says her stomach hurts. I'm making her tea."

The light bulb came on for Pippa.

"The tea is a sweet gesture, but I think she just needs some time with her mom," she said, stifling a grin.

"What am I missing here? What's so damn funny?"

"Shhh. Let me enjoy this moment," she said, closing her eyes.

"What moment? Dammit, Pippa!"

"When your lack of human interaction is counting against you."

"What do you mean?"

"She has her period, Blaze."

"We don't have that here! How—" he was about to ask when he realized the answer. "Oh."

He turned off the kettle.

"You want to do something nice for her? Make it hot chocolate. She'll appreciate that."

He nodded and went to it.

Pippa found Sienna sitting on the floor in the shower, hugging her knees to her chest and sobbing. The mangled framework of wings wrapped around her made her look even more pathetic. It broke Pippa's heart. She shook her head and sighed. "I do not miss those days."

She couldn't imagine what Sienna had been through. It was one thing, as a human, for those hormones to increase as you reached maturity. To have it all happen at one time? Blaze should consider himself lucky that his daughter didn't have a knife at her disposal when they were on their way home. She climbed in, sat down next to her daughter, and held her.

BLAZE HAD DONE AS SUGGESTED, WALKING INTO HER ROOM A half hour later with hot chocolate and cookies on a tray. Mother and daughter were snuggled together in her bed, asleep. He quietly set the tray down, leaned over, kissed them both, then crept out.

26

Trip was beside himself with pride as he and his son flew home. Caleb's decision to be an Avenger had him over the moon. The first thing they did was burn his leathers and start him with fresh ones. After that? It was sleep time. Caleb could barely keep his eyes open. Trip settled him in and returned to his living room to find his best friend sitting on his couch.

"Why aren't you home celebrating?" Trip asked him.

Blaze glanced around. "I don't see balloons and party hats up in here either."

"I made him go to bed. Look at me being a parent. A real one. Not that godparent stuff." He made a stern face and said, "Son, go to bed."

Blaze rolled his eyes. If only folks knew how much of a clown Trip really was. Unfortunately for him, Trip saved most of his antics for when they were alone.

"I told you mine, now what's your excuse?" Trip asked.

Blaze shook his head. "She doesn't want me there, besides, she's sleeping too. Pippa's with her. At least, now I know why everything I was saying was getting on her nerves."

Trip chuckled. "Dude, you need to get out more. A chick ragging has zero-tolerance for anything. You would know that if you had more human interaction. Imagine dealing with Pippa when she was human and on the rag. No thanks. She would have killed your ass."

"So what now?" he asked.

"You just wait 'til it's over. It shouldn't be long now. Maybe just another day or two. Oh, and feed her chocolate. It helps."

"You mean I'm gonna have to deal with daughterzilla for the next two days? Fucking shoot me now," Blaze said with a sigh.

Trip placed a hand on his shoulder. "You'll be fine. Besides, we've got more important issues to discuss."

Blaze frowned. "Which are?"

"Brother, you need to ease up."

"Ease up? With what?" Blaze asked, not sure if he wanted to hear the rest of this convo.

"Stryker," Trip said.

Now, Blaze *knew* he didn't want to hear the rest of it, but he also knew Trip would not let him off the hook. He shook his head. "You're not gonna change my mind on this one, Trip. I don't like him. And I really don't like the idea of him with Sienna."

Trip raised a hand. "For once in your life, will you just shut up and listen?"

Blaze sat back and crossed an ankle to his knee. "Fine, go."

"You need to understand something here. She likes him and the more you try to keep her from him, the harder she's going to try to be with him. You need to ease up. Do you trust her?"

"What do you mean, do I trust her? Of course, I trust her, it's him I—"

Trip cut him off. "Then you need to step back and allow her to make the right choice, on her own."

"And what do I say to him when he comes around to check on her?"

Trip shrugged. "Just be civil. You don't have to like it and you don't have to like him, but you have to be uh, 'nice' for her sake. Remember, the more you resist, the more she's going to want him. Sorry, brah, that's just how it is."

"Oh, and you know this because you have how many daughters?" Blaze asked, sarcastically.

Trip laughed. "I don't need to have a daughter to know how this works. Trust me, I've been the guy daddy didn't want his daughter around. I had a life before we met, you know."

"Christ, I can't even remember back that far anymore. I barely remember life before the cherubs."

"Funny how that happens, huh?"

"Listen to you. Like you've been a father for years and shit."

"I have and she's a girl. I didn't have to worry about anybody coming around her."

Blaze rolled his eyes. "It's not like you had to worry about the guy she liked taking advantage of her."

Trip shook his head. "No, I didn't, but I do now. And the situation gets even weirder."

Blaze nodded. "So I've heard. How's he doing?"

"He's exhausted," Trip said, shaking his head. "I still can't believe he came back."

"Why not? He seems like a good kid. Smart. Respectful. His mother did a pretty good job."

"For a human, right?"

"I didn't say that."

"You didn't have to, but, yes, she did. She was a schoolteacher."

A door opened down the hall, then a sleepy Lylac appeared, rubbing her eyes. "What are you guys doing up?" she asked.

"Just talking, babe. Sorry, if we woke you," said Trip.

She shook her head. "You didn't. How's our girl, Blaze?"

"As well as can be expected, given the circumstances."

"I'll be by tomorrow to see her," she said.

"I'll pass on the warning," he teased.

She flipped him off, then headed to Caleb's room.

"He's fine, babe, let him rest," Trip said.

"I just want to make sure," she said, then went in, closing the door behind her.

Trip shook his head. "She's crazy about him already."

"How does he feel about her?"

"Honestly? I'm not sure. The first time they met, his eyes practically fell out of his head. A mixture of 'damn Dad she's smokin' hot and what's with the purple hair and pointed ears?' He wasn't sure if he should be turned on or running for the hills."

"Venusians," Blaze said, standing up. "They're special."

"Ain't that the truth. You rolling?"

"Yeah, I want to look in on her before—"

"Before he shows up?" Trip asked with a raised brow.

Blaze scowled. "No. I was going to say before I turn in for the night."

"Whatever you say, Precious," Trip goaded.

"I say fuck you," Blaze responded, taking the bait.

"There's my kitten. I love it when you talk dirty." Trip blew him a kiss.

Blaze rolled his eyes. "You're an asshole. You know that?"

"All for you, baby, all for you," Trip retorted, then said. "Kiss her for me. We'll be over tomorrow, too. Caleb wants to know how to get there."

"Tell him he's welcome anytime. Later," Blaze said. They fist-bumped, then he left.

Trip hadn't heard Caleb come out of his room. He turned to find him standing in the hallway with an odd expression on his face.

"Do you always flirt with your best friend like that?" Caleb asked.

"Blaze and I have a special relationship. What are you doing up? Did Lylac wake you?"

"No, bad dream. Terrible. I'm really here, right? This part isn't the dream, is it? Please tell me I'm not dreaming right now," Caleb begged.

The look of borderline panic on his face broke Trip's heart.

"No, son, you're not dreaming. You're home and you're safe. I promise. What's happening to you is you're exhausted, but your body has gotten so used to being hyper-vigilant and it won't let you deep sleep. It's gonna take a few days. Tea?"

"Got anything stronger?"

Trip nodded. He made his son the tea, then spiked it with a healthy dose of spiced rum and a bit of butter. Caleb thought he'd never tasted anything so good as he gulped it down. Trip pulled out a deck of cards and started dealing them while he waited for the tea to do its job. It didn't take long. Caleb was soon nodding off. As Lylac had fallen asleep in Caleb's bed, Trip had to clear her out before returning his son to it. She woke as he was carrying her back to their bed.

"I'm sorry, babe, I fell asleep," she said.

"You don't say," he chuckled. "You okay alone tonight? He needs me."

She nodded. "Of course. You go to him. I'll be fine." She was back to sleep before he left the room.

When Trip returned to the kitchen, Caleb was asleep with his head resting on his arm, drooling. *Now that there is some good sleep,* Trip thought. He almost hated to disturb him. Gently, he lifted his son and carried him back to his bed. Then he climbed in with him and wrapped his arms and wings around him. Caleb struggled for a moment, crying out. Trip stroked his hair. "Shhh, shhh, shhh, it's okay, son. You're safe now. I'm here."

The words seemed to be enough to soothe as Caleb snuggled in closer to him. Then they both slept.

27

Stryker's homecoming was far from quiet. His brothers didn't hold back with their welcome, throwing him a huge bash complete with every spirit available by the keg, all of his favorite foods, and girls, girls, girls. Mainly for them. They had gotten Ebony to come for him. At least, that's what they were thinking. He knew that. Before he could greet her, his father cornered him.

"That was some kiss ye planted on the Reaper lass," Banger said.

Stryker nodded. "Well, I—"

"Now, forget about her. It will never work. She's a Reaper by blood and you're a Redeemer by blood. You know what that means," Banger clapped a heavy hand on his son's shoulder. "Leave her to the Avenger boy. They're more compatible."

Stryker was seething as he shrugged off his father's hand.

"Don't you mean their fathers are more compatible? This isn't about me or her, it's about you and Constantine and this stupid feud you've had all these years. If you want to fight with them, that's your prerogative, but I don't have to and I won't. I like her, Da. I like her a lot and I'm sorry if that offends you, but—"

Banger shoved his son back, then was poking him in the chest. "Listen to me, boy. I don't know where you think this little romance is going to lead, but I'm telling you, it's going nowhere. I won't allow it. And even if I were daft enough to go along with it, her father wouldn't be. You saw him come at me. It's a bad idea, Stryker, and it will only end in bloodshed. Let it go. Let her go. Trust me, she won't be the only damsel you save and you can't fall for all of 'em."

Stryker frowned at his father. "It's not like that, Da, and if you want me to be honest, I don't need, nor am I asking for your permission to see her. Now, if you'll excuse me, I'd like to greet my best friend."

He stormed off, leaving his father speechless.

Ebony saw the exchange between Stryker and his father. Whatever it was, it was huge. Both males were red in the face, and Stryker's angry exit only confirmed her suspicions.

She hugged him. "I missed you! Are you okay?"

He pulled back and nodded. "I'm fine. I missed you, too. Boy, do we have a lot to talk about."

"We sure do. So what was that about with your dad? Everything okay?"

He shrugged. "Same shit, different day. I'm tired of this feud he's got going with Constantine."

Ebony made a face. "That's not new, Stryker. Why should it matter now?"

"You obviously didn't hear about the debriefing?"

She shook her head. "Daddy's got everyone sworn to secrecy. I have no idea what went on. I was going to ask Sienna tomorrow when I go see her. I hear she's not feeling well?"

"Nah, female stuff."

She looked confused. "What female stuff?"

It was Stryker's turn to be confused. "You don't know? Your mother is human, and she never told you about it?"

"Until a month ago, my mother was a flying horse, so, no, it never came up."

Stryker's face was taking on a little more warmth than he would like. He did not want to discuss this with her. "Just ask her when you get home," he said. "And I suggest talking to her about it before you visit Sienna."

She shrugged. "Okay, if you say so. So what else happened. Why's your dad so up in arms?"

"I kissed her, at the debriefing, in front of everybody."

Ebony's eyebrows shot up. "Shut up! For real? What about Caleb?"

He bristled. "What about him?"

"Well, it's just that he likes her and—"

"What makes you think he likes her?" he asked, interrupting her.

"Well, he was saying about how pretty she was and how amazing her eyes are, I thought—"

"You thought wrong," he said, a little testier than he'd intended to.

"Well, sorry, I didn't mean anything by it. Maybe I should just go home. Let you get some rest."

He took her hand. "Don't go. I'm sorry. Give me a chance to explain. Let's go stretch our wings."

She agreed, then they hastily made their way to the door.

Banger watched as his son left with the king's daughter. Now, that was more like it. He always did like Ebony and her mother. According to Titus, it was Vanessa's idea for the two of them to play together ever since they were small. Back when she was still a winged horse and protective as all get out. He never had to worry when Stryker was in Titus's world playing with Ebony and frolicking with her mother. Vanessa had a way with the two little ones, and Stryker never failed to return home well spent. There were no tantrums to stay up on those nights. Maybe Ebony could talk some sense into him, or better yet, maybe she would finally give him the time of day.

※

Stryker and Ebony exited his father's kingdom and flew through the portal to Titus's world. They found themselves at the, now empty, stable her mother used to live in. It was their favorite place to sit and talk.

"I like the new leathers," she said, attempting to break the ice.

He smiled. "Thanks. Be glad you weren't there when the old ones came off."

"Oh, gods! I'm sure!" she laughed.

He grew serious. "I've liked you for a long time. You know that."

She nodded and looked down at her hands. "I know and I'm sorry I—"

"Don't be," he said. "Somewhere in the time we spent there, I kinda developed feelings for Sienna."

"Really?" Ebony asked, not sure whether to be happy for Sienna or sad for Caleb.

He nodded. "Yeah. Caleb said something that really drove it home for me."

"Oh? What was that?"

"He pointed out how graceful she was handling everything that was happening. The brunt of the shit fell on her and she just took it. Plus, she knew stuff about where we were. She knew about the creatures there and how to deal with them. And she even knew about the female stuff. Well, so did Caleb since it's a common occurrence where he's from. But, if it weren't for her spending so much time reading in the king's library? We would have been fucked."

"She's always carried herself well. She gets that from her mom. Pippa isn't one to kiss anyone's ass. Least of all, some guy. Blaze could tell you all about that," she laughed.

"Blaze, yeah right."

"What's wrong?"

"That's what that argument was about with my father. They don't like the idea of me and Sienna," he said.

She frowned. "Are you serious? This isn't about them. Nor is it about whether one is a Redeemer or a Death Angel. This could bring the two groups together. A grandbaby—"

Stryker put up both hands. "Whoa, whoa, whoa! Slow your roll there, princess! Who's talking about cherubs? We haven't even hooked up yet. Easy!"

Ebony laughed. "Just like a male to be afraid of the word 'baby'. Baby, baby, baby, baby."

"Keep it up. Each time you say it, my shit shrivels up more and more. I'm gonna tell Sienna it's your fault."

"Please, she's a virgin. She won't know the difference."

"Oh, yes, she would. She's already seen it."

Ebony gasped in surprise. "What?! When?"

"Let's just say a lot of shit went down there and we needed to wash our clothes and let them air dry. Modesty was probably the first casualty in that godforsaken place."

"I see. So does that mean you've seen her too?"

"Yes, but I'd seen a naked female before. You know, it's kinda not fair for other guys that I am the first male she's ever seen naked. She was even cool about it. Didn't make a big deal or anything. Just like Caleb said. The grace of a lady. And why are you laughing?"

Ebony had been stifling a guffaw. She let it out. "You are not the first male she's ever seen naked. Trust me."

"You know what I mean. The first one not related to her."

"Oh, okay," she giggled. "And you think you are, you know, intimidating?"

He scowled. "Shut up, Ebony."

And didn't that just make it even funnier? She was now holding her belly and tears were shimmering in the corners of her eyes.

"It's not that funny," he said.

"I'm sorry. I'm sorry. I'm sorry," she said, toning it down to a snicker.

"You're still laughing," he said, feigning hurt feelings.

This was a familiar game for them. "Whatever, player," she said.

He gave her a weak smile. "But seriously, it feels weird not having them around. I slept with her the entire time Caleb was gone. You know? I wasn't going to let anything else happen to her, Eb. I couldn't live with myself if it had."

"You wanna go see her?"

He sighed. "I told her I'd stop in and check on her, but I just want her to sleep. I want her to rest."

She nodded. "I'm sure she'll understand that."

"So what about you? How's it been catching up with your mom?"

"It's been great. She hangs out with the other human moms, especially Pippa's and Joel's."

He rolled his eyes. "Christ, Maxine. That's not awkward," he said, sarcastically.

She shook her head. "Actually, they're all cool with each other. They even joke about him and get this. Dinah's been coming around more, too."

"Shut the fuck up! You know it was her mother that started all this."

Ebony nodded. "So I've heard. Something about Isabel and fertilized eggs. I'm not sure I want to know."

"You don't. Trust me."

"It's all good. I'm just glad to have my mom back," she said.

He nodded. "That's cool. I have yet to meet her, well, as a human."

"Oh, that's right. Wanna go now?"

He shook his head. "Nah, I'm just enjoying my time here with you."

She placed a hand over his and squeezed. "I missed you, too."

They stayed up talking well into the night, eventually taking the reunion to her room. It was just like old times. They were in her sitting room finishing a bottle of vodka when he started yawning and Ebony noticed his blinks were getting a little on the long side. She stood and pulled him to his feet. He gave her his boyish grin. The same one that had all the girls swooning over him. The same one Sienna had fallen for way back when she was less than a septennium old. The same one that Ebony always considered herself immune to. So what was different now? Why did she suddenly want to kiss him? He was always trying to kiss her, and she was always turning him away. For a fleeting moment, she actually considered giving in to the urge and going for it, but she wouldn't do that to Sienna. Even if it was just a kiss.

He read her facial expression and said, "Maybe I should go home."

She shook her head. "You don't have to. You know you're always welcome to crash on the pullout bed."

"I told her I'd wait for her and I meant it," he said.

"Good, she deserves that, but I wasn't going to try anything, trust me."

"I know you wouldn't, but I've waited and wanted for so long. It's me I don't trust."

He kissed her hand, then her cheek, and for a moment she thought he was going to kiss her lips. Instead, he turned and flew out her window.

Ebony watched until he disappeared through the portal.

"Sleep well, dear friend," she said.

28

Sienna sat up and stretched. How long had it been since she slept that well? She couldn't remember. For that matter, exactly how long had she slept? The sun was already high in the sky. She had missed Sunrise Welcome, but she hadn't missed breakfast. The smell of pancakes wafted into her room. She laughed to herself, remembering the Bugs Bunny cartoons she liked to watch with her mother. The character floating through the air following his nose to whatever wonderful delicacy awaited. She went to get up and realized she was enshrouded from her neck to her knees in linen. Her wings! When had they done that? That would mean she had been out for at least a week, and that stupid period bullshit would be over. Thank the gods and good riddance! She worked her way out of the shroud and opened her wings. Good as new. A fresh set of leathers were laid out for her and she quickly pulled them on. Now, sustenance.

There were voices coming from the dining room.

"More pancakes, Caleb?" she heard her mother ask.

"Yes, please. Thank you, ma... um, Ms. Pippa."

"Ok, well, I guess that's better than ma'am, but there's no need to be so formal here, Caleb. You're family. Understood?"

"Yes… uh yes," he said.

When Sienna rounded the corner, they all stood. Lylac was the first one on her, squeezing her and covering her cheeks with kisses. Sienna giggled. Lylac had been doing it to her ever since she was a cherub. She could be one-hundred eons aged and it would never be old.

"I'm so glad you're okay," the purple-haired Venusian gushed. "We were so worried about you."

"Thanks, Aunt Lylac, it's good to be home."

Trip picked her up and spun her around. "He'll never tell you, but he was a mess," he whispered, "Don't ever scare us like that again."

She nodded. "As long as I can help it, I won't."

"Good enough. I'll take that," he said.

"How was your rest?" her father asked as they all sat down.

"It was great. I have to thank Allfather for fixing my wings. I'll stop over to see him after breakfast, then I think I'll go see Layka."

Blaze nodded. "Good idea. She stopped in. She'll be glad to see you."

There was a knock at the door. Blaze and Sienna stood up together. He pointed at her seat.

"Eat, I got it."

"Were you with me the whole time, Mom?" Sienna asked.

Pippa nodded. "Yup, right up until Sunrise Welcome today. I didn't have the heart to wake you for it."

Then they heard Blaze exchanging words rather heatedly.

"She's fine. I'll tell her you stopped by," they heard him say.

Sienna ran for the door just in time to see Stryker leaving.

"Wait! Daddy, what are you doing? Invite him in," she said.

"It's okay, Sienna," Stryker said. "I'll see you later. I'll go hang with Caleb."

"Caleb's here. Come in, we're having breakfast. Join us," she said. She reached for his hand to pull him in.

Stryker looked at Blaze, who was glaring at him. "No thanks. I already ate. I wouldn't want to impose. I'll catch you later."

"Are you sure?" she asked. "Why don't you come in and wait. We can hang out after breakfast."

"Didn't you hear him, sweetie?" Blaze said to her. "He doesn't want to impose. You'll see him later."

She frowned. "But how is it imposing if we invite him in?"

Trip was now leaning against the dining room archway. He cleared his throat and coughed. Blaze looked at him, then back at Stryker. Trip's previous words came to mind. By blocking her, he'll only make her want him more. But what if Trip's wrong? What if he does nothing about it and she starts seeing him on the regular? Not just that. What would his own father say about him allowing his daughter to get romantically involved with a Redeemer? What if things really heated up and Stryker made her his mate? Then there'd be cherubs. Oh. Hell. No.

"Sienna, go finish your breakfast," Blaze demanded.

"But, Daddy—"

"Now!"

He shoved Stryker out the door. "Listen to me. I understand you went through a traumatic experience with my little girl. I get that, but this thing you two think you have going on? It's not gonna happen, and I'd really appreciate it if you'd stop feeding into it."

Stryker was staring past him. Blaze sighed. Steeling himself for the hurt in her eyes, he turned to face her.

"Why Daddy?" she asked, quietly.

"It's complicated, Sienna. Go back inside."

"But how?"

"It just is. Inside. Now."

Stryker met his gaze and said. "With all due respect sir, your daughter is not a little girl. She's a lady. Even when we were in that horrible place, she still carried herself with the grace of one. So, I'll do as you wish. I'll leave her alone. For now. But not because you or my father is asking me to. But because I don't want a relationship with her that's tainted by the ugliness you two insist upon embracing."

With that, he turned and flew toward the palace. Blaze had almost forgotten. Stryker and Ebony were thick as thieves. Which meant there was absolutely nothing he could do about Stryker always being around. All he could do is put his foot down and keep his daughter away from him. It would start now. He went back inside and sat down. Everyone was quiet, staring intently at their plates and pushing their food around with their forks. Nobody was eating. Fine. May as well address it now.

"Sienna, I forbid you to see him anymore. Do you understand?"

She looked up at him, stunned. "But Daddy—"

"Do not argue with me. It is not up for discussion. As long as you live under my roof, I forbid you to see him. Do. You. Under. Stand?"

Her lip quivered as she said. "Yes, Daddy. May I be excused, please? I'm not hungry."

"Yes," Pippa said as Blaze said, "No." She glared at her

mate. "Really? You just broke your daughter's heart and you're going to make her sit here and entertain company?" She stood up. "Sienna, go to your room. Julian, take Caleb and go to yours."

It was a rule established when the twins were little. Don't fight in front of the kids. Blaze knew he was in for it, but she surprised him by addressing Trip.

"Do you think you could talk some sense into your friend? I can tell, he's not gonna listen to me."

Lylac started clearing the table, then disappeared into the kitchen.

"I don't know what you expect me to do," Trip said. "I already tried, and he ignored me." He pinned his friend with a glare.

"Don't look at me like that, Trip. What if you're wrong?" Blaze said, defensively.

"And what if I'm right?" Trip shot back.

"Well, she didn't argue, now did she? Obviously, the fact that I'm her father still counts for something," Blaze said.

Trip shook his head and scoffed. "Really? Have you forgotten who you're mated to?"

Blaze frowned. "What's that got to do with anything?"

Trip laughed. "Absolutely nothing! Why don't you go check on your daughter?"

"What—" Blaze began, then went and knocked on his daughter's door. No answer. "Sienna?" he called.

When she didn't answer again, he opened the door. The room was empty.

"She deliberately defied me," he said, angrily. Then he was heading to the front door.

"Where are you going?" Pippa asked.

"The palace. It's where Stryker was headed when I sent him away. No doubt going to hang out with your sister."

"Don't go yelling at her, Blaze, it won't help," she said, lifting off to follow him.

"Is this party just for two?" Trip asked, joining them.

Pippa rolled her eyes. "Oh, now you want to be helpful?"

Trip shook his head. "Helpful? Nah. I'm not going to miss seeing her take him on and win."

"What are you talking about?" Blaze asked.

Trip smiled. "You'll see."

Blaze barged into the king's office. "Is Sienna here? Have you seen her?"

Titus looked up from his work, surprised. "Good morning to you too, warrior, and yes, she's where she always is, in the library. Is there a problem?"

Blaze ran a hand through his hair. "Just a minor disagreement. I'm sorry to have disturbed you." He bowed, then headed off to the library.

Pippa was waiting for him outside the office but had heard every word. "A minor disagreement? Understate much?" she said.

He frowned at her. "I'm not the asshole here, Pippa. He is."

"Blaze, they're kids. All of them. Stryker, Ebony, Caleb, Julian, and Sienna. They're going to do 'kid' things. Every girl has that guy in her past that her father hated. And every girl I know continued to date the guy just to chap her father's ass. Is that what you want?"

"Now, you sound like Trip. Speaking of, where did he go?"

"He's probably already at the library. You see, my dear husband, Trip knows a little something about the female psyche. You'd do well to pay attention."

"Gods be damned! The next being to remind me of how little I know about girls gets throttled!" Blaze seethed.

The conversation piqued Titus's interest, and he followed them from his office. Clapping a hand on Blaze's shoulder, he said, "You know, warrior, you may need to, you know, rethink what you think you know about girls, hmm?"

Blaze stopped and just looked at him.

Titus shrugged. "Just sayin'."

"You know, I'm glad you're finding my irritation so damned amusing today."

Titus and Pippa started laughing. "Your irritation is always amusing, my love," Pippa said. "Even when it's directed at me."

"Especially when it's directed at me," Titus added.

Father and daughter hi-fived and fist-bumped.

Blaze shook his head. "I need my own realm."

Pippa was right. Trip was indeed waiting for them at the library entrance and he had heard Blaze's last words.

"Your own realm? You know black holes already exist, right?" he said.

"Fuck you, Trip," came the curt reply.

The library was just off the main atrium. A wide archway opened into a large room lined with fully loaded bookshelves and a reading area with cafe-style seating. There was no lack of light as the entire ceiling was glass. Another room, reserved for reference books and research, branched off from the reading room. In it was a long boardroom style table lined with chairs. The room was rarely busy, as everyone preferred the natural lighting. Sienna was sitting at one end, intently poring over an enormous book with a short stack sitting next to her.

"Go talk to your daughter, Blaze. Talk. To. Her," Pippa said.

He watched her from the archway, hoping she would look up. When she didn't, he went to her.

"Hey," he said.

She looked up and smiled. "Hi, Daddy."

He sighed. "Listen, I'm having a little trouble here."

She frowned. "Oh?"

He nodded. "Yeah. Somewhere along the way, you grew up on me. You're not a little girl anymore, though you will always be my little girl. Sorry."

"It's okay, Daddy. You were right. I'm living under your roof and as such, I'm subject to the rules of the house. I understand."

"Really? You're not upset?"

"Well, sure, I wish things were different, but as you said, it's complicated," she shrugged. "Guess there's not too much I can do about it, right?"

He paused. "I, too, wish things were different, for your sake. But I'm glad you understand."

She nodded. "I do."

"So, we're good?" Blaze asked his daughter.

"Sure, Daddy."

"Good," he kissed her forehead. "You ready?"

"For what?"

"To come home."

She looked down at her book. "Not yet."

"I see. You're still upset."

She said nothing.

"Okay, so we'll see you later on?" he asked.

She nodded.

"Sienna?"

She looked up at him. "Yes, Daddy?"

"I love you. I hope you know that."

"Sure, I do, Daddy."

"Okay."

The others could hear the conversation from the archway.

Trip shook his head and walked away, muttering under his breath. "Fucking clueless."

Titus looked at Pippa. "You want to bring me up to speed on what I'm missing here?"

She did so as they headed back to his office.

"So, how do you think it went?" Pippa asked Blaze when he joined them. She was seated across from her father's desk, arms crossed.

"I'm not stupid," he answered. "She's still pissed, but at least she's trying to be an adult about it."

"Is that what you think?" Trip asked.

"Well, yeah, you heard her. She was cool about it."

"So, you're still not considering what Pippa and I have told you?" Trip was incredulous.

"What? Why should I? She says she's cool with it. She'll have to get over her anger, but, hey. Eventually, she'll come around and see that I'm right. He's no good for her," he shrugged. "I'd still like to see her with Caleb. Why don't you—"

"I'm not getting involved with this, Blaze," Trip said, cutting him off. "You're making a big mistake. This shit's gonna blow up in your face. You watch."

"I don't see how," Blaze said. "I put my foot down, and she accepted my decision. Done."

Pippa and Trip exchanged a look.

"What?" Blaze demanded.

Pippa gave him a weak smile. "Whatever you say, Babe."

"I'm heading back," Trip said. "Lylac will rearrange your entire house if you let her. She's been alone for a while."

"Just talk to him, Trip. That's all I'm asking," Blaze said.

"No, Blaze, I mean it. Caleb's already interested in somebody and I will not interfere. If it works out, it works out, but if not? Well, ultimately it'll be his decision. *His* decision. Not mine. *His* life. Not mine. There's no question that he loves Sienna, but he's not *in* love with her. And more importantly, she doesn't feel that way about him. Get over it, Blaze, and suck it up, or you're going to alienate her. I'm not saying anything else on this. They've only been back a week. Be grateful she made it back okay. You and Banger seemed to have lost sight of that."

Before Blaze could respond, he took flight out the nearest window.

Blaze and Pippa left shortly afterward, leaving Titus to get back to his work. He was just settling in when he felt a pair of eyes on him from the open doorway. He glanced up to see his granddaughter standing there with a piece of paper.

He smiled. "I've been expecting you."

"Really?"

"Yes. Understand, Sienna, you are your father's only daughter. I have many daughters. Is it safe to assume that paper is an emancipation request?"

She nodded.

"Any particular reason why you waited until they left?"

"I didn't want him looking over my shoulder while I wrote it."

"I see. You realize he is going to be blindsided by this, right?"

"I'm giving him what he wants," she said.

"How do you figure?"

"He specifically said that as long as I'm under his roof, I'm forbidden to see Stryker. I took that to mean he didn't want me under his roof anymore. Maybe he got used to me being gone."

Titus chuckled. "That has got to be the biggest crock of shit that I've ever heard."

She shrugged. "It is what it is."

SON OF THE AVENGER

"Sarcasm. You know he will not take this lying down."

"If you honor it, he doesn't have a choice, now does he?"

Titus nodded. "True. Have you considered an alternative recourse if I don't?"

She sighed as she shook out her hair and raked her fingers through it. Titus couldn't help thinking how much like her mother she was. Not just in looks, but in resourcefulness. This whole stunt was definitely something Pippa would have pulled.

"Do you think this is going to make him change his mind?" Titus asked.

"I don't know, Allfather. But I don't want his stupid feud dictating my life. Does that make sense?"

"It does," Titus said. He took the paper, read over it, then signed it. "Normally, I'd have your mother deliver this. But under the circumstances, I think it'll be better if I deliver it myself. You're welcome to stay here. You can have your mother's old bedroom until we get this settled. All right?"

She nodded, vigorously. "Yes, sir. Thank you!"

"Don't thank me yet. I'm sure you'll be receiving a visit from him. Be ready."

She nodded, then went to her new bedroom.

29

Caleb and Julian were back in his room. "So, what's your dad's problem with Stryker?" Caleb asked.

"It's an old family feud. Been going on for a long time." Julian said, then he explained how Redeemers and Reapers had been at odds for centuries.

"Wow. So it really is like Romeo and Juliet," Caleb said.

Julian frowned. "I don't see Sienna committing suicide over it."

Caleb chuckled. "Neither do I. She's not built like that."

Julian shook his head. "No, she's not. She's more likely to do something like, I don't know, file for emancipation."

"So you guys have that here, too?" Caleb asked, surprised.

Julian nodded, then the two of them started laughing.

"Can you see her drawing up some sort of document and presenting it to your grandfather?" Caleb asked, still laughing.

"Oh, my gods! She'd do it with calligraphy and everything. It would be all official looking and she'd be beaming over that shit!" Julian added.

"I know, right? Then she'd march into the king's office and slam it down on his desk, demanding that he take her seriously," Caleb continued.

They went on laughing for a few more minutes, then Caleb grew serious. "Yo, you don't think she'd really do it, do you?"

Julian scoffed. "Pfft! Nah, she's got the smarts for it, but she doesn't have the balls to stand up to my dad all like that."

"I'm not so sure about that, Julian. Remember how she was just before Minerva took us?"

Julian nodded. "True, there is that. You think we should say something?"

"That depends," Caleb said.

"On what?" Julian asked.

"On how you feel about your sister seeing Stryker."

Julian shrugged. "I'm not against it if it makes her happy. That's all that matters to me."

Caleb smiled and offered a fist. "My man."

Julian bumped it.

Trip and Lylac were just leaving when Titus arrived. Trip glanced at the sealed document in the king's hand. *Fuck me, she actually did it*, he thought. A part of him wanted to stand by and enjoy watching it play out, but as stubborn as Blaze was being about the situation, Trip knew this would not go well. He thought about how he'd feel if it was Caleb. It would hurt his feelings, but he'd see it for what it was. A wake-up call. She's now an adult, according to the law, and he would no longer have a say about anything in her life. Trip shook his head. *It didn't have to come to this, Blaze,* he thought.

Pippa greeted her father with. "Didn't we just see you like ten minutes ago?"

Titus nodded. "Yes, I'm afraid I'm here on official business."

He handed the document to Blaze.

"What's this?" the warrior asked. He unrolled it and began to read. His tongue went to his cheek as he shook his head. Then he balled the paper up and angrily threw it across the room. His eyes were narrowed as he asked the king. "And you signed off on this?"

"I had to. She gave a perfectly logical argument, though, I think there may be some misunderstanding."

Pippa picked up the paper, flattened it out, and read it. She turned to Blaze, her face contorted in fury. The redheaded firing squad was now activated.

"What have you done?" she demanded.

"Me? She's the one—"

"No! Damn you, Blaze! All she wants is a chance to see him and see where it goes. They're not asking to get mated. They're simply asking to spend time together and if it leads to intimacy? Then so be it! You're the only one here who gives one flying fuck about that damn feud!"

"But I—"

"Shut up! No! You shut your mouth! I'm talking now and I'm telling you, you're going to take your stubborn ass back to the palace and you're going to apologize to her. And you are going to suck up to her, because she deserves it, Blaze. She's just been to Hell and back, literally! The very least you can do is give her this one thing if it will make her happy. Do you hear me, warrior?"

"And what if—"

"It's a yes or no question, Blaze," she seethed.

He scowled. "I heard you just fine, now you listen to me. What if it goes the whole way? What if they decide to get mated? Then what?"

Pippa scoffed. "And what if they do? It's not the end of

the world. Do you really love that feud more than you love our daughter?"

Blaze couldn't answer her. He hadn't thought of it that way. Was that how Sienna was seeing this? Was she questioning his love for her as her father? No, he couldn't let that happen. It was time to let go of the past. He would not lose his little girl over a prejudice he, his father, and Banger were harboring. It wasn't worth it. He looked at Pippa and nodded.

"I'll go talk to her," he said, resigned.

"Good and make sure you bring her back with you or I'm moving back to the palace with her," she said.

He nodded. "Will do."

"You want a wingman?" Titus asked.

Blaze shook his head. "No, I've got this, but thanks."

He bowed to the king, then took off for the palace.

Titus made eye contact with Trip, then nodded toward the door.

"On it," Trip said, then followed his friend.

Blaze heard Trip approaching.

"What part of 'I've got this' threw you?"

"You're welcome," said Trip.

Blaze already knew which window was hers. He'd slept in that very room many a night with Pippa. He was about to enter when he heard voices coming from inside.

"This isn't the way to go about it," he heard Stryker say.

"But, he wasn't getting it," Sienna argued.

"Sienna, he's your father. You can't go disowning him just because he pisses you off."

"I didn't disown him, I just emancipated myself from his rules. He was being unreasonable," she said, defensively.

"Really? And now who's being unreasonable?" he asked.

"I don't think I am," she answered.

He scoffed. "Of course you don't and I've got a news

flash for you. Neither does he. Did it ever occur to you that maybe he just needs to get used to the idea? You're forgetting, he still sees you as his little girl. Not to mention, I do have a reputation. He's just looking out for you."

Stryker's attitude surprised Sienna. "I thought you'd be happy," she said, then she looked down. "Have you changed your mind?"

He took her hand. "No, I want this too. Just as much as you do, but not like this, Sienna. This can only fuel his fire. He already hates me. This just gives him justification for it."

"So, what do we do in the meantime? Am I supposed to pretend I feel nothing?"

He took a deep breath. "If that's what it takes? Then yes."

That *so* was not what she wanted to hear and dammit she would not stand there and cry about it either. She pulled her hand from his. "Fine, I guess you'd better see your way out of my bedroom, then. Good day to you."

"Sienna, come on, don't be like that."

"Don't be like what?" she said, sharply.

"Don't be mad."

"I'm not mad, Stryker, you said it yourself. If it means me not feeling anything, then so be it. You can see yourself out," she went into the adjoining bedroom and closed the door, leaving him alone to ponder. *What just happened?*

Blaze punched the air with a fist, *Yes!* Trip frowned at him and smacked him in the middle of the forehead.

"What the fuck was that for?" Blaze asked, rubbing the spot.

Trip now had a finger in his face. "That's for your stupid ass thinking that you're now off the hook. You aren't. You still need to go in there and make things right with your daughter. And Stryker? He just did you a major solid. You need to be thanking him."

"How do you figure?"

"Blaze, he could have taken full advantage of this situation. Instead of hearing them facing off, we could have just as easily rolled up on them getting their groove on, but we didn't. He didn't do it and from what I just heard him say, it was out of respect for your dumbass. You've been nothing but, hateful and mean to him and he's been turning the other cheek like a motherfucker."

"So?"

"So after you apologize to her, I suggest you seek him out and apologize to him too."

"I'm not trying to be apologizing to *him* of all Redeemers," Blaze grumbled.

"You will if you want your daughter to stay a virgin a little while longer. Because she's ready to give it up. I know you don't want to hear it, but it's the truth, brother. And if you keep slapping him in his face, he's gonna get fed up and say 'fuck you' then he'll be ready to fuck her just to chap your ass on principle. Is that what you want? No father likes the idea of his daughter having sex, Blaze, but it's gonna happen, eventually. Do you want her first time to be with someone she cares about and who cares about her, or are you willing to make it into a situation where you've given bragging rights to a Redeemer. I'm telling you, that's exactly where this is headed. The ball is in your court, brother. What are you going to do?"

Blaze knew his friend was right. They heard the bedroom door open as she returned to the sitting room.

"All right," he said, then leaped to the windowsill.

Sienna was sitting on the couch facing the window as if she'd been expecting him. As if? Of course she was. The whole idea behind this stunt was to get his attention. Right?

She succeeded, and well. He stepped off the ledge and stood before her.

"Hey," he said, not sure where else to start.

"Hi, Daddy," she answered.

He looked around the room. She'd already changed it, putting her own stamp on it.

"It looks good," he said.

"Thanks, Daddy," she said.

"Sienna, you didn't have to do this. I'm right here. We could have talked it out," he said.

She shook her head. "No, we couldn't. You made your position painfully clear, and you left no room for compromise."

He sighed. "I suppose you're right. I can see why you'd feel that way. I'm sorry, Baby. I was only trying to protect you."

"No, Daddy, you weren't," she said. "You were trying to protect an outdated idea that you and his father aren't ready to let go of. And that's okay. That's why I did this. This way you can still cling to it without having to witness me and Stryker's friendship, because I'm not giving him up, Daddy. He's too important to me. And I hate that you put me in a position where I had to choose."

"And you chose him," Blaze said, sadly.

"No, I didn't choose him. I chose me. I don't want any part of your feud. I should be free to choose whom I want to love."

Blaze's eyebrows shot up. "Love?"

She nodded. "Yes, Daddy. I love him, but I also love Caleb. We all got to be very close."

Blaze suppressed a sigh of relief. "Oh, I see. You're right, sweetheart. It was selfish of me to infringe upon the relationship you'd developed with him. I had trouble seeing past my own ideas, forgive me?"

"Sure, Daddy," she said. Then she was in his arms.

He closed his eyes and held her. When he opened them, Trip was standing in the doorway with Stryker.

"You wanted to see me?" Stryker asked.

Fucking Trip, Blaze thought. He cleared his throat. "Um, yeah. Listen, I may have been a little hasty earlier. I, uh, underestimated how important the three of you had become to each other, and uh, well, please accept my apology," he offered a hand.

Stryker nodded and shook his hand.

"Accepted, sir."

30

As Caleb was now an angel, he had angel responsibilities. Trip took his son under his wing and showed him the ropes on being an Avenger.

"I can show you how and what to do as an Avenger, but if you really want to be like me? You're going to need warrior training. Even though I'm an Avenger by blood, I'm also part of Titus's army. The next class will be starting soon and from what I understand, Stryker wants to be in it. You two could be buddies, but it's imperative that you take it seriously."

Caleb nodded. "I know and we can. I still don't understand why he wants to take it. He's already a warrior."

Trip chuckled. "Yes, but he's not one of Titus's warriors. It's a whole new level. Plus, it's kind of a status symbol here. No shortage of pussy."

"Is that all you think about?" Caleb asked.

"And you don't?" Trip asked, genuinely astonished.

Caleb thought for a moment. "Okay, point taken, but I have a specific one in mind."

Trip covered his ears. "La la la la la la la!"

Caleb laughed. "Oh, great. Are you gonna be like your buddy about this?"

"No, unlike my buddy, I like the guy who's digging my girl. I'm just busting your chops, but since we're on the topic—"

Caleb covered his ears. "La la la la la la la!"

Trip gave his son a playful punch. "Seriously, what are you waiting for?"

Caleb shrugged. "She's cool and all, and we're friends, but I'm not so sure she's receptive to the idea. Sometimes it feels like she's still trying to hook me up with Sienna."

"Still?" Trip asked.

Caleb nodded. "Yeah."

"I see. Have you told her?"

Caleb's eyes grew wide. "No!"

"Why not?"

"What if... I mean... I don't... but..."

"I need a string of words that actually makes sense. You may have heard of it. It's called a sentence. Try again," Trip said, teasing.

"What if she doesn't like me?" Caleb asked, quietly.

Now Trip understood. The fantasy had become a part of his life and for her to spurn him would be the end. He wasn't ready to let it go.

"I get it," Trip said. "But, you'll never know if you don't try. I'm surprised Sienna hasn't just told her."

"I made her promise not to," said Caleb.

"Ahh, okay. Don't you think it's time you man up and handle your business?"

Caleb winced at his father's words. "I guess so."

"Let me ask you this, what are you like when you're around her?"

"What do you mean?"

"I mean, are you cute and cuddly like a puppy or are you more take charge as that puppy's dad would be? Which one do you think she'd be interested in?"

Caleb chuckled. "She'd probably like the puppy's dad."

"You're damn straight. Look at who her father is. She's used to being around males who are badasses. That's her comfort zone. Cute and cuddly is for cherubs. She's not a cherub anymore, and she's not one to take anybody's shit."

Caleb frowned. "Yeah, I noticed. She has no problem telling Stryker where to get off."

"Exactly! What's with the sour puss? Don't tell me that puts you off."

"No, not really. It's not that. It's just, I don't know."

Trip leaned back and gave his son an appraising look. "Are you afraid of her?"

Caleb's frown deepened. "No! Of course not! I'm no pussy."

"Just making sure, but for the record. Her bark is much worse than her bite."

Caleb grinned. "Kinda like her father?"

Trip stared at his son, mouth agape. "Excuse me?"

"I was just saying her father seems really cool."

Trip slowly nodded. "He is, but don't think for one minute that he's not dangerous, son. There was a time in our history when he was known as Titus the Terrible, and he lived up to that shit. He's the real deal, and he's no fucking joke."

"So what happened that he's all chilled and laid back now?"

"We're not at war."

"Oh, then he's the one I should be afraid of. What if he doesn't like me for his daughter?"

Trip laughed. "Sounds to me like you're looking for an

out. Look, he's fine with it. Just do it, Caleb. You're worrying for nothing. Go for it."

"I will. Soon."

Trip rolled his eyes. "Whatever. It's your life, but I wouldn't take too long if you're serious about warrior training."

"Why?"

"No sexual activities allowed while training. It's a distraction and you have to be focused. It's grueling and intense."

"Does he teach it himself?"

"Not since Blaze and I graduated, but from what I understand, yours will be the first class since then. Good luck. Titus is hard on his students, but you'll be ready for his army when he's done with you. I guarantee it."

"Oh, so once I become a warrior, I'm part of his army?"

"Yes, do you have a problem with that?"

Caleb shook his head. "No, but don't I need to swear some sort of allegiance to him?"

Trip grinned and nodded. "Easy killer, you're getting ahead of yourself, but yes. That'll come later."

"So, what can I expect?"

"Oh, no. I'm not telling you anything. Just know that once you commit, you're expected to finish."

"And if I don't?"

"Then we would leave this realm."

"Why?" Caleb asked. "That seems pretty drastic. Would he really kick us out?"

"No, I'd be too ashamed to stay."

Caleb's mouth fell open. "Are you serious?"

"I'm dead serious, son. So if you decide you want this, you'd better make damn sure that you really want it. There's no shame in choosing not to do it. But once you commit, it's a whole new ball of wax. So, do you want it?"

Caleb looked into his father's eyes and nodded. "Yes, I do."

Trip heaved a sigh of relief. "You didn't hesitate. Good."

"Why would I hesitate?"

"I just want it to be your decision. I don't want you to feel like you're doing it for me."

"But it is important to you that I do it, right?"

"I'd be lying if I said it wasn't, but please don't let that influence your decision. This is your life and you are always free to choose how you want to live it."

"Thanks for saying that. I don't want things to be the way it was with Sienna and her father."

"He's coming around. Remember, that feud has been going on for a long time. Hard feelings and bad blood run deep. It's going to take some getting used to for him. Plus, it's different for girls."

"Oh man, that's not sexist," Caleb said, sarcastically.

"It's the truth, sorry. Just how it is."

"Again, what's keeping Titus the Terrible from going all terrible on me over his daughter?"

Trip chuckled. "Please, Ebony is cherub seven hundred for him. He's got letting go down to a science."

"Seven... seven hundred? He's got seven hundred kids?"

Trip nodded. "Long story. I'll tell you about it sometime. Just know that you're good. He's cool with you as long as you make her happy."

"Well, there's no guarantee, but I'll try."

"Wrong attitude, son. You've got to be more positive. Be more sure about it. Claim it as if it's already yours. That little bit of belief is known as faith, and it has the strength to move mountains. The universe responds to a positive attitude. It has to. Remember that."

"Jeez, now you sound like a motivational speaker."

Trip grinned. "You found that to be motivational?"

His father was beaming with such pride, Caleb didn't have the heart to tell him he was being facetious. He nodded. "Sure Dad and I'll remember it."

"Good, you would do well to remember something else too."

"What's that?"

"You've already got something in your favor with her."

"Which is?"

"You've got my DNA, it gives you an advantage. You're her type."

"I don't think she sees it that way."

Trip shrugged. "So make her."

Caleb wasn't exactly sure what that meant, but his father had him thinking. Maybe he needed to be a little more assertive, but then again, look at Stryker. He'd been all over her for years and she never gave him the time of day. But Stryker didn't have his DNA, either. Hmm. The group of them were meeting up after lunchtime. It would be as good a time as any to test his father's theory.

31

The group ended up meeting over dinner instead of lunch, because, well, shit happens. Titus was telling Caleb about the birth of his father, over dessert.

"Word had spread that an albino was born. So, we all went to see him and he was so pale and his hair was white, but then he opened his eyes. They were icy blue, then they turned gray. There was no question. Definitely an Avenger."

"Disappointed?" Caleb asked.

Titus shook his head. "Not at all. He's one of the best warriors I've ever had the pleasure of training. You're following some major footsteps, son. You up for it?"

"Yes sir, I am," Caleb said. He glanced at his father, who was making quite the show of ignoring the conversation.

Titus looked at him appraisingly. "No hesitation. Eye contact. Good. You're gonna need that resolve."

Sienna, who was sitting across the table next to her own father, spoke up. "That resolve came in handy while we were in the wastelands, while he was still human. No peach fuzz on those bad boys."

"Sienna!" Blaze said, turning to his daughter.

"What? It's true. He was absolutely fearless the whole time." She made eye contact with Ebony, then quietly repeated, "The whole time."

Caleb wanted to kick her under the table, but she was too far from him.

"I'd like to hear about it sometime," Ebony said. "Stryker and Sienna have already told me what it was like for them. I would be interested to hear a human's perspective on it. I'm sure you remember."

Trip, who was sitting next to Caleb, continued eating with his left hand. Reaching under the table with his right, he gave his son a sharp poke in the ribs.

Caleb flinched. "Uh yeah. I do. I'll uh be glad to tell you about it uh sometime," he said.

Trip coughed into his fist. "Pussy!"

Caleb looked around the table to see if anybody else had heard. If they did, they weren't letting on. Faces continued to be buried nose deep in ice cream. His tongue went to his cheek as he shook off his father's accusation, then looked down the table at Ebony.

"How about after dessert," he said. "We could take a walk down by the stable?"

She nodded, emphatically. "Sounds great. You mind if I freshen up first?"

He shook his head. "Not at all."

She wiped her mouth with her napkin and said. "Daddy, I'm finished. May I be excused?"

"Me too?" asked Sienna.

Titus nodded and all the males stood while the two young ladies left. Then it was back to the serious business of eating ice cream. The silence that followed was broken when, without looking up the king said, "It's about time somebody manned up."

Trip snickered. "Damn, son, the king just put you on blast. You gonna take that?"

Caleb looked at Titus, who was now looking back at him expectantly. He looked back at his father and nodded. "From him? Yes."

That got the entire table roaring with laughter.

Titus winked at him. "Good answer, son. Good answer."

※

Ebony went back to her room with Sienna in tow.

"Why are you looking at me like that?" she asked her niece.

Sienna covered her mouth and giggled, adulthood be damned. Sometimes it was just fun to act like a teenager. "I'm not supposed to tell you."

"Then don't. Just sit there, quietly," Ebony said.

Caleb wasn't the only one feeling hesitant. Ebony had heard that he was interested, but she still couldn't be sure. And if he was, why didn't he act on it? Maybe he saw her as a spoiled bitch. No doubt, Trip had filled him in on their past.

Sienna plopped down on her bed and quietly watched her touch up her lipstick and liner. Yeah... she was quiet, alright, but she still had a goofy grin on her face.

Ebony stopped what she was doing. "What?"

Sienna bit her lip and shook her head.

Ebony rolled her eyes. "It's killing you, isn't it?"

Sienna nodded, vigorously. "It really is, please?"

"On one condition."

"Anything! What?" Sienna asked.

"If he asks me, I get to tell him it was you who let the cat out of the bag."

Sienna thought for a moment, then decided she could live

with that. "Okay, but since you just said that means you already know or at least suspect, right?"

Ebony sat down next to her. "Yes, I knew. I've known all along."

Sienna gasped in surprise. "But, what about all those times you were trying to steer him towards me?"

Ebony shrugged. "I guess if he had someone else to be interested in, it would let me off the hook."

"But why would you want to be? Do you have any idea how many of my friends want to hook up with him?"

Ebony laughed. "Oh, come on! Your friends want to do Stryker, too."

Sienna feigned a frown. "True, they're just gonna have to wait for their turns."

Ebony raised an eyebrow. "Turns? There's more than one?"

Sienna made a face. "You know there is. He's hot as fuck. I don't know how you resisted him all those years. Honestly? I questioned whether you were homosexual or just blind."

"I can assure you, I prefer junk of the swinging variety, thank you very much, but I have kissed a chick or two."

Sienna waved her off. "Who hasn't?"

Ebony's mouth fell open. "Listen to you, sounding all grown up and shit!"

"Seriously? How old were you?"

Ebony paused. "Good point. Time flies. I guess I still see you as a little girl sometimes."

"So does daddy. Honestly? I'm not sure I'm ready for it. Not even with Stryker."

"He knows," Ebony assured her.

"So, how come you never hooked up with him?"

"I don't know. I just didn't see him in that light."

"Even now? After what we've been through. I know

we've changed. You don't go through something like that and come out unscathed. I don't care who you are. You can't tell me there wasn't ample opportunity."

Ebony looked away. "Yeah, there is something different about him now. I can see it, but... I couldn't do that to you."

Sienna squeezed her hand. "It would have been okay. I would have been okay with it."

Ebony nodded. "I suspected as much, but *he* wasn't okay with it. And in my book, that makes him a great guy. He really has changed."

"He always was a great guy in my book," Sienna said, beaming.

"I know, but understand. Back in the day, the flash of a smile along with the promise of ass was enough to get his attention."

"Oh, so it's not just Julian?" Sienna asked with obvious sarcasm.

Ebony laughed. "You're so much older than you let on." She grew serious. "You don't really expect him to wait, do you?"

"No. The idea is sweet, but the reality is the body has its needs and I don't expect him to starve himself for me."

"That's an interesting way to put it," Ebony said. "It's very mature of you to see it that way."

"Just being realistic. It's not like we're naturally monogamous. The only relationships I see here that are, are comprised of a human and an angel. My mom and dad and your mom and dad. Everybody else..." She shrugged.

"What about Trip and Lylac?"

Sienna gave her aunt an *oh please!* expression. "You know they're a special breed of freaky. And they get that about each other. Because they connect on that level. I don't think anybody else could tolerate being mated to either of them, you?"

Ebony laughed and nodded. "True, even when I was crushing on him, I never had a problem with Lylac. I could sense that. I think they're the true definition of soulmates. Even if they were to split up, you know—"

Sienna completed it with her. "—they'd eventually find their way back to each other."

Ebony nodded. "Exactly."

She went back to the mirror and started fussing with her tresses. Even in Titus's perfect world, curly hair had a mind of its own and it wasn't behaving today. She finally grabbed a scrunchie and bound it into a bun, leaving a few haphazard stragglers that insisted upon falling loose and hanging next to her face.

Sienna sighed as she watched her. She always knew Ebony had a beauty of the breathtaking kind, hence the mad crush Stryker had on her. Who could blame him? Even Trip. She couldn't help wondering, for Ebony's sake, if things had been different, could it have happened? Who knew? One thing was for sure. Caleb was finally getting his chance. A part of her wanted to witness it, but as long as she was there, nothing would happen. Better to give the two of them their time. Ebony stopped what she was doing and turned to her.

"You're doing it again," she said.

Sienna frowned. "Doing what?"

"Looking at me as if it's the last time you're gonna see me. It's not like we're leaving the kingdom."

"I know, but..." Sienna smiled her crooked little grin. It was just like her father's and it was every bit as cute on her as it was on him.

Ebony gave her a knowing smile. "Oh, I see. You think tonight's the night, huh?"

Sienna covered her cheesy grin and nodded.

"No, that's so not happening tonight, if ever."

"But what if it does? And what do you mean 'if ever'? Don't you want to?"

"Of course, I'm just not sure it'll be him, that's all."

Sienna wasn't convinced. "But if it does?"

"I'll tell you what," Ebony said. "If, and that's a big 'if', if it happens tonight, I'll come back and give you all the juicy details. Fair enough?"

Sienna squealed with delight and resisted the urge to stand up and start chanting, *Caleb's gonna get some, Caleb's gonna get some.* Instead, she said, "Agreed! Just so you know. I'm sleeping over."

Ebony laughed. "I kinda figured. The room's all yours. Do not rearrange it! I know how you and Lylac are."

"Fine! I won't! But, can I try on some of your clothes?"

It was nice to have an aunt the same height and build, well almost the same build. Sienna had way more going on in the bust department, and Ebony beat her hands down with more booty.

"Now what kind of aunt would I be if I said no?"

Sienna didn't even wait for her to leave. She let out a whoop, followed by, "Sweet!" Then she disappeared inside Ebony's closet.

Ebony shook her head and laughed, then headed out to the stable.

32

Caleb went back to the house to change clothes. The weather that day had been extremely mild. When the king was in a good mood, the weather was glorious. But when he was pissed off? Look out. Then there was all manner of thunder and lightning going on. He changed into a t-shirt with a pair of cargo shorts and sandals. It reminded him of home. The only thing missing was the surf. He was going through the same third degree with his father that Ebony had with Sienna. Trip was leaning against the bathroom door frame watching him groom. Caleb picked up his razor.

"Don't." Came the emphatic demand from the doorway.

"Why not? It's a day and a half old," Caleb said, rubbing his face. "And scratchy."

Trip's eyes twinkled. "Exactly. Trust me on this one. She likes the beard. Leave it. And while we're on topic, you know how to locate the man in the boat, right?"

His father was now standing in the mirror with him and waiting for an answer. Caleb applied conditioner to his stubble and frowned.

"Locate the man in the—" then he realized what he was being asked. "I'm so not having this conversation with you."

He turned to walk out of the room. Trip blocked his exit. When your father is almost seven feet tall and built like a Norse god, there's not too much you can do when he's standing in the doorway, and filling it up. Caleb crossed his arms and waited.

"I'm not moving," Trip said. "And yes, we are having this conversation. I'd be remiss as your father if I didn't make sure I properly prepared you."

"Really? I'm having a hard time picturing Blaze and Julian having this talk."

Trip chuckled. "Well, for your information, they did. I was there for it. You want me to invite him over for this one?"

"No!"

"Then talk. It's just you and me. I promise you, I'm not trying to be nosy and I'm not out to embarrass you. I just want to make sure everything's perfect."

Caleb looked up at him. "For her?"

Trip nodded. "Yes, for her. I just want to make sure you know what you're doing and that you're not gonna be sloppy about it. Because trust and believe, there's a female friend waiting to hear all the details afterward. And that information will spread like wildfire."

"I see, then it will reflect on you, right?"

"Yes, that's the reality of it. I know things are different in Terra-3, but—"

"I'm not in Kansas anymore?"

"Right."

Caleb ran a hand through his hair. "Okay, what do you want to know?"

Trip threw back his head and laughed. "Damn, that almost sounded like *you* had something to teach *me*."

Caleb shrugged. "Maybe I do."

"Go on! I've got four hundred years on your newbie ass! What could you possibly show me that I haven't done?"

Caleb thought for a moment then said, "I could show you how it feels to be a proud father."

Gotcha. Trip had to admit he was right. He looked into his son's eyes and said, "You already have."

Then father and son had the talk of all talks, and Trip was pleasantly surprised to find that his son did actually know a thing or two about the female anatomy. There was only one problem. Caleb had never been with a virgin before.

Trip's eyes narrowed. "Is that the real reason you've been dragging your feet?"

Caleb nodded. "I don't want to hurt her and I don't want you to be mad at me for it."

"First of all, everything you've got down there, you got from me. Short of surgery, there's nothing you can do about that. You're not down for having your dick altered, are you?"

Caleb's eyes were wide. "No!"

"Good. As for the second part, I wouldn't be mad at you for that. Truth be told, she's a little old to be a virgin here. That shit's usually taken care of around Sienna's age."

"I don't think Blaze got that memo."

"Christ, with females, Blaze missed all the memos. He's never had a virgin, either."

"What?!" Caleb exclaimed, surprised.

"It's true. His choice. He doesn't deal well with emotions and the last thing he wants is some chick crying after he's gotten his rocks off."

"What about you?"

"Of course, I have. Lylac was a virgin when we first hooked up."

"Really?"

"Yep, to let her tell it, I split her ass, leaving her unable to crawl out of bed for three days. A gross exaggeration on her part, for sure, because guess who she chose to hook up with at the next party?"

"You?"

"Damn straight. Again, in her words, it was because I was sweet about the whole thing. I stayed the night with her. We did it again the next morning."

"Are you serious? Why would you do that if she was already sore?"

"Hey, it was her choice. She was on a mission. She was just trying to get past the whole 'getting used to it' stage. And the rest, as you know, is history."

"What do you mean 'as I know'? How the fuck would I know?"

Trip shook his head and laughed. "You can't tell me you've never heard us shouting down the walls up in this piece."

The pink that tinged Caleb's cheeks said he sure had.

Trip continued, "Yeah, that's what I thought. Listen, the big thing to remember with a virgin is to go slow. Take your time. Allow her body to get used to the feeling of you being inside. Remember, here, there is no menstruation, so unless she masturbates with a dildo or with her fingers on the inside, she's had nothing in there."

"What if she doesn't masturbate?"

Trip laughed. "Everybody masturbates. Get that in you. Guarantee you won't be giving her her first orgasm, but you'll be the first she shares one with. You ready?"

Caleb nodded. "Yeah, I am. I think."

"Questions?"

"One. Since there're no periods here, does that mean I don't need a condom?"

"That's exactly what it means, but it only goes for here. If you were to leave the kingdom, you would need one. Make sense?"

"Yeah, I guess I'm living proof, huh?"

"That you are, but if I had it to do again? I wouldn't change a thing. I'm glad you're here."

"Thanks, Dad."

"Go get 'em, tiger."

33

Ebony's heart pounded in her ears as she made her way to the stable on foot. She could have flown, but she wanted the extra time to think. Was this really it? Was it going to happen tonight? She'd saved herself all those years for a fantasy, albeit a childish one. And now that the fantasy was shattered, was she selling out for the first candidate? It didn't feel that way. But the question that truly begged to be answered was, did she feel the same way about him as he did for her? She saw the way he looked at her, the way he acted around her, not to mention, no matter how hard she tried to distract and redirect him with Sienna, it hadn't worked. But, who was she really trying to redirect and distract? Herself? Maybe. She thought about that for a moment. So if tonight turned out to be the night, wouldn't it be better if they were in her bed? No. She didn't want it to happen under her father's roof. Especially if it ended up hurting as bad as some of her friends said it did. She looked out across the fields surrounding the stable. There was no sign of him. All was quiet. The half-moon limited the light. Maybe he was already inside. She approached the large door and swung it open. It felt strange being there after her mother's transformation. She had wanted to remove it altogether, but Vanessa had insisted it stay, citing sentimental reasons. Stay, it did.

"Caleb?" she called out, tentatively. No answer. She let out a long breath. Was that a sigh of relief? Maybe this wasn't such a good idea. The small amount of luminescence the moon was shedding cast a long, dim shadow as she pulled the door open. Then there was a second shadow cast next to hers.

"Hey," he said, quietly.

She turned to face him and damn if he wasn't right there. Right. There. Close, real close. Like 'you're invading my space' close and he wasn't moving. She took a step back.

"Sorry, I'm late," he said, taking a step forward.

She shook her head. "You're not, I just got here myself."

She looked and noticed he had a sleeping bag rolled up under one arm and a bottle in the other. Ohhhh, he came prepared to hook up.

"A sleeping bag? A little presumptuous, don't you think?" she asked.

"Let's not play that tonight, okay?"

"Play what?"

"Play like we're not attracted to each other. We've been dancing around it since I got here. Say we haven't."

He was right. Ebony didn't know what to say. There really was no argument, but that didn't mean she couldn't play hard to get. "And what if I say no?" she challenged, stepping back.

He shrugged and tossed the sleeping bag behind her. "Then I guess I'll be sleeping out here alone," he said, stepping forward.

"You're kind of invading my personal space, right now. Hasn't anyone ever told you that's rude?" she asked, taking another step back. This time she stepped out of her flip-flops. He kicked them aside as he stepped forward, his eyes never once leaving hers.

"Nope," he answered. "Guess that makes me something of a Neanderthal, huh?"

She shook her head. "I didn't say that."

He was so close she could smell his shampoo. He smelled crisp and clean—and masculine. Like his father. *Oh, boy*, she thought, *I'm in trouble here. This really is going to happen, isn't it?*

She figured she must have looked panicked because his next words were, "Ebony, we're not gonna do anything that you don't want to, okay?"

She nodded. "Okay."

He looked up at her hair and smirked.

She frowned, suddenly feeling self-conscious. "What?" she asked, reaching up to fix whatever he was finding so damned amusing.

"Nothing. It's just that your hairband is failing you. Here, let me."

He reached up and snagged the scrunchie, jailbreaking all those unruly curls and allowing them to spill down over her shoulders and back. A low growl escaped his lips. "That's better," he said, his eyes boring into hers.

Holy shit! He's seducing me, and well, she thought. This was not the sweet, shy Caleb she was used to. Hell no, quite the opposite. And wasn't that the point, here? From the moment he arrived, he was well on his game tonight. That her insides felt like smoldering embers were a testimony of it. She broke eye contact and glanced down at his hand.

"So, what's in the bottle?"

He chuckled as if to say, *wouldn't you like to know?* then unscrewed the cap and offered it. "Bourbon."

She nodded in agreement. "We can do bourbon."

She took the bottle and chugged down three healthy gulps. Wincing, she handed it back to him. He followed suit without the wince, eyes still locked on hers. She went to step back once more, but there was a bale of hay there. Her arms started windmilling as she struggled to re-establish her balance. He reached out and caught her, pulling her in. And there they were. The two of them on the precipice. In that moment, she knew. It was time to stop "faking the funk" as Joel would say and admit to herself that, yes, she felt the same way about him and yes, she was more than okay with him being her first. She was in his arms, his face inches from hers with his whiskey tainted breath, and who knew that was sexy? His eyes went to her lips as he licked his own. Just as she was about to lean in and kiss him, he did it first and oh what a kiss it was. Nothing at all like the one he'd given Sienna, as Sienna had inadvertently given her the details whilst comparing him to Stryker. Just goes to show you can't fake passion. No, sir. And those smoldering embers were now blazing white hot and entering into molten lava territory. Oh yes, this night was definitely going to end with them sharing that sleeping bag. Caleb Trip Lawson was no longer stuck in the *friend zone*, oh no boys and girls, he was now in the realm of desirable badass and the possibilities were endless. Ebony had also worn shorts and a t-shirt. He grabbed the tail and tugged it over her head. He loved watching the curls as they cascaded over her shoulders and down her back. He couldn't resist anymore as he tangled his fingers in them and pulled her in for another kiss, more aggressive this time. And she liked it, a lot. She returned the favor of pulling his shirt over his head, the two of them parting just long enough for it to come off. Then they were at each other again. The next thing to go was her bra. He was pretty adept at getting it off with one hand. That impressed her, but she was far too busy to stop and tell him so. It was time for those cargo shorts to come off. But was he like all the other males around her? None of them had a clue what underwear was. Judging by the way his were hanging off his hips and there was no sign of a waistband? Commando. Before she could go for them, his hands were at her waist and opening hers, then they were hitting the floor. She stepped out of them and looked up at him.

"Your turn," she said.

"Why don't we get in the sleeping bag first," he said.

"Why? Is there something you don't want me to see?"

"No, of course not."

"Are you afraid you're gonna scare me?" she asked, coyly.

"I'm your first, aren't I?"

She nodded. "So?"

"So, maybe I'd like us both to have something to open when we climb in."

She nodded. "Fine, but just so you know, I want to see it before we... you know."

He gave her a cocky grin. "Oh, you'll see it all right."

"Okay."

They unfolded the sleeping bag together, then stretched out on top of it. His hands went to her hips as his lips found hers again. Then he was working his way down the length of her body. She closed her eyes, enjoying the sensation of his fiery breath and lips against her bare skin. But when his mouth found her nipples, it was all over for her. It felt so good. She sighed, then her fingers were in his hair as he slid a hand inside her panties. She froze and grabbed his wrist.

"What's wrong?" he asked.

"I don't know. It's just that nobody has ever touched me there."

"Not even you?"

"Of course, I have! I shower every day."

He slowly shook his head. "That's not what I meant."

She looked at his chest and quietly said, "I know what you meant."

Despite her own broken filter, it was a topic she wasn't comfortable discussing with a male. Even Stryker had tried to steer the conversation on more than one occasion, making it quite clear it was something he visualized regularly. It was way more than she had ever needed to know about him.

"Are you okay?" he asked.

She nodded. "Yeah, I just needed a minute to get used to the idea."

He snuggled in closer. "You sure?"

"Yes," she said, then leaned in to kiss him. She had to admit, he was a damn good kisser. Not that she really had anybody to compare him to, and that thought just made her feel sorry for the next guy or girl. This time both hands were at her waistband. She lifted her hips, allowing him to slide them off. He sat kneeling, staring at her. Oh great, was he disappointed now? She wondered.

"What's wrong?" she asked.

"Absolutely nothing," he said, and the look he was now giving her said it all. From here on out there would be no more interruptions. He stood up to remove his shorts, thus releasing his erection from its confines. It was huge, at least to her. Sure, males who were shameless about being nude surrounded her, but they were never erect in her presence. She realized he was watching her for a reaction. She looked at it again, then up at him, eyes wide and mouth slack-jawed.

"Is it too late to change my mind?" she asked.

He shook his head. "No. I told you, we're not gonna do anything you don't want to. If you're not ready for this, we can wait." He stretched out next to her. "I'm perfectly happy just being here with you, but that doesn't mean there aren't other things we can do."

She shook her head. "No, let's do this."

He propped his head on an elbow. "Are you sure?"

She nodded. "I'm sure. Can I touch it?"

"Of course."

She reached out, wrapping her fingers around it. "Is this okay?"

"Yes," he whispered.

Then she slid her hand up the length and rubbed the head with her thumb. He hissed and closed his eyes. The skin was so smooth and tight. A single drop of clear fluid appeared at the slit, and she couldn't help wondering what it would taste like. She licked her lips at the thought. She looked into his face. His eyes were open again, albeit hooded. He gave the slightest of nods. That was all the permission she needed she leaned over and swirled her tongue around that bad boy. He gasped and let out a low moan. She liked that reaction. So she did it again, savoring the slight saltiness and enjoying the satiny feeling of his skin against her tongue. He rolled onto his back. And if that wasn't a blatant invite she didn't know what was. She kneeled between his legs and started running her tongue up and down the length. He had his eyes closed and was rubbing her shoulders. She stopped to look at it with admiration. Just because she was a virgin didn't mean she was ignorant. She recognized that she was simply inexperienced. And what was the best way to gain experience? Participation. She moved in closer, this time noticing his balls. She smiled.

"What are you grinning at?" he asked, amused.

"They're actually kinda cute," she said.

"Cute? Um... not sure I've ever heard them described like that before, but I can tell you this. If I were to stand up and bend over, 'cute' would be the last word to come to mind."

She laughed. "You think?"

"Trust me, I know."

"Really? Do you make it a habit to look at yourself from behind in the mirror while bending over?"

"No. Every male knows that 'the mountain goat' is his most unattractive angle."

"Mountain goat?" she asked and started howling with laughter.

He sat up. "It's true."

"So show me."

"Hell no!"

"Come on."

"Nope."

"Pleeease?"

"Uh-uh, not gonna happen. At least, not deliberately. Now, you've had your fun and your chance to explore. It's my turn."

He rolled her onto her back and started kissing her hipbone. She giggled and squirmed.

"What are you doing?" he asked, laughing.

"It tickles!"

"Oh, really?" he asked, then he parted her thighs and was kissing her along the hairline.

She stopped and looked down at him. He looked back at her and wiggled his eyebrows.

"So tell me..." he began.

She could feel his fingers parting her lips and then his hot breath was right there next to that most sensitive bundle of nerves. She swallowed in anticipation.

"Tell you what?" she asked, quietly.

His eyes locked onto hers. "Do you touch yourself?"

Ebony was grateful for the lack of light as the heat made its way up her neck and spread across her cheeks. Slowly, she nodded.

"See? That wasn't so hard, now was it?" he asked, then blew on her skin causing her to gasp then let out a shuddering breath.

She shook her head and answered. "No, I guess not."

Her response fell on deaf ears as he had resumed his own exploration and was now kissing her there with the same fervor he'd had when kissing her mouth. She cried out and arched her back. He spread her thighs farther and dove in, tongue first while she laid back and closed her eyes. Touching oneself didn't hold a candle to what he was now doing. She hissed and shuddered each time his tongue passed over her clit. She couldn't help it. It felt so damned good, too damned good. She was already close to coming. She felt his fingers again. This time he slid one inside. She froze. She'd never had anything there before, not even her own. The sensation was a bit strange. He withdrew his finger then slid it in again, a little further this time all the while his tongue was moving faster and faster. She was now teetering on the edge of one powerful orgasm. She could hardly stand the buildup. Soon, she was holding her breath and pounding the ground with her fist, exactly what Caleb was waiting for. In one move he sucked her clit into his mouth, completely engulfing it as his tongue swirled around and around and up and down, this time his finger went in the whole way, then he was moving it in a *come hither* motion stroking that hard little bean. It was a tip his father had given him, and it worked like a charm. She cried out and started bucking against his face. Normally, he would have stopped at that point, but his father had said,

"What do you mean stop? Dude, you're just getting started. You keep up that motion until she's speaking in tongues and begging you to stop. Trust me on this. If you can pull that off? She'll keep coming back." So he did. Ebony had never considered herself multi-orgasmic. She had thought about trying just to experiment, but would always fall asleep after the first one. Caleb wasn't about to let her fall asleep and in no time she was building up to a second one and damn if it wasn't more powerful than the first. Caleb now had two fingers inside her working his magic, but she barely noticed as he continued going for a third. She was gasping for breath, not sure if her body could take much more.

"St... st... stop!" she stammered. He didn't. Instead, he increased what he was doing. Faster, faster, faster... then it happened. And Ebony saw stars. She tried to crawl out from under him, but he followed her, still licking and sucking and stroking. *One more, just one more...* was the mantra in his head. He was damn near close to coming himself, and if she didn't stop moving, the friction against the sleeping bag would be just enough to finish him. No way he was going out like that. In a mighty move, he hooked both arms around her thighs and pulled her back, continuing his onslaught causing her to cry out. Then his face was being drenched. Oh yeah, number four. Sometime he was going to have to tie her down and see just how many he could get out of her in one night, he thought. But not tonight. His balls were aching. It was time to satisfy himself. He rose over her and positioned himself at her opening. As wet as she was, he should have no trouble working his way in. He was right, but it still hurt for her. He could see it in her face. She was no longer riding the ebb of an orgasm, but grimacing and gritting her teeth. There was no getting around it. *I don't care who you are, two fingers does not a dick make. A*gain, his father's words. It was in her favor that he was almost ready to come. It wouldn't take long. He started rocking his hips. It would still get him there without beating her cervix to hell and back. Save that for a night when he could bend her over and take her from behind. It was an image he'd used many a night while furiously working himself over with his left hand. It never failed to send him over the edge and now was no exception. He buried his face in her neck as his hips bucked forward and he stiffened.

He gasped then whispered. "Jade…"

She wrapped her arms around him and kissed his neck, clinging to him until the final shudder. Then he stilled, his hot breath heaving against her neck. He gave her earlobe a playful nip, causing her to squeal and wriggle away. He rolled off her and propped himself on an elbow again. Then he saw that her face was tear-streaked.

He looked at her, alarmed. "You're crying. I hurt you. I'm so sorry."

She shook her head. "Don't be. There's nothing you could have done about it. It's okay."

"Are you okay?"

She nodded. "I will be."

"Will be?"

She nodded. "I'm not gonna lie, Caleb. It hurt. But nothing that a good night's sleep won't fix."

"Come on, let's get comfortable," he said.

They climbed into the sleeping bag and cuddled together, spooning. He was playing with her hair. Pulling a curl and watching it spring back when released.

"You still awake?" he asked.

"Yes."

"Still sore?"

"Gods, yes!"

He winced. "Sorry."

"Would you stop already? I told you, it's fine. I'll be fine."

"Okay," he said, kissing her neck.

"Caleb?"

"Yeah?"

"Do you know you called me Jade while your were coming?"

"Did I?"

She nodded, then rolled over to face him. "Yes. It's my middle name."

"I know."

"How? Oh, Uncle Trip, but how would he know to tell you?"

Caleb told her about the sketchbooks and the dreams he had of her. "In my dreams, your name is always Jade. I hope I didn't offend you."

She smiled. "Of course not. I like it."

"You do?"

"Yes. Kinda like a term of endearment."

"Term of endearment? I like that," he said, smiling.

And what a beautiful smile it was. She snuggled in closer to him. They lay together, neither one speaking. She was thinking about all the details Sienna was going to grill her for, and he knew his father was going to be expecting a report of some sort. As far as he was concerned, his father didn't need details. Ebony fell asleep first. He could feel her warm, even breaths lightly on his skin. He kissed her forehead, then closed his eyes. His last thoughts before sleep overtook him were of looking into his father's eyes and simply saying *mission accomplished*. It was enough. It would have to be. Besides, his father shouldn't expect anything less from him, after all, he too had Avenger blood in his veins.

34

Vanessa and Titus made love like there was no tomorrow. It was just like old times. Buttons flying around the room, the sound of ripping fabric followed by a soft whisper as it landed on the floor. The moans, the shouts, the tangled sheets, the sweat; the scratching and hair-pulling, mainly done by Vanessa, and finally the breathless afterglow. They both lay holding hands and staring up at the ceiling, well spent and trying to catch a fleeting breath. The mattress was completely stripped and a little off-center. Monkey sex at its finest. If the sheets were still on the bed, then you didn't do it right. Vanessa spoke first.

"That was beyond monkey sex," she said, still out of breath.

"Aye, that it was," Titus agreed. "I believe we've graduated to baboon status."

They laughed and fist-bumped.

She rolled onto her belly, then leaned in to kiss him. He reached up, placed a hand behind her head, and pulled her in. He moaned as her tongue slid between his teeth, teasing.

"I see how it is," he said. "Fuck that baboon. We're going for the orangutan!"

She laughed and rolled away. "No! We're going for a shower," she said.

He sat up. "Works for me. You know I can have bars installed in there. Make things more interesting. Just a thought."

"Okay, Trip," she laughed.

He shook his head and followed her in. "Can you imagine what their en suite shower looks like? Probably a swing."

"Right? With spikes and whatnot."

Titus closed his eyes and waved his hands. "Stop, stop, stop. Remember, his mate is one of my daughters. That visual is a bit much. Not to mention ours is currently in the stable with his son. Who knows if he's like his father? Hmm. Maybe I should go check on them." He started for the door, naked. Vanessa laughed and pulled him back.

"Stop! She's fine. You'll only embarrass her," she said.

"I was kidding, but maybe you could do something to keep me busy so I don't wander off."

She grabbed him as he pretended to head for the door again.

"Busy, huh?" she said.

He glanced up, and a bar appeared just below the ceiling. "Orangutan?"

She covered her face. "No, you didn't!"

"What? Why not?" He turned on the hot water and grabbed the soap. "Shall I wash your back?" he asked, his voice an octave lower. Ahhh, seduction.

She giggled. "Oh no! Not the child molester voice!"

He feigned hurt feelings. "I was going for Barry White, but okay. I've got ca-a-a-ndy-y-y…"

"Oh, god! You're making it worse! My back, yes please and thank you."

She faced the wall, and he moved in.

He lathered up his hands and began rubbing her body. Down her shoulders and across her breasts.

"That's not my back, sir!" she said.

He leaned in and kissed her neck, then ran his tongue up to her ear. She shuddered and leaned back into him.

"That's still not my back," she whispered.

He kissed her shoulder, then soaped her back and below. He ran his hand across her left butt cheek and paused, frowning.

She sighed. "Don't. It's okay, really."

"No, it's not. And it's my fault. I'm so—"

She turned to face him. "I swear if you apologize to me again, we're gonna have problems that monkey sex won't fix, Mr. Walker," she said, resorting to the nickname she had given him in their previous life.

"He marked you, Vanessa. Permanently. You should've never been there," he said.

She glanced at the scar on what would have been her flank in horse form. Back then, it was hidden under her fur, but now? It practically glowed, showing up almost white against her dark skin.

"And why does it look like it's getting lighter?" he asked.

She shook her head, giving him a nervous laugh. "Guilt does crazy things to the imagination, Titus. Forgive yourself. Let it go. I'm here with you now and that's all that matters."

She placed her hands on either side of his face. "I forgave you a long time ago, Titus. Everything happens the way it does for a reason. It's time you forgave yourself. As your queen, I'm ordering you to forgive yourself and to never mention it again. What's done is done and now we move on. Hmm?"

"You're ordering me?" he asked, giving her a weak smile.

"I am. No more about this. You open your mouth to speak on it and I am walking away. You hear me?"

He nodded. "Yes, ma'am," he said, and this time the dimples were engaged. Much better.

"So touching it doesn't hurt, right?" he asked.

She frowned. What kind of question was that? "No, of course, not. Why?"

"So if I did this—" he asked, giving it a slap.

"Oooh!" she exclaimed, then glanced up at the new bar. "Don't be starting shit, Mr. Walker. You could find yourself in a world of trouble."

He pulled her in for a kiss. "Oh, I'm starting shit."

Cue the orangutans.

THE HALF-MOON CAST ITS DIM GLOW ACROSS VANESSA'S face. She started and sat up, touching her cheek. Had someone just touched her? She glanced over at Titus, who was on his back with an arm over his head and mouth wide open. Thank the gods he didn't snore, but damn that open hatch could catch a lot of spiders. The moonlight was dim, but it was being reflected around the room via the myriad of mirrors. Vanessa caught her reflection and froze. She was dreaming. She had to be. Staring back at her from the mirror was a black horse! Titus groaned and shifted positions. She glanced down at him to make sure he was still asleep. He confirmed it as he ground his teeth together, then licked his lips. Vanessa cringed at the sound. He really needed to find some method of stress relief. Maybe the new warrior class would help. Who was she kidding? There was no sex during that time, and she knew her angel. He'd be insatiable in the days that followed. She looked at the mirror again and was disappointed to see the horse gone. But why would she be disappointed? Because she missed it. She missed flying. Funny how that worked. When she was a pegasus, she'd felt like a human trapped in the creature's body, and now she felt like a pegasus trapped in a human body.

That's because you are, a voice inside her head said. Great. Now she was losing her mind.

She glanced around the room, expecting someone to be there, but no. Then she caught her reflection again. This time there was a black unicorn. She leaped out of the bed. The creature turned its head and winked, then nodded. *You know,* said the voice within.

"I know," Vanessa repeated as her eyes turned black and she became entranced. She reached for her hooded robe and padded out of the room.

VANESSA HAD INSISTED ON KEEPING THE STABLE FOR sentimental reasons, she'd said. But that wasn't the whole truth. She made her way to the structure and stared in.

Ebony and Caleb slumbered inside a sleeping bag spooning. She smiled to herself, so proud of her daughter, no longer a cherub. How quickly does time fly? *Fly. Fly. Fly.* She continued on to the meadow, shedding the robe along the way. She stopped and closed her eyes, feeling the night air on her skin, inhaling the fresh scents of the foliage and something else. A human-like smell. She glanced around, seeing no one she looked up at the moon and spread her arms, then she was feeling the rush of air as she took flight. It was glorious! Gods, how she had missed this! She flew the entire perimeter of the kingdom and returned, landing next to her robe. She put it back on, then quickly made her way back to the palace, back to her bed. She climbed in and settled under Titus's arm. Soon her even breathing matched his as she fell into a deep sleep. Oblivious.

Oblivious to the fact that she still shared a body. Oblivious to the fact that she had been walking to the meadow every night and flying around the kingdom in pegasus form. Oblivious to the fact that the scar was indeed becoming more visible after each flight. Oblivious to the fact that she had a secret, unrevealed, even to her. A secret that could lay ruins to an entire realm or be the salvation of a kingdom.

And oblivious to the fact that someone had seen her.

AND LAST, BUT NOT LEAST...

The dragon lifted its head, his feelers firing off all kinds of notifications. A ripe female! And she was close. But, if he could sense her, so could any of his brothers in the vicinity. He needed to move fast. He took flight, searching. Wherever she was, she wasn't moving. A shame. It would make her harder to find. He looked below. She was there. He knew it, but he still couldn't see her. All good. All he had to do was wait for a groundsweeper to find her then follow it. The wait wasn't long. The black cloud matriculated out of thin air with a shriek and started rolling along the ground. BINGO! The dragon made a beeline for the creature, and there she was. The contrast of her pale skin against the darker ground made her easier to see up close. He landed next to her and turned his tail to the groundsweeper. Just as it opened its mouth, he released a gas ball, instantly smoking the creature to ash. He leaned in and sniffed. His olfactory was for shit, but up close he could he catch the faintest hint. Running his nose along the length of her body, he savored her fragrance. Roses, rain, and pheromones. Instinctively, he knew the dark thatch of hair *was where the party was. He would stay with her as long as she continued to release pheromones and he would mate with her repeatedly marking her with his own scent. Then once her pheromones dissipated, it would be safe to leave her alone, to heal... and gestate.*

DRAGO SAT IN HIS OFFICE, FROWNING. MINERVA'S LAME-assed plan had failed. Titus and his cronies had swooped in at the last minute and saved the day. Whoopdedoo. He still had fertilized eggs in need of surrogates. Minerva would have a two-headed cow if she knew. He chuckled to himself as he thought of it. That would be kinda fun to watch. Alas, there was no time to enjoy the fantasy. Where to find a surrogate? Preferably a human one. Terra-3 Earth would be good, but why go through all the trouble when Hedon was just on the other side of Purgatory? He could get a humanoid body without all the human issues. Such whining! It was too bad that dragons didn't have uteri. Even if they did, most of the beasts would eat the young as soon as it was born. Not good. He needed to think. One of his favorite places to go for that was the Wastelands. He thought himself to the spot where they had last been and found Minerva lying on the ground, healing. Whoa. She wasn't dead?

There was a sudden movement to his left, and a dragon was bearing down on him, roaring. What the fuck? Since when did any of his sons challenge him? He roared back, and the beast stopped and stared at him. That wasn't right. It should have bowed. What was going on here? The only thing that would cause this behavior would be a successful mating. It would protect its unborn. Drago looked down at Minerva's body. Holy shit! Had his son impregnated her while she was healing? He threw back his head and guffawed. It was so epically poetic! And so... useful, he thought while stroking his chin. Hmmm. Not only was she humanoid, but she was an angel. Her body was superior in every way. She would make the perfect surrogate! What more could a grandmother do than to help her grandchild make its way into this world. You couldn't make this shit up. He looked at the young dragon, which was still standing its ground. He cooed at it, soothingly. The beast bowed to him. Nice. He approached it and stroked its head.

"You did well, my son. I couldn't be prouder," he said. Then he leaned in and whispered, "Sleep."

The beast fell to the ground, snoring. Drago lifted Minerva into his arms and returned with her to his lab. If he did this properly, she would never know.

She wasn't dead. She wasn't dead! She. Wasn't. Dead. Minerva sat up and looked at her body. Her skin was healthy and pink. She turned her hands over, examining both sides. She touched her face. Healed. Her hair. Healthy and flowing over her shoulders. Exactly how long had she been down? What did it matter? She survived! She opened her wings and shook them out. Not perfect, but it was nothing a good shower and grooming wouldn't fix. She was lucky. At the time of the torching they had been tucked into her skin, protected. She stood up and stretched. That felt good. Now to test her wings. She lifted off with no problems and set down on an upper branch, surveying her surroundings. Was she really stuck there? She concentrated, pulling energy from the air around her body, then projected her thoughts to her home. The scenery changed, and she was standing in her garden. It worked! She was home! She could have fallen to the ground weeping in gratitude. She was home, dammit! Fuck Titus and fuck Drago too. But she still needed those fertilized eggs. She couldn't afford to have any of them survive. There was only one being left she could turn to, and he was truly a last resort. They hadn't spoken in almost seven hundred years. Back then, she had wanted only one thing from him and, of course, he had wanted one thing from her. And she had given it to him, twice. Chances are he would want it again. She showered and shaved. Everything. Because that was how he liked it. And if she was going to him for help? She was going prepared to pay the price. She tied her hair up in a sash and spritzed it with rose water. Another thing he liked. She took a deep breath, then thought herself to his palace.

He was standing with his back to her when she arrived. Things had changed a lot since she'd last been there. He wasn't wearing his toga. No. Today, he was wearing a white tailored suit. Not what one would expect from a god, but hey, whatever floats your boat. Right? Ramsis turned to her and smiled, "Good morning, Minerva. I've been expecting you."

THE END

NEXT UP

Thank you so much for hanging in with me, so far! Never fret, dear reader, The Last Daughters of Titus Series is not over. Our story continues with Book 6, **Kindred of the Guardian** please enjoy this excerpt:

"Gentlemen, welcome to day one of warrior training," said the king. His latest recruits stood before him in various states of dress, each representing the house of his father. There were sixteen in all. Two of which were from his own kingdom. His grandson, Julian and Caleb, Trip's son. The others were fortunate enough to be hand-picked from surrounding sovereigns. When the greatest warrior of the Upper Realms decides to personally train a new class of warriors pandemonium ensues as everybody wants *their* son in *that* class.

It had been centuries since Titus had last trained a class himself. He'd been tied up, busy even, what with being sentenced to dole out and share the pain of seven hundred heartbreaks each resulting in the creation of an offspring. Yeah, that'll keep someone busy for quite some time, almost a millennium. Then The Master had turned things around on him by allowing his heart to be the one broken in the end. That sucked major balls. Big time. And he'd acted like a complete ass about it, banishing his beloved queen, Vanessa, to an undeserved season in Hell. Not one day went by that he didn't regret his actions. Oh, well, lessons learned, water under the bridge and all that jazz. She had eventually returned to him going so far as to even forgive him. But her return had more strings attached to it than a marionette. First of all, she came back as a winged horse. Oh, but she was the most majestic, beautiful creature he'd ever seen. Her black coat so shiny one could see rainbows reflected in the light of it. Second, she had to keep this form until their daughter, Ebony, was able to earn her own wings. After which, Vanessa could choose to go back to human form, which brings us to the thickest string of all. Titus was to be celibate during the entire wait.

Twenty-two years. A drop in the bucket for an angel over a thousand years in age, but still, inconvenient as hell. Oh, and she could talk, but only he could hear her. Yes, well, that caused the king to be on the receiving end of a few this-motherfucker-done-lost-his-mind looks until everyone figured out what was going on. Now that his punishment had finally come to an end, he could get back to what he loved most. Churning out the best of the best protectors of the Upper Realms.

Things had been peaceful between the Upper and Lower Realms for a long time, but it was just a matter of time before something would pop off. Titus could feel it and he wasn't one to wait for shit to go down and not be prepared for it. So, here he was. Back to training warriors and just as excited about it as his students. The poor saps had no idea what they were in for. There was a reason he was nicknamed Titus the Terrible. This entire class was too young to know about those days, but they were going to learn and he had no qualms about telling them so.

He continued, "Forget everything you think you know about me. I know I've hung out with all of your parents and even some of you, but recreation is recreation and this? This. Is. Not. Recreation." He paused for effect. It worked. All eyes were on him and all mouths were shut. Good.

"I'm sure you all noticed the new building next door. That's where you'll be staying for your duration here. Any questions?" Crickets. Swell.

He proceeded to pick up an eighteen inch length of bamboo and started smacking his palm with it as he walked back and forth. "When you make your way to the barracks you will find a cot and a footlocker with your name on it. Inside your lockers you will find your new training leathers. This is not a boot camp, gentlemen. When your fathers applied for you they were given specific instructions as to what condition I expected you to be in upon arrival. My time is far too valuable to be wasted getting you into shape for training. Now, training will start tomorrow morning first thing after Sunrise Welcome. No breakfast. Is that understood?"

He was answered with various heads bobbing, a few 'yeses' and one resounding 'Sir! Yes, sir!' Titus cocked an eyebrow and looked at that last one. He was the smallest boy in the class. And damn if his little ass wasn't standing at attention. Titus chuckled, not surprised.

Beylan, son of Gamesh, shared his father's dark brown skin and golden eyes. At only five feet eleven inches he was short for an angel. It was obvious he hadn't hit his second septennium growth spurt yet. To be in Titus's training class, one had to have at least two septennia under one's belt.

Beylan had just made it, making him fourteen in human years. Most of the candidates were closer to celebrating their third septennia, a few already surpassing. None of that mattered to Titus. If one was ready to be a warrior, it didn't matter how old he was as long as he no longer had status as a cherub, hence the two septennia rule. Titus couldn't help being impressed with the little badass. The boy stood with his head held high, serious as a heart attack. His father had prepared him well. Judging by the tribal markings extending up the boy's neck and across his shaved scalp, he was being groomed to replace his father. Again, impressive. Should he successfully complete Titus's course, he'll earn warrior markings down his right arm. They all would and Titus himself would be applying them. He addressed the group.

"Everyone here could take a lesson from the youngest lad here as he's the only one of you that addressed me properly."

Somebody muttered, "It's not like his nose ain't already brown, right?"

Titus froze. Pinning the group with a steely-cold glare, he asked, "Who said that?"

Everyone looked down at the floor and shuffled their feet, then a tall, pale angel with hair the color of a fire engine stepped forward. "I did, sir. I didn't mean anything by…"

Titus didn't allow him to finish. "Alrid! The only thing saving you from being sent back to your father right now is the fact that you came forward without making me ask twice. Not only was your comment rude and uncalled for, it was racist in nature. There's no room for any form of prejudice here. Racially, sexually or otherwise. Do you understand?"

Alrid snapped to attention. "Sir, yes sir!"

Titus addressed the group. "That goes for all of you! Beylan, step forward please." The boy did as he was told. Titus said, "Shake hands with your new bunkmate, Alrid. From here on out you two are partners." He paused waiting to see if there'd be any argument from either one. Neither one did. Though, Beylan's eyes were narrowed as he shook hands with his new 'friend'. The two got back in line standing next to each other, guarded. Titus would be watching them closely. He knew it was just a matter of time before they would be best of buddies. He'd seen it before.

"Gentlemen, take a look around you. Look at each other. I mean, really, look at each other. I am not your mother, your father, your friend or even," he made eye contact with Julian, "your allfather. I am your teacher and you are my students and this is going to be hell. That guy standing next to you is now your brother. This group, right here, right now is your family. You will look out for each other, you will build bonds and trust amongst yourselves. Trust me, I'll be watching closely. Anybody who cannot fall in line and function as part of a group will be sent home. We have no need for showboats or glory hounds here, so if you know this to be true about yourself, please save your and my time by excusing yourself now." He waited. No takers. Moving on.

"How many of you have parents or older siblings that trained under me?" he asked. A few hands went up. He nodded. "Did they tell you what to expect?" A collective 'no sir'. "Good. They upheld their vows. What happens here, stays here. Though your parents will be receiving weekly emails on your progress and I will be keeping an individual personal account of each and every one of you. When you leave, I will present that report to you so you can see how far you came from beginning to end. Any questions?" Silence.

"Alright, then. First things first. We have one last bit of business here then you will be done for the day. You're to go to the barracks and find your lockers. Unpack, unwind, and relax. Now, take a seat on the first bleacher. You'll notice there's a bench in front of it. Shoes and socks off and feet up on the bench, now."

He waited while the group complied. When he was standing in front of a row of sixteen pairs of bare soles resting in front of him, he continued.

"For this training to work. There must be a system of discipline in place. I direct your attention to the board on the wall to your left. On the left side of the board is a list of offenses. On the right you will see a number. That number is how many strikes that offense is worth. Actions have consequences. If you feel that you can withstand the punishment…" He shrugged. "…by all means, offend away. Though, I will tell you this. Three of those offenses in one day will get you sent home. That tells me you're not with the program and as I said, I ain't got time for that."

He studied their faces. Only one of them appeared to know what was coming. Beylan. No surprise there. Gamesh was no joke. The boy was already bracing himself for it. Good. That's where he'd start. He walked over to Beylan.

"Just so we're clear. It is imperative that you know what said punishment feels like before you get any ideas on how well you think you can withstand it. Now, is when you'll begin to hate me."

Without warning he swing the cane, smacking Beylan solidly on the sole of his foot. The boy didn't flinch, but Titus saw his jaw tighten and he swallowed. Now he had their attention.

"He is the youngest one of you and he took that like an adult. No tears. No crying out. It's one strike. If this little guy could take it," he rested a hand on Beylan's shoulder, "so can you."

He then proceeded down the line, demonstrating the punishment they could expect should they step out of line. When he was finished he looked back at them. Each one had one very red foot and not one lip was trembling. Oh, yes, this was a good group. Titus's heart swelled with pride. It was going to be a pleasure training them. He was about to churn out sixteen certified badasses.

ACKNOWLEDGMENTS

First and foremost, allow me to thank my beta readers. Y'all know who you are. You keep me on my toes. I can't thank you enough! A special shout out to Betty Updike, thank you so much for all you do and all the time you spend helping me. I want to thank Michael Irizarry who allows me to bounce ideas off of him no matter the hour of the day or night. Dude! You have no idea how much that means to me! Your enthusiasm helps stoke the flames when I'm feeling low. Daniela Gabrielle, my own private motivational coach and cheerleader. LOL Girl, you inspire me on the regular in so many ways! Stay extra! Last but, certainly not least, Detra Williams and Natalie McCleary, the other Knights of the Round Table, for reminding me who I am, when I forget. It happens to the best of us and sometimes a swift kick to the rear end is in order. I appreciate you wearing soft shoes.

ABOUT THE AUTHOR

A D Hunter is a huge fan of all things paranormal and romantic. From angels to unicorns, vampires and werewolves. If it's got a little magic, fantasy or just plain ol' love, it is definitely her thang! When she's not conjuring up hot, fantastic stories about mischievous angels, she can be found in her kitchen conjuring up hot goodies because everyone knows nothing beats good pie with great coffee! Her husband claims that when she's writing, smoke comes out of her ears. That can't be confirmed nor denied.

Let's keep in touch!

>Email me: adhunter@worldofadhunter.com
>Visit my website: http://worldofadhunter.com

ALSO BY A D HUNTER

The Last Daughters of Titus Series:

Book 1: Face of an Angel

Book 2: Body of a Venus

Book 3: Heart of Stone

Book 4: Fate of the Reaper

Book 5: Son of the Avenger

Coming soon:

Book 6: Kindred of the Guardia